THE CREEPS

Also by John Connolly

The Charlie Parker Stories
Every Dead Thing
Dark Hollow
The Killing Kind
The White Road
The Reflecting Eye (Novella in the 'Nocturnes' Collection)
The Black Angel
The Unquiet
The Reapers
The Lovers
The Whisperers
The Burning Soul
The Wrath of Angels

Other Works
Bad Men
The Book of Lost Things
The Wanderer in Unknown Realms (eBook)

Short Stories
Nocturnes

The Samuel Johnson Stories (For Young Adults)
The Gates
Hell's Bells

The Chronicles of the Invaders (*For Young Adults*)
Conquest (*with Jennie Ridyard*)

Non-Fiction (as editor, with Declan Burke)
Books To Die For: The World's Greatest Mystery Writers
on the World's Greatest Mystery Novels

THE CREEPS
JOHN CONNOLLY

HODDER &
STOUGHTON

First published in Great Britain in 2013 by Hodder & Stoughton
An imprint of Hodder & Stoughton
An Hachette UK company

I

A CIP catalogue record for this title is available from the British Library

Hardback ISBN 978 1 444 75182 6
Trade Paperback ISBN 978 1 444 75183 3
eBook ISBN 978 1 444 75184 0

Typeset in Stempel Garamond by Palimpsest Book Production Limited,
Falkirk, Stirlingshire

Printed and bound by Clays Ltd, St Ives plc

Hodder & Stoughton policy is to use papers that are natural, renewable
and recyclable products and made from wood grown in sustainable forests.
The logging and manufacturing processes are expected to conform to the
environmental regulations of the country of origin.

Hodder & Stoughton Ltd
338 Euston Road
London NW1 3BH

www.hodder.co.uk

For Cameron and Alistair

Picture Acknowledgements
© Alamy: 28, 127, 160
© Shutterstock: 113, 263

CHAPTER I

In Which a Birthday Party Takes Place, and We Learn That One Ought to Be Careful With Candles (and Dangling Prepositions).

In a small terraced house in the English town of Biddlecombe, a birthday party was under way.

Biddlecombe was a place in which, for most of its history, it seemed as though nothing very interesting had ever happened. Unfortunately, as is often the case in a place in which things have been quiet for a little too long, when something interesting did happen it was very interesting indeed; more interesting, in fact, than anybody might have wished. The gates of Hell had opened in a basement in Biddlecombe, and the town had temporarily been invaded by demons.

Perhaps unsurprisingly, Biddlecombe had never really been the same since. The rugby team no longer played on its old pitch, not since a number of its players had been eaten by burrowing sharks; the voice of the captain of the Biddlecombe Golf Club could still occasionally be heard crying out from somewhere at the bottom of the fifteenth hole; and it was rumoured that a monster had taken up residence in the duck pond, although it was said to be very shy, and the ducks appeared to be rather fond of it.

But the creature in the pond was not the only entity from Hell that had now taken up permanent residence in Biddlecombe, which brings us back to the birthday party. It was not, it must be said, a typical birthday party. The birthday boy in question was named Wormwood. He looked like a large ferret that had suffered a severe attack of mange[1], and was wearing a pair of very fetching blue overalls upon which his name had been embroidered. These overalls replaced a previous pair upon which his name had also been embroidered, although he had managed to spell his own name wrong first time round. This time, all of the letters were present and correct, and in the right order, because Samuel Johnson's mother had done the stitching herself, and if there was one thing Mrs Johnson was a stickler for[2], it was good spelling. Thus it was that the overalls now read 'Wormwood' and not 'Wromwood' as they had previously done.

Wormwood was, not to put too fine a point on it, a demon. He hadn't set out to be a demon. He'd just popped into existence as one, and therefore hadn't been given a great deal of choice in the matter. He'd never been very good at being a demon. He was too nice for it, really. Sometimes folk just end up in the wrong job.[3]

---

[1] For those of you unfamiliar with mange, it is an ailment that causes a loss of fur. Think of the worst haircut you've ever received, and it's a bit like that, but all over your body.

[2] Technically, that sentence should read 'if there was one thing *for which* Mrs Johnson was a stickler', as nobody likes a dangling preposition, but I said that Mrs Johnson was a stickler for good spelling, not good grammar.

[3] Such as Augustus the Second (1694–1733), King of Poland and Grand

A chorus of voices rang out around the kitchen table.

'Happy Birthday to you, Happy Birthday to you, Happy Birthday dear Woooorrrrrmmmmmwooo ood, Happy Birthday to you! For he's a jolly good, um, *fellow* . . .'

Wormwood smiled the biggest, broadest smile of his life. He looked round the table at those whom he now thought of as his friends. There was Samuel Johnson and his dachshund, Boswell. There were Samuel's schoolmates, Maria Mayer and Tom Hobbes. There was Mrs Johnson, who had started to come to terms with having demons sitting at her kitchen table on a regular basis. There were Shan and Gath, two fellow demons who were employed at the local Spiggit's Brewery as beer tasters and developers, and who were responsible for a fifty per cent increase in the brewery's profits, as well as a 100 per cent increase in the number of

---

Duke of Lithuania, also known as Augustus the Strong. He managed to bankrupt his kingdom by spending all of its money on bits of amber and ivory, lost a couple of battles that he really would have been better off winning, and fathered over 300 children, which suggests that, in between losing battles and collecting trinkets, he had a lot of time on his hands, but his party piece consisted of gripping a horseshoe in his fists and making it straight. He would probably have been very happy just straightening horseshoes and blowing up hot water bottles for a living, but due to an accident of birth he instead found himself ruling a number of kingdoms. Badly. You should bear this in mind if your dad or mum has a name beginning with the words 'His/ Her Royal Highness', and you are known as 'Prince/ Princess Something-Or-Other'. Unless, of course, your name is really 'Something-Or-Other', in which case you don't have anything to worry about (*about which* to worry – darn it) as your parents didn't care enough about you to give you a proper name, and you are therefore unlikely to amount to anything. Sorry.

explosions due to the instability of the still-experimental Spiggit's Brew Number 666, also known as 'The Tank-buster', which was rumoured to be under consideration by the military as a field weapon.

And then there was Nurd, formerly 'Nurd, the Scourge of Five Deities' and now sometimes known as the Nurdster, the Nurdmeister, and the Nurdman, although only to Nurd himself. Nobody else ever called Nurd anything but Nurd. Nurd had once been banished to the remotest, dullest region of Hell for being annoying, and Wormwood, as his servant, had been banished with him. Now that they had found their way to Biddlecombe, Wormwood preferred to think of himself as Nurd's trusty assistant rather than his servant. Occasionally, Nurd liked to hit Wormwood over the head with something hard and memorable, just to remind Wormwood that he could think of himself as anything he liked just as long as he didn't say it aloud.

But in the end Nurd, too, was one of Wormwood's friends. They had been through so much together, and now they worked alongside each other at the Biddlecombe Car Testing Institute, where Nurd tested the safety of new cars, aided by the fact that he was immortal and hence able to walk away from the worst crashes with only the occasional bruise for his trouble.

Wormwood had never had a birthday party before. Until he arrived on Earth, he didn't even know there was such a thing as a birthday. It seemed like a very good idea to him. You got cake, and gifts, and your friends sat around and sang about what a jolly good fellow you were. It was all quite, quite splendid.

The singing ended, and everyone sat waiting expectantly.

'What do I do now?' asked Wormwood.

'You blow out the candles on the cake,' said Samuel.

When they'd asked Wormwood how old he was, he'd thought that he might just be a few billion years younger than the universe itself, which made him, oh, about ten billion years old.

'The cake's only a foot wide!' Mrs Johnson had pointed out. 'He can't have ten billion candles. They won't fit, and if we try the whole town will go up in flames.'

So they'd settled on one candle for every billion years, which seemed like a reasonable compromise.

Nurd was seated directly across the table from Wormwood. He was wearing a red paper party hat, and was trying unsuccessfully to blow up a balloon. Nurd had changed a lot in the time that they'd been in Biddlecombe, thought Wormwood. His skin was still green, of course, but not as green as before. He now looked like someone who had just eaten a bad egg. His head, which had formerly been shaped like a crescent moon, had shrunk slightly. It was still long and odd looking, but he was now able to walk the streets of Biddlecombe without frightening too many children or causing cars to crash, especially if he kept his head covered.

'This balloon appears to be broken,' said Nurd. 'If I blow any harder, my eyes will pop out. Again.'

That had been embarrassing. Samuel had used a spoon to retrieve them from Nurd's glass of lemonade.

Wormwood took a deep breath.

'Make a wish,' said Maria. 'But you have to keep it to yourself, or else it won't come true.'

'Oh, I think I've got the hang of the balloon now,' said Nurd.

Wormwood closed his eyes. He made his wish. He blew. There was a loud *whoosh*, followed by a *pop* and a distinct smell of burning.

Wormwood opened his eyes. Across the table, Nurd's head was on fire. In one of his hands, he held the charred, melted remains of a balloon.

'Oh, thank you,' said Nurd, as he tried to douse the flames. 'Thank you very much.'

'Sorry,' said Wormwood. 'I've never tried to blow anything out before.'

'Wow,' said Samuel. 'You have inflammable breath. I always thought it smelled like petrol.'

'The cake survived,' said Tom. 'The icing has just melted a bit.'

'I'm fine,' said Nurd. 'Don't worry about me. I love being set on fire. Keeps out the cold.'

Samuel patted Nurd on the back.

'Seriously, I'm OK,' said Nurd.

'I know. Your back was on fire, though.'

'Oh.'

'There's a hole in your cloak, but I expect Mum will be able to fix it.'

Mrs Johnson cut the cake and gave everybody a slice.

'What did you wish for, Wormwood?' asked Tom.

'And if you tell me that you wished my head was on fire, we'll have words,' said Nurd.

'I thought I wasn't supposed to say,' said Wormwood.

'That's before you blow,' said Tom. 'It's all right to tell us after.'

'Well, I wished that everything would stay the way it is now,' said Wormwood. 'I'm happy here. We all are.'

Shan and Gath nodded.

And in the general hilarity and good cheer that followed, nobody noticed that it was only Nurd who had not agreed.

CHAPTER II

In Which Someone Sees a Ghost. (Yawn.)

As has already been established, the town of Biddlecombe was a lot odder than it once had been, but the curious thing about Biddlecombe was that it had always been ever so slightly strange, even before the attempted invasion from Hell. It was just that people in Biddlecombe had chosen not to remark upon its strangeness, perhaps in the hope that the strangeness might eventually grow tired of being ignored and just go and be strange somewhere else.

For example, it was well known that if you took a right turn on Machen Street, and then a left turn on Poe Place, you ended up back on the same corner of Machen Street from which you had recently started. The residents of Biddlecombe got round this peculiar geographical anomaly by avoiding that particular corner of Machen Street entirely, instead using the shortcut through Mary Shelley Lane. Visitors to Biddlecombe, though, tended not to know about the shortcut, and thus they had been known to spend a great deal of time moving back and forth between Machen Street and Poe Place until somebody local came along and rescued them.

And then there was the small matter of the statue of Hilary Mould, Biddlecombe's leading architect. Nobody could remember who had ordered the statue, or how it had come to be in Biddlecombe, but the statue had turned up sometime in the nineteenth century, shortly after Mould disappeared under circumstances that might have been described as mysterious if anyone had cared enough about Mould to miss him when he was gone, which they didn't because Mould's buildings were all ugly and awful.

The statue of Hilary Mould wasn't much lovelier than the buildings he had designed, Mould not being the most handsome of men, and it had often been suggested that it should quietly be taken away and lost. But the statue of Hilary Mould had a habit of moving around, so there was no way of knowing where it might be from one day to the next. It was usually to be found near one of the six buildings in Biddlecombe that Mould had designed, as if the architect couldn't bear to be separated from his work.

As with so many of the strange things about Biddlecombe, the townsfolk decided that the best thing for it was to ignore the statue and let it go about its business.

Which was, as we shall come to learn, a terrible mistake.

As it happened, the statue of Hilary Mould was, at that moment, lurking in a still and silent way near what appeared to be an old sweet factory but which now housed a secret laboratory. Inside the laboratory, Brian, the new tea boy, had just seen a ghost.

The effect this had on Brian was quite considerable. First of all he turned pale, so that he bore something of a resemblance to a ghost himself. Second, he dropped the tray that he was carrying, sending three cups of tea, two coffees, and a plate of assorted biscuits – including some Jammie Dodgers, of which Professor Stefan, the Head of Particle Physics, was especially fond – crashing to the floor. Finally, after tottering on his heels for a bit, Brian followed the tray downwards.

It was only Brian's second day on the job at the secret Biddlecombe annexe of CERN, the advanced research facility in Switzerland that housed the Large Hadron Collider, the massive particle accelerator which was, at that very moment, trying to uncover the secrets of the universe by recreating the moments after the Big Bang. The Collider had been notably successful in this, and appeared to have confirmed the existence of a particle known as the Higgs Boson, which was believed to be responsible for giving mass to the universe.[4]

The Biddlecombe annexe had been set up to examine the strange goings-on in the town in question, which had so far included the dead coming back to life, an attempted invasion by the Devil and all of his demonic hordes, and the abduction to Hell of a small boy, his dachshund, a number of dwarfs, two policemen, and an ice-cream salesman. It was clear to the scientists that Biddlecombe was the site of a link between our universe and another universe that wasn't half as nice, and they had decided to set up an office there in the hope that something else very bad might happen so they could watch and take notes, and perhaps win a prize.

☠ [4] It was, to put it simply, the stuff that made stuff stuff.

The problem was that the good people of Biddlecombe didn't particularly want scientists lurking around every corner and asking hopefully if anyone had been abducted, possessed, or attacked by something with too many arms. The people of Biddlecombe were hoping that whatever hole had opened between universes might have closed by now, or been filled in by the council. At the very least they wanted to forget about it because, if they did, then it might forget about them, as they had quite enough to be getting along with, what with rescuing tourists from the corner of Machen Street and avoiding walking into old statues.

The result was that the scientists had been forced to sneak into Biddlecombe and cleverly hide themselves in a secure location. Of course, Biddlecombe being a small place, everyone in the town knew that the scientists had come back. Now they could only pray that the scientists might blow themselves up, or conveniently vanish into another dimension.

The location of the secret facility was slightly – well, considerably – less spectacular than CERN's massive operation in Switzerland. The annexe was housed in the building formerly occupied by Mr Pennyfarthinge's Olde Sweete Shoppe & Factorye,[5] unoccupied ever since a tragic accident involving Mr Pennyfarthinge, an

---

💀 [5] There is a certain type of shop that just loves sticking the letter 'e' on the end of words in the hope it will make said shop appear older and more respectable. Businesses selling candles, sweeties, Christmas decorations, and models of fairies are particularly prone to this, although in reality the only thing that the 'e' adds is ten per cent extra on to the price of everything. Mr Pennyfarthinge's fondness for the 'Olde E' was so extreme as to qualifye as a forme of mentale illnesse.

unsteady ladder, and seventeen jars of gobstoppers. To keep up the pretence, the scientists had reopened the sweete shoppe and took it in turns to serve sherbet dabs, liquorice allsorts, and Uncle Dabney's Impossibly Sour Chews[6] to various small persons for an hour or two each day.

Technically, Brian was not, in fact, a tea boy, but a laboratory assistant. Nevertheless, as he was the new kid, his duties had so far extended only to boiling the kettle, making the tea, and keeping a close watch on the Jammie Dodgers, as Professor Stefan was convinced that someone was stealing Jammie Dodgers from the biscuit tin. Professor Stefan was wrong about this. It wasn't 'someone' who was stealing Jammie Dodgers.

It was everyone.

Brian's proper title was 'Assistant Deputy Assistant to the Assistant Assistant to the Assistant Head of Particle Physics', or 'ADAAAHPT' for short.

Which, oddly enough, was the last sound Brian made before he fell to the floor.

'Adaaahpt,' said Brian. *Thump*.

The noise caused Professor Stefan, who was concentrating very hard on a piece of data analysis, to drop his pen, and Professor Stefan hated dropping pens. They

---

[6] Uncle Dabney's Impossibly Sour Chews were banned in a number of countries after the sheer sourness of them had turned the faces of several small boys inside out. See also: Uncle Dabney's Dangerously Explosive Spacedust (tooth loss due to explosions), Uncle Dabney's Glow-In-The-Dark Radiation Gums (hair loss due to radiation poisoning), and Uncle Dabney's Frog-Shaped Pastilles (mysterious disappearance of entire populations of certain frogs). The late Uncle Dabney was, of course, quite insane, but he made curiously good sweets.

always managed to roll right against the wall, and then he had to get down on his hands and knees to find them, or send the Assistant Deputy Assistant to the Assistant Assistant to the Assistant Head of Particle Physics to do it for him. Unfortunately, the ADAAAHPT was now flat on his back, moaning softly.

'What is ADAAAHPT doing on the floor?' said Professor Stefan. 'He's your responsibility, Hilbert. You can't just leave assistants lying around. Makes the place look untidy.'

Professor Hilbert, the Assistant Head of Particle Physics, looked at Brian in puzzlement.

'He appears to have fainted.'

'Fainted?' said Professor Stefan. '*Fainted?* Listen here, Hilbert: elderly ladies faint. Young ladies of a delicate disposition faint. Assistants do not faint. Tell him to stop all of this nonsense immediately. I want my Jammie Dodgers. He'll have to get some fresh ones. I'm not eating those ones after they've been on the floor. We can give them to the numbskulls in Technical Support.'

'We don't have any Technical Support,' said Professor Hilbert. 'There's only Brian.'

He helped Brian to sit up, which meant that Professor Hilbert was now technically supporting Technical Support.

'Guh—,' said Brian.

'No, it's not good,' said Professor Hilbert. 'It's not good at all.'

'Guh—,' said Brian again.

'I think he may have bumped his head,' said Professor Hilbert. 'He keeps saying that it's good.'

'You mean that he's bumped his head so hard he thinks

good is bad?' said Professor Stefan. 'We can't have that. Next he'll be going around killing chaps and asking for a round of applause as he presents us with their heads. He'll make a terrible mess.'

Brian raised his right hand, and extended the index finger.

'It's a guh—, it's a guh—, it's a guh—'

'What's he doing now, Hilbert?'

'I think he's rapping, Professor.'

'Oh, do make him stop. We'll have no hip-hoppity music here. Awful racket. Now opera, there's—'

'IT'S. A. GHOST!' shrieked Brian.

Professor Hilbert noticed that Brian's hair was standing on end, and his skin was covered in goose-bumps. The atmosphere in the lab had also grown considerably colder. Professor Hilbert could see Brian's breath. He could see his own breath. He could even see Professor Stefan's breath. He could not, however, see the breath of the semi-transparent young woman, dressed as a servant, who was standing in a corner and fiddling with something that only she could see. Her image flickered slightly, as though it were being projected imperfectly from nearby.

Professor Hilbert stopped supporting Brian, who duly fell backwards and would have banged his head painfully had not some Jammie Dodgers absorbed most of the impact.

'So it is,' said Professor Hilbert. 'I say, it's another ghost.'

Professor Stefan peered at the young woman over the top of his spectacles.

'A new one, too. Haven't seen her before.'

Professor Hilbert carefully approached the ghost.

'Hello,' he said. He waved his hand in front of the

ghost's face, but she didn't seem to notice. He considered his options, then poked at the woman's ribs. His finger passed right through her.

'Bit rude,' said Professor Stefan disapprovingly. 'You hardly know the girl.'

'Nothing,' said Professor Hilbert. 'No response.'

'Just like the rest.'

'Indeed.'

Slowly, the image of the girl began to fade, until finally there was only a hint of vapour to indicate that she had ever been there at all, if, in fact, she *had* ever been there at all. Oh, she was certainly somewhere, of that Professor Hilbert was sure. He just wasn't convinced that the somewhere in question was a laboratory in twenty-first-century Biddlecombe.

Brian had managed to struggle to his feet, and was now picking pieces of Jammie Dodger from his hair. He stared at the corner where the girl had been.

'I thought I saw a ghost,' he said.

'Yes,' said Professor Hilbert. 'Well done, you. And on only your second day too. You can't go around fainting every time you see one, though. You'll end up on the floor more often than you're upright if you do.'

'But it was a *ghost*.'

'Just make a note of it, there's a good chap. See that big hardbacked notebook on the desk over there?' He pointed to a massive black volume, bound in leather. 'That's our record of "ghost sightings". Write down the time it began, the time it ended, what you saw, then sign it. Professor Stefan and I will add our initials when you're done. To save yourself some time, just turn straight to page two hundred and seventy-six. That's the page we're on now, I think.'

Brian looked like he might faint again.

'Page two hundred and seventy-six? You mean that you've filled two hundred and seventy-five other pages with ghost sightings?'

Professor Hilbert laughed. Even Professor Stefan joined in, although he was still disturbed at the loss of so many perfectly good Jammie Dodgers.

'Two hundred and seventy-five pages!' said Professor Stefan. 'Young people and their ideas, eh?'

'Two hundred and seventy-five pages!' said Professor Hilbert. 'Dear oh dear, where do we get these kids from? No, Brian, that would just be silly.'

He wiped a tear of mirth from his eye with a handkerchief.

'That's volume three,' he explained. 'We've filled *one thousand*, two hundred and seventy-five pages with ghost sightings.'

At which point Brian fell over again. When he eventually recovered himself, he added the sighting to the book, just as he had been told. He noted down everything he had seen, including the hint of black vapour that had hung in the air like smoke after the ghost had disappeared. Had Professors Hilbert and Stefan taken the time to read Brian's note, they might have found that black vapour very odd.

Outside, the statue of Hilary Mould stared, solid and unmoving, at the old factory. A cloud passed over the moon, casting the statue in shadow.

When the moon reappeared, the statue was gone.

CHAPTER III

In Which We Travel to a Galaxy Far, Far Away, But Since It's Not a Long Time Ago the *Star Wars* People Can't Sue Us.

Some things are better left unsaid. Among them are 'This situation can't really get any worse,' which is usually spoken before the loss of a limb, a car going off a cliff, or someone pushing a button marked DO NOT PUSH THIS BUTTON. EVER. WE'RE NOT JOKING; 'Well, he seems like a nice person,' which will shortly be followed by the arrest of the person in question and the removal of bodies from his basement, possibly including your own; and finally, and most better-left-unsaid of all, 'You know, I think everything is going to be just fine,' because that means everything is most assuredly not going to be fine, not by a long shot.

So. Everything is going to be fine. Are we clear on that?

Good.

In another part of the Multiverse, a couple of dimensions from Biddlecombe, a small green planet orbited a slowly dying star. The news that the star was dying might have proved alarming to the inhabitants of the planet had any of them been sufficiently advanced to be capable of understanding the problem, but so far the planet had not produced any form of life that was equipped to do anything more sophisticated than eat while trying not to be eaten itself. Much of the planet was covered by thick coniferous forests, hence its colour from space, although it also boasted some very nice oceans, and a mountain that, at some point in the future, representatives of some species might try to climb because it was there, assuming the star didn't die long before then.

The creature that moved through the depths of one of the planet's oceans didn't have a name since, as we have established, there was nobody around with the required intellectual curiosity to give it one. Also, as the creature was very large, very toothy, and very, very hungry, any contact with it would have gone somewhat along the lines of 'Look, a new species! I shall name it – AAARRGHHH! My leg! Help, help! No, AAARRGGHH! My other leg!' etc., which doesn't tend to look good in history books.

There was very little in the oceans that the creature had not encountered before, and nothing that it had so far not tried, successfully, to eat. But on this particular occasion its attention was caught by a small bright glowing mass, a clump of atoms that vaguely resembled a cluster of blue fish eggs. The creature, always hungry and open to trying new foodstuffs, wolfed the blue mass down and proceeded on its none-too-merry way, already on the lookout for even more tasty and interesting things to eat.

It had been swimming for a mile or so when it began to consider what all of this hunting and eating was about, really. I mean, it swam so it could eat, and it ate so it could keep swimming, and that was the sum of its existence, as far as it could tell. It wasn't much of a life when you thought about it, which it hadn't until only moments before, and there had to be more to it all than that. What would happen, it wondered, if it sent other creatures out to hunt on its behalf while it put its fins up and made plans for the future, among which were the enslavement of the planet's population – hey, we're on a planet? – followed by the building of space-ships and the further enslavement of lots of other planets' populations, upon which it could then feed to its belly's content? That sounded great! Oh, and apparently the star – star? – around which its planet was orbiting was dying, so the sooner it got started on this whole business of building spaceships, whatever they were, the better.

Before it could get to work on the fine print of its grand design, a larger, even toothier, and even hungrier monster bit it in half, and the creature's brain had just enough time to think, Oh, well that's just great, that is, before its divided body was chomped to mincemeat and began the great journey through the digestive tract of another.

Whereupon *that* large, hungry creature began to wonder about the nature of good and evil, and how evil seemed much more fun, all things considered, and so this might have continued for a very long time until there was an unfamiliar popping sound in the ocean's depths, and into existence popped a wobbly being with one eye. It was wearing a very fetching top hat tied with a piece of elastic beneath what passed for its chin, just to ensure that its hat didn't float away, as it was very fond of that hat.

The massive ocean monster, all teeth and gills and eyes and horns and scales, looked at the new arrival, opened its jaws, and prepared to chew, but before it could start chomping the little hat-wearer shot into its mouth and down its gullet. The monster gave a kind of fishy shrug and swam on, distracted from the peculiar appearance of its latest meal by all of this evil stuff, which sounded just fascinating.

Deep inside the monster's gut, the gelatinous mass, whose name was Crudford, Esq. began searching through half-digested flesh and bone. It stank something awful in there, but Crudford, cheerful and contented by nature, didn't mind. In fact, he even whistled a happy tune just to pass the time. Eventually, somewhere in the newly consumed remains of a giant segmented eel, he found what he had been looking for: a small group of atoms that glowed a bright blue. Crudford lifted his hat, the elastic stretching as he did so, and retrieved from the top of his head a glass bottle. The bottle was sealed with a cork, and the blue atoms in the monster's belly found a kind of reflection in a similar, but larger, cluster already contained inside. Crudford removed the cork and carefully added the new atoms to the old before resealing the bottle and placing it safely under his hat. His jellied features split into a deep smile, and he patted his hat happily.

'There you are, Mrs Abernathy,' he said. 'We'll have all those bits of you back together again in no time.'

With that, he popped out of existence again, and the huge sea creature that had recently swallowed him forgot all about being evil and simply went back to eating things, which was probably for the best.

There were many advantages to being an entity composed entirely of transparent jelly. Actually, there weren't, but Crudford, Esq., who was a creature of boundless optimism, tried to find the bright side of any situation, even his own, which was very *un*bright. Looked at from the outside, he appeared to be on the same level as slime[7], and in possession of only a single hat. But in Crudford's own mind he was a slug-like object on the rise, a wobbling thingummy on the way to greater things. Someday, an opportunity would present itself, and there would be only one gelatinous demon for the job: Crudford, Esq.

Amazingly enough, that day had come when Mrs Abernathy, the Great Malevolence's left-hand demon, had suddenly found herself with each of the billions and billions of individual atoms that made up her body separated from its neighbours and scattered through the Multiverse, all because she had messed with Samuel Johnson, his dog, two policemen, four elves, and an ice-cream salesman.[8] Oh, and four of her own demons,

---

[7] Which was probably to be expected, given that the slime was usually his own. 'I've produced more slime, sludge, glop, gunk, mucus and mire than you've had hot dinners,' he would boast proudly to anyone who might listen. Which would usually be enough to put someone about to sit down to a hot dinner right off the idea.

[8] An adventure described in *Hell's Bells*, available from all good bookshops

including Nurd the Scourge of Five Deities, who everyone had thought so useless at being a demon that even Crudford was more terrifying than him, and Crudford couldn't help but be nice to everyone he met.

Crudford imagined that being blown apart at the atomic level must have hurt a lot. Unfortunately for Mrs Abernathy, as Crudford had come to realise, she hadn't just been blown apart at the atomic level: the protons, neutrons and electrons that made up her atoms had also become separated from one another, and then the particles *within* the protons and neutrons, known as quarks, had been scattered for good measure. There were three quarks within each proton and neutron, bound together by other particles called gluons, and all of those various bits and pieces were now scattered throughout the Multiverse. Being blown apart on the sub-atomic level must have hurt an awful, awful lot, thought Crudford. Still, look on the bright side: at least Mrs Abernathy was seeing new places.

But cometh the hour, cometh the congealed, hat-wearing jelly being. It turned out that Crudford had always been very good at squeezing into small spaces, and oozing through tiny holes. No one in Hell was entirely sure what Crudford was made from, exactly, but it was remarkable stuff, and there was no other creature remotely like him in that awful place.

And Crudford couldn't just squeeze through cracks

---

and some bad ones. If you haven't read it, please find a copy and turn to the second footnote in Chapter One, which will wag a finger disapprovingly at you for picking up the later books in a series without first reading the earlier ones.

in rocks and wood and metal: no, Crudford could ooze through the rips and tears in universes, the holes and flaws between dimensions. It made him the perfect candidate to search for, and gather up, Mrs Abernathy's quarks and gluons and occasional reconstituted atoms so that the process of putting her back together again could begin. At last, Crudford had found his purpose. The recreation of Mrs Abernathy was his responsibility, and his alone. He was searching for subatomic needles in the universal haystacks of the Multiverse, and he loved it.

He could even explore those spaces between universes, although Crudford didn't like hanging about there for long. Like everyone else in Hell, he had always felt that the Great Malevolence, the foulest, most evil being in the Multiverse – but probably a lovely demon once you got to know it, Crudford tried to believe – was the cherry on the cake when it came to entities of which one ought to be frightened.

But Crudford had come to learn that there were things in the gaps between universes that made the Great Malevolence look like a small flowery unicorn that pooed fairy dust. At least you knew where you stood with the Great Malevolence. Admittedly, that was on the edge of an infinite fiery pit or a cold, bottomless lake of ice, into either of which the Great Malevolence might plunge you if the mood took it, but there was no mystery about the old GM: it hated everything that breathed, especially everything that breathed on Earth, and ultimately it wanted to torment the living for eternity and turn the Multiverse into a realm of ash and fire. Fair enough, thought Crudford. Aim high. Everybody needs an ambition.

But between universes there were entities that didn't feel anything at all, not even hatred. They had no form, and barely a consciousness. They existed only to bring about nonexistence. They put the 'thing' in 'nothing'. When Crudford came close to their non-kingdoms, he was aware of their non-attention coming to rest upon him, their complete and utter uncaring-ness, and even his relentless optimism would start to flag somewhat.

But the worse of the unknowable entities dwelt in the Kingdom of Shadows. They had taken the concept of nothingness – the aching absence of absolute emptiness – and added one simple ingredient to the mix.

Darkness.

And not just any old Darkness either, but a dense, suffocating blackness that coated the body and the mind and the soul, a Darkness like eternal drowning, a Darkness from which all hope of light had fled because it came from a place in which light had never been known. Even calling the place in which they lurked the 'Kingdom of Shadows' was a kind of mistake because shadows required light to form. The Great Malevolence, who had seen so much and recorded it all, had shown Crudford the fate of universes invaded by the Darkness, and it had always begun with shadows where no shadows should have been.

So Crudford moved carefully through the spaces between universes, and he carefully watched every shadow. He listened too, for Crudford could hear the rips widening in the fabric of universes, just as he could see the light through the new gaps. Now, as he moved through the Multiverse to return to Hell with his shiny blue prizes, he became aware of a rhythmic, pulsing sound coming from somewhere distant. It was familiar to him.

It was a heartbeat.

Crudford's senses were so keen that he could tell the beating of one heart from another, for each heart had its own unique beat. But this was a very special heart. He alone, sensitive beyond any other demon, had heard its secret rhythm in Hell. It was a human heart through which no blood flowed, only malice.

Somewhere in the Multiverse, Mrs Abernathy's heart was beating.

CHAPTER IV

In Which We Go Shopping, and Rather Wish That We Hadn't.

L et's drift back through Biddlecombe on this cold dark night, drift like smoke.

Like Shadows.

Wreckit & Sons had once been the largest shop in Biddlecombe. It sold almost everything that anyone could possibly want: pins and pots, bread baskets and bicycles, televisions and tea trays. It was four storeys tall, took up an entire block of the town's centre, and its shelves stretched for miles and miles. Its basement was so huge and poorly lit that a man named Ernest Tuttle had once got lost there while trying to buy a tennis racket and a socket wrench, and promptly vanished. His ghost – a pale, moaning figure – was said to haunt the store, until it was discovered that it was not, in fact, Ernest Tuttle's ghost but Ernest Tuttle himself. He had spent two years trying to find a way out, and couldn't understand why people kept running away from him. When they pointed out that he was pale and moaning, he replied that they'd be pale too if they'd been trapped in a basement for two years living only on rice cakes, and they'd probably moan a bit as well. His feet hurt, he told reporters, and he believed that the mice had adopted him as their king. He still hadn't managed to find a tennis racket or a socket wrench either.

The store was another of Hilary Mould's buildings, but it wasn't quite as offensively awful as the others. There was something almost grand about Wreckit & Sons. In the right light – somewhat dim, a bit murky – it resembled a cathedral, or a temple. Arthur Bunce, the man who had originally asked Hilary Mould to design the store, took one look at it and promptly went mad. Instead Mould bought the building himself, and he disappeared shortly after. The building remained empty for many years until a gentleman named Wreckit took a fancy to it, and opened his department store there.

But if Wreckit & Sons sold a lot of things that people might want, it also tried to sell a lot of things that nobody could possibly want. As he grew older, Mr Wreckit became more and more eccentric. He began calling it Wreckit & Sons for starters, which annoyed his daughters greatly, as he didn't have any sons. His buying habits changed. For example, he bought two thousand three-dimensional Chinese-made photographs of the man on the next page. (We put him there so that you can prepare yourselves for the shock when you turn over. Ready? Are you sure? Okay then. Don't say we didn't warn you . . .)

The man's name was Max Schreck, and he was famous for playing the vampire in an old film called *Nosferatu*. Max Schreck was so strange-looking that it was whispered he might even be a *real* vampire. The 3D nature of the photos bought by Mr Wreckit meant that Max Schreck's eyes followed you around the room, and NOBODY wanted this man's eyes following them around the room. Mr Wreckit sold precisely one of the pictures, and that was to himself. He kept it hidden under a blanket.

Mr Wreckit also bought 100 unicycles, but it was only when they were shipped to him that he discovered they were not actual unicycles but merely bicycles that were missing one wheel. If it is hard to ride a unicycle, it is significantly harder to ride a bicycle that is fifty per cent down in the wheel department. Mr Wreckit tried. The resulting bang on the head made him even stranger.

He bought teapots with no spouts, sieves with no holes, and steel piggy banks with a slot for the money to go in but no way of getting it out again. He bought televisions that only picked up signals from North Korea, and radios that tuned into frequencies only dogs could hear. He sold gloves for people with six fingers, and gloves for people with three fingers, but no gloves for people with four fingers and a thumb. His fire extinguishers started fires, and his firelighters wouldn't light. His fridges boiled milk, and his ovens were so cold that when a penguin escaped from Biddlecombe's Little World of Animal Wonders, it was later found to be living in one of them, along with its entire family and a single confused chicken.

Nobody seemed able to reason with Mr Wreckit. He had simply gone bonkers. He was nutty as a fruitcake. Still, as he was the sole owner of Wreckit & Sons due to the absence of any real sons, and refused to talk to his daughters because they weren't men, he was free to run the business into the ground and there wasn't anything anyone could do to stop him.

So Mr Wreckit did, in the end, wreck it. The store went out of business. Mr Wreckit, broke and crazy, retired to a cottage on the Devon coast. When asked what had possessed him to destroy his own business, he replied, strangely, 'That's a very good question. What *did* possess me?'

But he had no answer. On his deathbed, he apologised to his daughters. His last words were: 'The Voice in the Wall made me do it.'

Nobody wanted to take over Wreckit & Sons after that, and the building stayed empty. It stood at the end of Biddlecombe's main street, a great block of not-quite-nothing, for it always seemed as though the spirit of the great old store was still present, infusing its bricks and mortar, its wood and its windows, waiting for the moment when its doors might be opened again, and people could get lost in its basement.

But nobody came, and the spirit slept.

*   *   *

So it was that the store had been closed for what seemed like a very long time – and was, actually, a very long time.[9] Two generations of Biddlecombe children had grown up without any memory of Wreckit & Sons being anything other than an empty shell, its ground-floor windows boarded and its doors locked. Eventually people just stopped noticing it, although strangers would sometimes pass through the town and gaze up at it. And when they asked who had designed such a building, the residents of Biddlecombe would shrug their shoulders and point at the statue of Hilary Mould, assuming they could find it.

But if the history of Wreckit & Sons was odd, its oddness didn't stand out quite so much when monsters and demons began invading Biddlecombe, even if they

---

💀 [9] Well, long in human terms, which is all that concerns most people. That's a little narrow-minded, though, and if you only think in those terms then perhaps you should take a long, critical look at yourself in the mirror. Frankly, you're not the centre of the Multiverse, no matter what your mum and dad might say, or your nan, or your Auntie Betty who never got married – mainly because, according to your dad, nobody could get her to shut up long enough to ask her – but comes around to 'babysit' occasionally and just seems to drink a lot of your parents' sherry before falling asleep.

Sorry, where were we? Oh yes, long lives. *Anyway*, what seems like a long time to you is the blink of an eye to lots of other species. The Llangernyw Yew is the oldest tree in Europe, and is reckoned to be 4,000–5,000 years old, while certain specimens of black coral have been found to be over 4,200 years old. Meanwhile, the giant barrel sponge *Xestospongia muta*, which lives in the Caribbean, is one of the longest-lived animals on earth, with some such sponges now over 2300 years old. Mind you, they don't do a lot of shopping, your black sponges, and so couldn't really have done much to help Wreckit & Sons stay open. Then again, Wreckit & Sons did *sell* sponges, so the black sponges, had they known, would probably have been quite pleased to see it close. Things that live for thousands of years tend to have long memories, and know how to hold a grudge.

didn't leave a lot of proof behind once they went away again, monsters in ponds and spectral voices from golf courses excepted. Psychiatrists spoke of mass hysteria, and comedians made jokes about the townsfolk. Experts arrived and took readings. They dug in the ground, and tested the air, and poked at people who didn't want to be poked, thank you very much, and warned that, if the experts continued to poke them, they'd find their poking sticks stuck somewhere the sun didn't shine.[10] With so much strangeness going on, suddenly Mr Wreckit's old store began to seem not so strange after all. But it was. It was very, very strange, and strange things have a habit of attracting more strangeness to them.

In the basement of Wreckit & Sons, something moved. It was pale and naked, but it eventually managed to find a suit that fitted it, and a shirt that wasn't too yellowed, and a smart grey tie. As thousands of eyes followed it round the room, it wiped the dust from an old mirror and smoothed its hair.

'What is my name?' it asked.

The Voice in the Wall told him.

You shall be called Mr St John-Cholmondeley.

'How do you spell that?'

The Voice in the Wall spelled the name.

💀 10 'In a cave?'
No.
'In a very deep ocean?'
No.
'Hmmm. Up someone's bottom?'
Possibly.

'But you say it's pronounced Sinjin-Chumley?'

Yes.

'Are you sure that's right?'

Yes.

The Voice in the Wall sounded a bit miffed. It was so difficult to find good help these days.

The newly animated Mr St John-Cholmondeley looked doubtful.

'If you say so.'

I do.

The Voice in the Wall directed Mr St John-Cholmondeley to a safe, and told him the combination. Inside the safe was a great deal of gold, along with details of secret bank accounts. The bank accounts were all in the name of St John-Cholmondeley, even though they had been set up more than a century earlier.

'What do you want me to do?' asked Mr St John-Cholmondeley.

The Voice in the Wall told him, and Mr St John-Cholmondeley set to work.

Wreckit & Sons was about to reopen for business.[11]

☠ [11] Are you on the edge of your seats now? If we had a soundtrack to this book (of which more later) that kind of ending to a chapter would come with a three-note theme along the lines of 'Dun-dun-*dah!*' About that edge-of-the-seat business: in a sense, we are *always* on the edge of our seats because of electromagnetic repulsion, which means that the atoms that make up matter never actually touch one another. The closer atoms get, the more repulsion there is between the electrical charges of each atom. It's a bit like trying to make the same poles of a pair of magnets touch: it just doesn't work. So you may at this moment think that you're sitting in a chair reading this footnote, but you're actually hovering ever so slightly above it, suspended by a force of electromagnetic repulsion a billion billion billion billion times stronger than the force of gravity. You are officially a hoverperson.

CHAPTER V

In Which We Go on a Date – Well, Not 'We' as
in You and I, Because That Would Just Be
Awkward, But We Go on a Date with Other
People. No, Hang On, That's Still Not Right. Oh,
Never Mind. Just Read the Chapter.

There may come a time in your life – I hope that it
does not come, for your sake, but it might – when you
realise that you may be with the wrong person. By this
I don't mean being in Russia with Napoleon just as the
weather starts to turn chilly, or on a raised platform
while a chap with a hood over his face raises a big axe
and looks for a way to make you roughly a head shorter,
although neither of those things would be good.[12]

No, what I mean is that you may ask someone out
on a date, and during the course of the date you may
discover that you have made a terrible mistake. You
may even get a clear signal that a terrible mistake has
been made. The person sitting across the table from
you, or next to you in the cinema, may announce that

[12] Similarly, a century ago you would not have been happy to find that
one of the passengers on your ship was Violet Jessop. Ms Jessop, a stewardess
and nurse, was on the *Titanic* when it sunk in 1912. She was also on the
Britannic, which was hit by a mine in 1916, and she was onboard the *Olympic*,
the *Titanic*'s sister ship, when it collided with HMS *Hawke* in 1910. If Violet
Jessop was one of your fellow passengers on a voyage, you might as well have
jumped overboard at the start just to get the whole business out of the way.

she wasn't sure that she was going to make the date because she was certain the jury was going to find her guilty, even though she hadn't really murdered anyone because her last boyfriend had simply tripped and fallen on the knife she just happened to be holding at the time, ha-ha-ha, what a silly boy he was, and DON'T EVER MAKE ME MAD! Other subtle signs that you may have erred in asking someone out for an evening include: shooting the waiter for spilling the soup; laughing very loudly any time anyone dies in a film, especially if they die horribly, and everyone else in the cinema is weeping; or telling you that they've never gone out with anyone quite like you before, and when you ask them what that means you get the reply, 'You know, a real person. One that I didn't imagine, or build from Lego.'[13]

Samuel Johnson was having one of those moments. In fact, he'd been having them for quite some time, but had hoped that things might get better. After all, he'd had a crush on Lucy Highmore for so long that he couldn't actually remember a time when he *didn't* have a crush on her. Occasionally in life we will wish for something that may not be very good for us simply because we think it will make us feel better about

---

💀 [13] To quote the title of a famous song, 'Breaking Up is Hard to Do', and people find all sorts of ways to do it. If someone is breaking up with you, they may tell you that 'it's not you, it's me'. This will be a lie. If someone says that it's not you in order to stop going out with you, then it is you. It doesn't matter if they tell you that they want to go off and help little orphans in some obscure part of the world, or sign up for an experimental space mission, or become a monk or a nun, and this is why it's not you, it's still you. You, you, you. Believe me, I know. I'm not bitter though. Not really. OK, maybe a bit.

ourselves, or make us seem more important in the eyes of the world. This is why people buy expensive cars that they don't need, or wear gold watches bigger than their heads. It is also why people will often date someone simply because he or she is wealthy, or famous, or beautiful. In case you didn't already know – and if you're clever enough to be reading a book, and have managed to get this far without stumbling over any words longer than five letters, then you probably *do* know – let me explain a truth to you: it doesn't work. You're trying to fix a flaw in yourself by shoving the problem on to someone, or something, else. It's like having a cut on your finger and bandaging your toe instead. It's like feeling hungry, and hoping that you'll feel less hungry by buying yourself a hat.

A wise man once said that you should be careful what you wish for, because you might get it. Samuel wanted to meet that wise man and ask him why he hadn't been there to advise Samuel when he'd started wishing that Lucy Highmore would go out with him. That was the trouble with wise men: they were never around when you needed them, and by the time you became a wise man yourself it was too late to use any of your wisdom on yourself, and nobody else wanted to listen to you.

Lucy Highmore didn't particularly like Samuel's friends. She didn't like where he lived, and she didn't like how he dressed. She didn't like the sunlight because it damaged her skin, and she didn't like the cold because, well, it made her feel cold. She didn't like going out, and she didn't like staying in. (When Samuel suggested that they could just stand at her front door with one foot inside and one foot outside, she had looked at him in a troubled way.) She didn't like Samuel's dog, Boswell, because he smelled funny. Boswell, who understood people better than people understood him, found this very unfair, as he wasn't one of those dogs inclined to roll in stuff that smelled bad. He had yet to find a dead animal or a pile of deer poo that made him think, Wow, now why don't I have a bit of a spin in that because I bet everyone will want to hug me after, and there's no way they'll make me take a bath that I don't want. Furthermore, Lucy Highmore smelled funny to Boswell too, but there wasn't much that he could do about it. She smelled of peculiar perfumes with French names that sounded like *Mwah-mwoh*, or *Zejung*, names that were only impressive when spoken by an invisible man with a deep voice. She also smelled slightly of vegetables because that was all she seemed to eat. She could live for a week on a stick of celery and half a carrot, and there were camels that consumed less liquid.

On their first date, Samuel had taken Lucy to Pete's Pies. Everyone loved Pete's Pies. It was a small pie shop run – and you're ahead of me here – by a man named Pete. Pete's pies were perfect pastry constructions filled with meat and vegetables, or just vegetables if you were that way inclined, and just meat if you really, really liked meat. The pastry was as golden as the most perfect dawn, the filling never too hot and never too cold. Pete also made what he called his 'dessert pies', triangles of apple, or rhubarb, or pear that made grown men weep for their sheer loveliness, and grown women weep with them. There was nobody – I mean, nobody – who didn't like Pete's pies. No one. You'd have to be mad not to like them. You'd have to be impossible to please. You'd have to be –

Lucy Highmore.

On that first date, Lucy had politely declined to share a pie, and had simply sipped delicately at a glass of water – so delicately, in fact, that natural evaporation caused the level in the glass to drop more than Lucy's sips.

Now, months later, she and Samuel were still together, but both of them were starting to think that they shouldn't be, although neither could quite find the words to say it. They were also back in Pete's Pies. Since Lucy never seemed to eat much, it didn't really matter where they went. She could choose not to eat in Pete's Pies just as easily as she could choose not to eat anywhere else. They were the only people in the pie shop apart from old Mr Probble, who now spent his days reading the *Oxford English Dictionary* in order to improve his word power. He'd started at 'A', and was reading a page a day. This meant that conversations with Mr Probble tended to involve exchanges like the following:

'Hello, Mr Probble. Nice day, isn't it?'

To which Mr Probble might reply, 'Aardvarks amble awkwardly.'[14]

Samuel stared into Lucy's eyes, and Lucy stared into his.

☠ [14] Until he moved on to the letter 'B', when the reply became 'Aardvarks amble awkwardly *but briskly* . . .'

'You know,' she said, 'you ought to get new glasses.'

'Really?' said Samuel.

'Yes, those ones make your face look a funny shape. They also make you seem like you have trouble seeing things.'

'But I do have trouble seeing things,' said Samuel.

'But you don't want everyone to know, do you?' said Lucy. 'It's like ugly people and hats.'

'Is it?' said Samuel, not sure where ugly people came into it, exactly, or hats.

'Of course, silly.'

Lucy patted Samuel's arm. To be honest, 'patted' might have been an understatement. There were wrestling champions who would have screamed 'Ouch!' after being patted by Lucy Highmore. She had quite a swing on her for a thin girl.

'Ugly people wear hats so that people can't see how ugly they are,' explained Lucy. 'The hats cast a shadow, and so they hide their ugliness, and pretty people don't have to feel so bad about being pretty.'

'But . . .' said Samuel, rubbing his arm. He tried to find his train of thought, but it had departed the station long before, with a fat lady on the back waving goodbye with a handkerchief and leaving Samuel stranded on the Platform of Confusion. 'But don't pretty people wear hats too?'

'Yes, sillikins,' said Lucy, and Samuel just prayed that she wouldn't pat his arm again. He still couldn't feel his fingers. 'But they wear them for a different reason. Hats on pretty people make them look prettier! Everything looks prettier on pretty people. It's a law.'

'Right,' said Samuel. If you followed that statement to its logical conclusion, then Samuel's glasses should have made him look prettier – er, more handsome – but only if he was pretty – er, handsome – to begin with. But if they didn't make him look more handsome – there, got it right third time – did that mean he wasn't handsome at all? Samuel sort of guessed that he wasn't, but he was hopeful that the situation might change as he got older. The fact that Lucy Highmore had agreed to go out with him had fuelled that hope.

In a way, both Lucy and Samuel had made two versions of the same mistake. Lucy had agreed to go out with Samuel because, despite what some of the folk in Biddlecombe might have thought or said, he was a kind of hero. He had faced down the hordes of Hell. He had fought demons. He might have been visually challenged, and distinctly awkward, and so attached to his dog that it accompanied him on dates, but he still wasn't like most of the other ordinary boys in Biddlecombe, and Lucy Highmore felt less ordinary for being with him. It was the same reason that she always made sure her hair was perfect before leaving the house, and always wore the prettiest and most fashionable clothes, and always surrounded herself with people who were slightly less pretty and perfect than she was. She did it because, deep inside, she suspected that she wasn't as interesting, or clever, or even as pretty as she liked to believe, but if she acted like she was, and shielded herself with boys and girls who were even more insecure, she might just convince everyone that she was better than they were. If she tried really, really hard, she might even convince herself.

But the main reason that Lucy had agreed to go out with Samuel was because Maria Mayer, one of Samuel's closest friends, was more than a little in love with him. Everyone knew this – everyone, that is, except Samuel, who was a bit thick when it came to girls. If Maria wanted Samuel, thought Lucy, then there must be something there worth having, even if Lucy wasn't entirely sure what that was.

And Samuel? Well, Samuel had always been happy with himself. I don't mean that he was smug, or self-satisfied. He knew he was awkward, and didn't see very well without his glasses, and that, in his case, his best friend really was his dog, but he didn't mind. He got on well with his mum, and with his dad, most of the time, even if his dad now lived in Norwich with a lady called Esther who wore so much make-up that, when she smiled or frowned, or even when she spoke, cracks appeared in her face and cosmetics avalanched to the floor. She had kissed Samuel the first time that they met, and the left side of his face had turned brown.

But he had looked at Lucy Highmore, who had never so much as glanced at him before all of that demon business, and wondered if being with her might make him feel just a bit less awkward, and a little less like an outsider. Who knew, she might even help to make his hair do what he wanted it to do. (Samuel's hair never seemed to want to do anything other than slouch lazily on his scalp like a flat, yellow animal; he had tried using gel on it once, and it had ended up looking like a flat, yellow animal that had somehow become frozen in place just as it was about to attack someone from the top of a small boy's head.) She could advise him on how to dress so that his shirt matched his trousers, or his shoes matched his jacket, or even so one sock matched the other. In the end, Samuel had wanted Lucy to make him better than he was, ignoring the fact that he was doing perfectly well just being himself. The result was that, because she was secretly more unhappy than he was, she had just ended up making him feel worse: about his hair, his clothes, his friends, himself, even about Boswell.

Lucy Highmore wasn't a bad person. She was slightly vain, but she wasn't mean. Samuel wasn't a bad person either. He was just insecure, and tired of being the odd kid out. Together, they were a small mistake that was rapidly becoming a bigger, more complicated one.

'If you like,' said Lucy, 'I'll go with you to help you choose your new glasses. It'll be fun.'

Boswell, lying on the floor of Pete's Pies beside his beloved master, put his head between his paws and sighed a long dog sigh.

CHAPTER VI

In Which We Are Reunited with Some Old Friends, and Keep a Close Watch on our Wallets.

The citizens of Biddlecombe woke one morning to find the windows of Wreckit & Sons blacked out. From inside the store came sounds of drilling and hammering, but nobody knew what construction company was in charge, and no one was seen either entering or leaving the building. But the work went on, day and night, and from somewhere in the depths of the store orders were placed for dolls, and games, and model trains.

The rumour was that Wreckit & Sons was about to reopen as a toyshop.

Sometimes, Dan wondered if he was right to be so upbeat all of the time. He had always had a sunny disposition. If life gave him bruised fruit, he made jam. The glass was always half full, even when it wasn't, because Dan would get down on his knees and squint at it from a funny angle until it appeared fuller than it was. Even if there was no glass at all, Dan assumed this was only because someone had taken it away to fill it up again. If he had been told that the world was ending tomorrow, Dan would have shrugged his shoulders and assumed that something would turn up to prevent it from happening. The asteroid that was about to destroy the Earth could have been visible as a flaming ball in the sky and Dan would have had a scone ready on the end of a fork so he could toast it without switching on the toaster.

Lately, though, it had been hard for Dan to keep a smile on his face. He had been a happy undertaker for many years[15] but had grown tired of having nobody to talk to. (Well, he did have people to talk to, but they didn't answer back, and even Dan might have been a bit concerned if they had started to.) He had then bought an ice cream van on the grounds that he had always liked ice cream, and lots of other folk liked ice cream too, and therefore he was likely to spread good cheer by selling it to them while his chimes played 'How Much Is That Doggie in the Window?' over and over. At the very least, it was likely that people would buy his ice cream just so that he would move on and they wouldn't have to listen to 'How Much Is That Doggie in the Window?' any longer.

Unfortunately for Dan, he and his ice cream van had been dragged to Hell and, although both had returned, the van had been a great deal the worse for wear when it got back, and Dan's insurance didn't cover unexpected trips to Hell. But, as always, something had turned up.

---

[15] This was not necessarily a good thing. There are many professions that might benefit from a smile and a hearty laugh, but undertaking is not one of them. The last thing people want as they arrive, red-eyed and weeping, to send their beloved Auntie Ethel on her way to the next life is to find someone in a black suit grinning like a loon and opining that it's a lovely day for a funeral. That way, frankly, lies a punch in the face.

Actually, four of them had turned up: Jolly, Dozy, Angry and Mumbles, known collectively as Mr Merryweather's Elves, or Mr Merryweather's Dwarfs, or by whatever name the police were NOT looking for them at any particular moment in time. Currently, they were known as Dan's Dwarfs, which had seemed like a good idea, Mr Merryweather having abandoned the dwarfs for a number of reasons, but mostly because he hated them.

So now Dan drove the dwarfs round, and tried to find them work. And keep them sober. And stop them from stealing. All of which was a lot harder than it sounded, and it already sounded quite hard.

Today, Dan's Dwarfs were on their way to the grand opening of Honest Ed's[16] Used Car Showrooms just outside the town of Biddlecombe. Why Honest Ed felt that a quartet of surly dwarfs would help him sell more dodgy cars was unclear, but Dan took the view that his was not to reason why, but just to take the money and run before something bad happened which, when the dwarfs were involved, it usually did.

This was why, as Dan drove the dwarfs around in a

---

[16] A quick word here about people who put words like 'Honest' or 'Cheerful' before their names: they usually aren't. Anyone who has to advertise the fact that he's cheerful is probably sadder than a bird without a beak in a birdseed factory, while someone who has to boast about how honest he is will steal the eyes from your head while you're cleaning your glasses. Mind you, this doesn't mean that someone who calls himself Dishonest Bob, for example, is automatically honest. He's just honest about being dishonest, if you see what I mean. Vlad the Impaler (1431–76) still went around impaling people, and Henry the Cruel of Germany (1165–97) was still cruel. They just believed that it paid to advertise. Generally speaking, then, if someone adds a good quality to their name, they're probably lying, and if they add something bad, then they're probably telling the truth.

battered old van, he was wondering if one could really continue to be upbeat when you were responsible for four dwarfs who appeared set on proving that good things did not always come in small packages.

'Lot of traffic today,' said Jolly, who often wasn't.

'It's moving fast, though,' said Angry, who often was.

'Anyone in a car that's moving fast mustn't have bought it from Honest Ed,' said Dozy, who often was as well. 'His cars are so old, they come with a bloke to walk in front of them waving a red flag.'[17]

'Nwarglesput,' said Mumbles, which is self-explanatory.

'Listen, lads,' said Dan. 'Let's not have any trouble, right? We go in, we dance around the cars, we look happy, we collect the cheque, and we leave. It doesn't have to be any more complicated than that.'

'What do you mean, "we"?' said Angry. 'You're not going to be dancing around in a funny hat, only us. There's no dignity to it.'

'There's fifty quid each to it,' said Dan.

'I suppose so,' said Angry. 'It's still no job for a grown man.'

'You're not a grown man,' said Dan. 'That's the point. If you were a grown man, they wouldn't be paying you to dance around a car showroom wearing a hat with

---

💀 [17] Curiously, the British Locomotive Act of 1865 (also known as the 'Red Flag Act') required that no self-propelled vehicle (which included cars) could travel faster than four miles per hour in the country, and two miles per hour in the city. Each car was also required to have a crew of three, one of whom had to walk 180 feet in front of the car carrying a red flag. In 1878 the whole flag business was made optional as cars became faster, probably because someone in a car got tired of travelling at two miles an hour and ran over the bloke with the flag, making it hard to recruit replacement flag wavers from then on.

bells on it and a shirt that says "Honest Ed's Cars – The Lowest Prices Around!"'

'We're not actually low,' said Jolly. 'We're small. There's no reason why we should be wearing shirts advertising low prices. Small prices maybe, but not low ones.'

'You're small *and* low,' said Dan. 'You're low to the ground. Can you reach things on high shelves without standing on chairs? No. So you're low.'

'Still don't like it,' said Jolly.

'Never mind that,' said Dan. 'We're nearly there. The local newspaper is sending someone along to take pictures, and a disc jockey from Biddlecombe FM radio – "The Big B!" – will be playing tunes and giving away prizes.'

'What kind of prizes?' asked Jolly.

'Mugs. Stickers. Pens,' said Dan.

'Fantastic,' said Angry. 'I can just see someone winning a pen and dying of happiness.'

'Or a mug,' said Jolly. 'There'll probably be some old lady who's dreamed all her life of having a mug to call her own. She's been drinking tea out of holes in the ground for all these years, and suddenly – bang! – she wins a mug. They'll write songs about it, and people will tell their children of it for generations to come: "You know, I was there the day old Mrs Banbury won a mug."'

Dan tightened his grip on the steering wheel. He tried to find something to be upbeat about, and decided that there was a limit to the amount of trouble that the dwarfs could cause at Honest Ed's. There'd be no beer, and they didn't have weapons. What could possibly go wrong?

* * *

'Well, that went all right,' said Jolly some time later, as the van drove away at speed. 'Sort of.'

Behind them came the sound of an explosion, and a Volkswagen Beetle – 20,000 miles on the clock, one lady owner, perfect motoring order – flew up into the air like a big, fat firework, trailing smoke and burning fuel. A second explosion, larger than the first, quickly followed, as the rest of Honest Ed's stock went up in flames.

'I told you I smelled gas,' said Angry. 'Very dangerous stuff, gas.'

'Absolutely,' said Jolly. 'You can't go messing about with gas.'

'Can't take chances with it.'

'Absolutely not.'

They were silent for a moment or two. In the distance, the horizon glowed in the light of the flames from Honest Ed's former car dealership.

'Probably shouldn't have gone looking for it with a lighter, though,' said Dan. He was driving faster than was safe, but it seemed like a good idea to put as much distance between the dwarfs and Honest Ed as possible. When last they'd seen him, Honest Ed had been looking for a gun.

'Well, the torch was a bit small,' said Angry. 'And it didn't light things very well.'

'I think we solved that problem,' said Jolly. 'It looks like Honest Ed's is lit perfectly well now.'

'Did we get paid in advance?' Angry asked Dan.

'We always get paid in advance,' said Dan. 'If we didn't, we'd never get paid at all.'

They drove on. The dwarfs sang. Dan went back to trying to be optimistic. Things, he thought, could only get better, mainly because they couldn't possibly get any worse.

In the basement of Wreckit & Sons, Mr St John-Cholmondeley sat at a desk and wrote what the Voice in the Wall told him to write.

WANTED

he wrote.

FOUR DWARFS FOR STORE WORK.
EXCELLENT PAY AND PROSPECTS.

Mr St John-Cholmondeley stopped writing.
'Do they really have excellent prospects?' he asked the Voice in the Wall.
Yes, replied the Voice in Wall. *They have the most excellent prospects.*
Of dying.

CHAPTER VII

In Which We Have a Musical Interlude.

The following morning, Dan gathered the dwarfs in the yard behind the offices of 'Dan, Dan the Talent Man, & Company', as he had recently renamed himself and the business. The '& Company' referred to the dwarfs, who each had an equal share in the talent management company, and therefore an equal say in its affairs. This made the monthly company meetings noisy, stressful and, in the case of Mumbles, difficult to understand. Behind Dan was a vaguely van-shaped object covered in a white tarpaulin.

'Now,' said Dan, 'you'll remember that, at our August meeting, we decided that we should buy a new van.'

The dwarfs vaguely remembered this. They didn't pay a lot of attention at the company meetings. They just liked shouting and arguing, and sticking their hands up to vote for things that they didn't understand.[18] They might well have voted in favour of buying a new van. Then again, they might have voted

18 This is how parliaments work.

in favour of buying a spaceship, or invading China. For little people, the dwarfs didn't pay much attention to small print.

'Just remind us: why are we buying a new van again?' asked Jolly.

'Because we can't keep repainting the old one,' said Dan. 'And you didn't want to be known as "Dan's Dwarfs" any more, or even "Dan's Elves".'

'That's because elves don't exist,' said Angry. 'It's like being called "Dan's Unicorns", or "Dan's Dragons".'

'Exactly,' said Dan.

'And we're not "your" elves,' said Jolly. 'It makes us sound like slaves. Which we're not.'

You're definitely not, thought Dan. Slaves might do a bit of work occasionally.

'You don't like being called "little people",' said Dan, 'and you're not sure about "dwarfs", so I had to think up a different name, which I did. I now present to you – the new van!'

Dan whipped away the tarpaulin, and the van stood revealed. It was bright yellow, and very shiny.

Dan glowed.

The van glowed.

The dwarfs did not glow.

'What's that?' said Angry.

'It's a van,' said Dan.

'No, not that. *That!* The writing on the side.'

'It's your new name: Dan's Stars Of Diminished Stature.'

Dan was very proud of the new title for the dwarfs. He'd spent ages thinking it up, and he'd visited the painters every day that they were working on the job just to make sure they got the details right. The words flowed diagonally down both sides of the van. They'd even found a way to continue the writing over the windows without obscuring the view. The van was a work of art.

DAN'S
Stars
Of
Diminished
Stature!

The dwarfs looked at the van. Dan looked at the dwarfs. Dan and the dwarfs looked at the van. Dan's eyesight wasn't very good, and things might have gone on like that until night fell had Angry not said, 'So, nothing strikes you as odd about the van?'

'No,' said Dan.

'Nothing at all?'

'Maybe the letters aren't big enough. Is that it?'

'No, no, the letters are more than big enough. Too big, some might say. It's more how they read that bothers me, so to speak.'

Dan looked again. He spelled out the words, moving his lips. He took a step back. He squinted.

He saw it.

'Oh,' he said.

'Yes, oh,' said Angry. 'In fact, not just "Oh", but "Ess, Oh, Dee, Ess". The side of our van reads "Dan's SODS!"'

'That's not good,' said Dan.

Definitely accurate, he thought, but not good.

The dwarfs and Dan sat in Dan's office. They did not present a happy picture. The van was just the latest in a series of disasters. They had caused a major gas explosion, and they now owned a van that described them as sods.

Oh, and they had recently been dragged to Hell for a time. Let's not forget that.

But their main problem at the moment was that, while they owned a talent agency, it didn't have any real talent to promote.

'What about Wesley the Amazing Tightrope Walker?' said Dan. 'We have him. He's a genius! He can walk along a length of spider web without falling off.'

'He's afraid of heights,' said Dozy. 'It's hard to get excited about a man who can only walk a tightrope that's six inches off the ground. Even then he looks a bit nervous.'

'Jimmy the Juggler?' suggested Dan. 'You've got to admit that the man can juggle.'

'He *can* juggle,' said Jolly. 'He has a gift. He'd be better if he had two arms, though. Strictly speaking, he doesn't juggle: he tosses.'

'Bobo the Clown?'

'He gets angry with children. It's one thing throwing a bucket of confetti over them, but he's not supposed to throw the bucket as well.'

'And then there's, well, *them*,' said Dan.

'Them!' said Jolly, shaking his head.

'Them!' said Angry, casting his eyes to heaven.

'Them!' said Dozy, putting his head in his hands.

'Arble!' said Mumbles.

Which said it all, really.

They followed Dan down a steep set of stairs to the basement and walked along a hallway to a large padlocked door. Dan fumbled in his pocket for the key.

'Do you really need to keep them locked up?' asked Jolly.

'It's for their own good,' said Dan. 'They wander off if I don't.'

'They were never very intelligent,' said Angry. 'It's a wonder they lasted as long as they did.'

'It's sad, really,' said Dan. 'You know, they wouldn't survive a day in the wild.'

He placed the key in the lock and turned it.

'Careful now,' Dan warned. 'They react to the light.'

He removed the padlock and pulled the bolt. The door began to open with a creak. The room beyond was big and comfortable, but very dark. As the door opened further, a rectangle of light appeared on the floor and grew wider and wider, like the beam of a spotlight tracing its way across a stage.

A figure jumped into the light, followed by a second, and a third, and a fourth. They all looked a little bleary-eyed. Their spangled shirts had seen better days, and their trousers bore food stains. Their voices also sounded somewhat croaky, but that was nothing new.

'Hi,' said the first. 'I'm Starlight.'

'Oh Lord,' said Jolly.

'And I'm Twinkle,' said the second.

'Good grief,' said Angry.

'I'm Gemini,' said the third.

'They never stop, do they?' said Dozy.

'And I'm Phil,' said the fourth. 'And together we're—'

'BoyStarz!' they all cried in unison, and performed a small twirl before they began doing to a perfectly innocent song what grape-crushers do to grapes.

'Make them stop,' said Jolly, his hands pressed to his ears. 'Please!'

'It's very hard,' said Dan. 'They see a light and they start performing. I've tried electric shocks, but that just seems to make them livelier.'

These were hard times for the BoyStarz. For a start, they were no longer as young as they were, but 'MenStarz' didn't have the same ring to it. Phil in particular looked like a doorman at the kind of nightclub where people got killed on a regular basis, while Sparkle, Twinkle and Gemini had only enough hair between all three of them for two people to share. Their career had never recovered from vicious rumours that the BoyStarz could not sing, and they simply mimed along to songs recorded by more talented vocalists. This led to the BoyStarz signing up for a special tour to prove the doubters wrong. In this it was successful, to a degree. The tour did prove that the BoyStarz could sing.

Horribly.

One critic compared the sound of BoyStarz singing live to the final cry of a ship's horn as it sinks beneath the waves with the loss of everyone on board. Another described it as only marginally less awful than being trapped in a room with a flock of frightened geese that kept honking in panic as they bumped into the walls. A third wrote: 'If Death had a sound, it would sound like BoyStarz.'

The BoyStarz kept trying. They turned up for the opening of shopping malls, but nobody came. Then they started showing up for the opening of individual stores, but still nobody came. Eventually they grew so desperate that if somebody opened a newspaper, or a packet of crisps, BoyStarz would pop up beside them and start warbling about how love was like a flower, or a butterfly, or a sunny day. People started complaining. Where once the BoyStarz had been driven everywhere in limousines, they now rode bicycles, or they did until someone stole the bicycles to stop them from showing up unexpectedly. It was all very sad, unless you actually liked music and songs being sung in tune, in which case it wasn't very sad at all.

The dwarfs felt partly responsible for the run of bad luck that BoyStarz had endured because it was they who had ruined the filming of the video for BoyStarz's Christmas single 'Love is Like a Castle (Built for Two)'. They had done this by taking bits of the castle in question and flinging them from the battlements until the castle built for two looked like a shed built for one. When the dwarfs had decided to set up a talent agency with Dan, it seemed only right and proper that they should try to find work for the BoyStarz. So far, the only work they'd found for them was in a hamburger restaurant, and even then they'd only lasted a day because they insisted on singing about how love was like a lettuce leaf, or a chicken nugget, or a bun.

'All right, boys,' said Jolly, 'the song's had enough. Time to put it out of its misery.'

The BoyStarz stopped wailing.

'Has you got work for us?' asked Gemini.

'Is we going to be stars again?' asked Twinkle. As he said the word 'stars', he tossed fairy dust in the air.

'Where do they get that fairy dust from?' asked Angry. 'They never seem to run out, do they?'

'I've searched their cell – I mean, their *room* – and I can't find a trace of it,' said Dan. 'I think they just produce it from their pores, like sweat.'

'What are you feeding them?' asked Dozy.

'Mostly cheese.'

'Well, that doesn't explain it. Whatever you get from eating lots of cheese isn't going to look like fairy dust, or smell like it either.'

'When is we going to sing again?' asked Starlight.

'What does he mean, "again"?' asked Jolly. 'And why can't they tell singular from plural?'

'I think they're becoming a single entity,' said Dan. 'Except for Phil, of course.'

'Ah.'

They all looked at Phil, who bore the same relationship to the other three as an emu might to three ducks. Every boy band had to have a Phil in it. It was a rule.

'What are we going to do with them?' said Angry. 'We can't keep them down here forever. Eventually somebody is going to come looking for them.'

'Really?' asked Jolly.

Angry thought about it.

'Possibly not,' he said. 'Still, we have to find something for them to do or else we'll just end up with four old people living in our basement who can't sing, smell of cheese, and appear to be made partly of fairy dust.'

There was a soft thud from above them as a copy of the *Biddlecombe Evening Crier* dropped through the letter box.

'Maybe there'll be a job for them in the newspaper,' said Dozy.

'Unky,' said Mumbles.

'You're right,' said Dozy, 'it is highly unlikely, but you never know. Sometimes good things happen to good people.'

'And what about us?' said Angry.

'Sometimes good things happen to us too,' said Dozy, 'although only by mistake. Or through theft.'

They closed the door on the BoyStarz.

'Goodbye, little men,' said a voice. It might have been Starlight's. Nobody knew for certain. They all looked the same.

Except for Phil.

And through the door came the sound of four voices singing loudly, if not terribly well, about how love was like a little man.

The dwarfs sat in Dan's office and thought about their future. It looked bleak.

'This is terrible,' said Jolly. 'We're broke, and we have a talent-free talent agency.'

'Maybe we could sell the BoyStarz into slavery,' said Angry.

'They wouldn't make very good slaves,' said Jolly. 'They're too delicate. Except for Phil.'

He looked at Dan.

'So?' he said. 'Is there by any chance a job for the BoyStarz in the newspaper?'

Dan beamed at him. At last, a bit of good luck.

'No,' he replied, 'but there's a job for all four of you!'

CHAPTER VIII

In Which the Forces of Law and Order Encounter the Forces of Lawlessness and Disorder.

Sergeant Rowan and Constable Peel were enjoying a nice pot of tea and a couple of pea and chutney pies at Pete's Pies. The sun was shining, the pies were good, and all was well with the world.

'Hello, Sergeant,' said a passerby, walking his dog. 'Criminals taking a day off today, are they?'

Sergeant Rowan smiled. When he chose to use it, he had a smile like a fatal gunshot.

'Do you have a licence for that dog?' he said, and the man hurried quickly along.

Constable Peel sipped his tea.

'Do you think criminals actually take days off, Sarge?' said Constable Peel. 'I mean, if they're on holiday and someone leaves a car unlocked or a wallet unattended, do criminals think, no, I'm not stealing that, I'm on my holidays?'

Since he'd been dragged to Hell, and then escaped, Constable Peel had begun to take a philosophical view of life. His philosophy was that any day that didn't involve demons, the undead, or being hauled off to Hell was a good day as far as he was concerned.

'I don't know, Constable, but here comes a criminal. Let's ask him.'

Sergeant Rowan stretched out a hand and gripped a passing dwarf by the collar.

'Bless my soul,' he said. 'If it isn't Mr Jolly Smallpants, off to find something that isn't nailed down.'

'All right, Sergeant Rowan. Always nice to see you,' lied Jolly, his toes almost touching the ground.

'My colleague here was wondering if criminals ever take holidays,' said Sergeant Rowan. 'I thought you might be able to help him with an answer.'

Jolly thought about the question.

'I once stole a yacht. Does that count?'

Sergeant Rowan reminded himself never to shake hands with Jolly Smallpants, or, if he did, to count his fingers afterwards just to make sure that they were all still there.

'When I said "taking" a holiday, I did not mean stealing one,' he said. 'I meant spending time not engaged in criminal behaviour, if you could imagine such a thing.'

'Oh no, Sergeant,' said Jolly. 'If you have a gift, you ought to take it seriously. We're like the law: we never rest. Well, except for you and Constable Peel. You like a rest. And *arrests*.' He chuckled. 'See what I did there?'

'I did,' said Sergeant Rowan, 'and if you do it again I shall drop you on your head. So where were you off to in such a hurry before I felt your collar? Somebody leave a bank vault open? Is there a cow standing in a field with bricks where its legs used to be?'

'No, Sergeant,' said Jolly. 'I'm off to get a job.'

Sergeant Rowan was so shocked that he let Jolly

go, and Constable Peel began choking on a piece of pie until Jolly helped him by slapping him a bit too enthusiastically on the back.

'Thank you,' said Constable Peel, once he could feel his spine again.

'Give him back his whistle, Mr Smallpants,' said Sergeant Rowan sternly.

'Sorry,' said Jolly. 'Force of habit.'

He handed Constable Peel his whistle and, as he was feeling generous, also returned his notebook, his pencil, and his hat.

'You mentioned a job,' said Sergeant Rowan, while Constable Peel tried to store away his belongings until he realised that Jolly had stolen one of his pockets.

'Yes,' said Jolly.

'An honest, paying job?'

Jolly looked slightly ashamed. 'It's only temporary. Desperate times, and all that.'

'And what would this job involve?'

'Christmas elf at Wreckit's,' said Jolly. 'A chance to make children happy, and to lighten the hearts of their parents.'

'Lighten their pockets by stealing their wallets, more like,' said Sergeant Rowan.

'Speaking of pockets . . .' said Constable Peel.

Jolly handed over a scrap of dark blue material.

'Sorry again,' said Jolly. 'Sometimes I don't even know what my own hands are doing.'

At that moment he was joined by Angry, Dozy, Mumbles and Dan, who greeted the two policemen with cheery smiles and the theft of the remains of their pies.

'Don't you lot have a new van?' asked Sergeant Rowan. 'I seem to recall seeing it being delivered yesterday.'

He frowned and tapped a finger to his lips.

'Now what did it say on the side? Was it "Dan's Twits", or "Dan's Thieving Little Gits"? No, wait a minute, don't tell me, it'll come. Ah, I've got it now. "Dan's Sods"! At least you can't be accused of false advertising.'

'Very funny,' said Dozy. 'Cost us a fortune, that van did, and we can't afford new paintwork. How are we supposed to get around now? We only have little legs.'

'It'll just make it harder for you to run away when we come looking for you,' said Sergeant Rowan.

'Why would you be looking for us, Sergeant?' asked Angry.

'Because the last time you lot worked as Christmas elves there were some very nasty incidents, and don't think that I've forgotten about them. That reindeer probably hasn't forgotten about them either.'

'We were just feeding it a carrot,' said Dozy.

'Carrots go in the other end, the mouth end.'

'It was dark in that stable,' said Jolly. 'It wasn't our fault.'

'And then there was the poor bloke playing Father Christmas.'

'We were sure that beard wasn't real,' said Angry. 'I mean, ninety-nine per cent sure. I'd have put money on it.'

'But you didn't put money on it, did you?' said Sergeant Rowan. 'You put *glue* on it. You glued it when he wasn't looking and then asked a child to give it a tug. You thought you'd end up with a small boy with a beard stuck to his hand, but instead you got a Father Chrismas with a small boy stuck to him. Father Christmas had to have his beard cut off, and the kid ended up with hands that looked like the paws of an elderly werewolf.'

'It won't happen again, Sergeant,' said Dan. 'They're changed men.'

'The only thing that will change that lot is Death,' said Sergeant Rowan. 'Even then, they'll probably try to steal his scythe.'

Dan began to hustle the dwarfs along.

'Well, we must be off,' he said. 'We're running late as it is. Good to see you again. Maybe we'll all meet up at the Grand Opening!'

'I can hardly wait,' said Sergeant Rowan.

He turned his chair to face Constable Peel.

'We need to watch them, Constable. We need to watch them like hawks. No, not just like hawks, but like hawks . . . *with binoculars*. We—'

He paused.

'Where's the rest of my pie gone?' he said.

'Sergeant,' began Constable Peel, as an engine started up.

'And my tea. And the teapot!'

The engine was followed by a burst of sirens, but they were quickly silenced.

'Sarge—'

'They've even taken the cups!'

'Sarge!' said Constable Peel with some force.

'What is it?'

'I think they've stolen our car.'

CHAPTER IX

In Which Clever Disguises Are Adopted.

Nurd trudged back to Mrs Johnson's house, his head low. Wormwood had chosen to stay late at the car testing centre. There had been some spectacular crashes that day, and Wormwood liked nothing better than rebuilding crashed cars.

Nurd was wearing a bulky jacket, and a hood covered his head. His hands were plunged deep into his pockets. It looked like rain, but he had decided not to take the bus because taking the bus meant being near people. Even though Nurd's appearance had changed a great deal in his time on Earth, he was still strange enough to attract startled glances from passers-by and fellow passengers. Small children sometimes cried at the sight of him, and he had lost count of the number of elderly ladies whom he had caused to faint with fright. It was easier just to walk home, even if it did take him an hour.

Home. Nurd grimaced at the word. Mrs Johnson's house wasn't home. Oh, it was comfortable, and Samuel and his mother did all that they could to make Nurd and Wormwood feel like part of the family, but as time went on Nurd just became more and more aware of how different he was. Earth was better than Hell, but Nurd still didn't belong there, and he didn't think that he ever would.

A bird sang from a nearby tree. Nurd stopped to watch, and listen. The bird took one look at him, let out a startled squawk, and suddenly decided to fly south for the winter, even though it wasn't a migratory bird.

Nurd adjusted his hood until only a tiny circle of his face was visible, and walked on.

Once they had retrieved their car – following a long lecture from Sergeant Rowan to Jolly about the difference between 'borrowing' and 'stealing', which Sergeant Rowan suspected went in one ear and out the other, but not before being relieved of any valuables – the two policemen decided to drive over to Mr Pennyfarthinge's to see what the scientists were up to in their Secret Laboratory That Everybody Knew About. It was part of the Biddlecombe constabulary's weekly routine: pop in, say hello, pretend that the scientists were simply sweet manufacturers working night and day to perfect new types of sherbet, and make sure that they hadn't opened any portals between worlds.

'We should have arrested them for stealing our car,' said Constable Peel as they neared Mr Pennyfarthinge's.

'Some things aren't worth the time or the trouble,' said Sergeant Rowan. 'At least we got it back before they sold it.'

'You're very tolerant of them.'

'Spending time in Hell with people will do that to you.'

'Spending time with them is Hell anyway,' said Constable Peel. 'Spending time with them in Hell was just Hell squared.'

'You know, I think they like you,' said Sergeant Rowan.

Constable Peel couldn't help but feel pleased despite himself.

'What makes you say that, Sarge?'

'Have they burgled you yet?'

'Not that I know of.'

'There you have it. Stands to reason, doesn't it, that they must like you if they haven't burgled your house?'

'I don't think they know where I live.'

'Really? Well, be sure not to tell them, then. You wouldn't want to put temptation in their way.'

They pulled into the yard of Mr Pennyfarthinge's. The factorye – sorry, factory[19] – occupied a big gloomy Victorian monstrosity designed by Hilary Mould. All of Hilary Mould's buildings were gloomy, thought Sergeant Rowan. They might not have started out that way on the plans, but that's how they ended up. Hilary Mould could have designed a Wendy house and made it look like a mortuary. His buildings were the kind of places that were probably advertised in newspapers in the Afterlife:

💀 [19] It reallye is catchinge.

FOR IMMEDIATE OCCUPATION: Building looking
for ghost to haunt it. All Dark Corners, Weird
Carvings, Creaking Doors, Sinister Paintings of
Relatives Of Whom Nobody Speaks, and Secret
Rooms Not Listed On Original Plans entirely intact.
Would suit ghoul, spectre, poltergeist or other
incorporeal entity. Available for eternity, although
shorter leases will be considered. Enquiries to the
wailing, demented spirit of Hilary Mould.

Why Mr Pennyfarthinge had originally chosen a
'Mould' for the location of his business was something
of a mystery, but it had certainly thrived there. Its
success was helped by the fact that Mr Pennyfarthinge
and the mysterious Uncle Dabney were one and the
same person, a detail that only emerged following Mr
Pennyfarthinge's death by gobstopper. The basement
of his factory was found to contain thousands of
boxes of unsold Uncle Dabney products, including
prototypes for some that had not yet been unleashed
on the public: Uncle Dabney's Orange Bombs (which
turned out to be actual bombs, with a hint of orange
essence); Uncle Dabney's Chocolate Bullets (real bullets
covered in rich dark chocolate: not less than fifty per
cent cocoa and fifty per cent gunpowder); and Uncle
Dabney's Nuclear Blast Toffees (of which the less said
the better). There were also samples of Uncle Dabney's
Cough Drops, which caused coughing instead of curing
it, and enough sachets of Uncle Dabney's Flu Powder
to count as a potential epidemic. It was said by some

that the building had driven Mr Pennyfarthinge mad. All things considered, it was a very good thing that the jars of gobstoppers had landed on Mr Pennyfarthinge's head when they did, for who knows what he might have ended up inventing if he hadn't been killed.

None of this, of course, concerned the scientists. They were just happy to find a place that they could rent cheaply, and the sale of sweeties – including the remaining Uncle Dabney products that had not been destroyed or classified as weapons – helped to fund their operations. To ensure that their cover remained intact, they had taken to wearing large beards to disguise their faces, for both Professors Hilbert and Stefan had visited Biddlecombe in the past, and were worried about being spotted by locals. Their assistant, Dorothy, also enjoyed wearing a beard. The scientists were not sure why, and didn't like to ask.

Thus it was that, when Sergeant Rowan and Constable Peel knocked on the side door of the factory, they were greeted by three people wearing false beards, one of whom was clearly a woman. Behind them was Brian, the new tea boy. He was not wearing a beard, which was unfortunate as it might have helped to cover some of his very pale, very frightened face.

To their credit, the policemen did not even blink at the peculiar appearance of the scientists. Sergeant Rowan had learned long ago that, if you started each day expecting people to behave strangely, then you would not be disappointed, surprised, or shocked in any way.

'Hello, er, sweet-makers,' said Sergeant Rowan.

'Hello!' said the three scientists in the excessively

cheery manner of people who have something to hide and are doing their best to make sure that it stays hidden.

'Everything all right here, then?' said the sergeant.

'It's all fine, absolutely fine,' said Professor Stefan.

'Nothing strange going on? No unexplained portals opening? No demons looking to take over the Earth?'

'Ha, ha, ha!' didn't laugh Professor Hilbert. 'Jelly babies don't cause portals to open.'

'Ho, ho, you don't get demons from clove drops,' said Professor Stefan.

'The only strange things here are the shapes of our caramels,' said Dorothy, in a voice that started out high and finished suddenly low, in the manner of a skier plummeting from a mountain.

'And we haven't seen any ghosts!' said Brian.

There was an awkward silence.

'Ghosts?' said Constable Peel.

'Yes,' said Brian, realising his error just a little too late, like a lion tamer entering a lion cage only to find himself wearing a coat made of meat. 'The ghosts that we haven't seen. We haven't seen them. Those ones. Can I go now? I don't feel well.'

Brian went away.

'Has he been drinking?' said Sergeant Rowan.

'No,' said Professor Stefan.

'Do you think he should start? I'd give him a stiff brandy, if I were you, especially if he's *not* seeing ghosts.'

Sergeant Rowan, who was a tall man, leaned over Professor Stefan, who was not tall, so that the professor appeared to be standing in the shadow of a collapsing building.

'Because,' said Sergeant Rowan, 'if I were to hear that innocent sweet manufacturers, who are not – I say absolutely *not* – scientists, were having strange experiences in my town and didn't see fit to tell me then I might get very, very annoyed. Do I make myself clear?'

'Yes, Sergeant,' said Professor Stefan. 'Very clear.'

'Right. We'll be off then. Do keep me posted if you continue not to see ghosts, won't you? Have a nice day sir, and you sir, and you, er, miss.'

'Sir,' said Dorothy.

'Don't,' said Sergeant Rowan, raising a finger in warning. 'Just – don't.'

He and Constable Peel got back in their car, and drove away.

'Ghosts?' said Constable Peel, as Mr Pennyfarthinge's receded into the distance.

'Ghosts,' said Sergeant Rowan.

'It's lucky they're not seeing any, isn't it?'

'Very lucky, Constable.'

'Because, if they were, we'd have to do something, wouldn't we?'

'Indeed we would, Constable.'

'And what would that be, Sarge?'

'We'd have to be afraid, Constable. We'd have to be very afraid.'

CHAPTER X

In Which We Pay a Brief Visit to Hell.

The Mountain of Despair was the tallest peak in Hell. It dominated the landscape of that terrible place in the way that only something really, really terrible can do, given the general terribleness of the place in which it happened to be. Even though no sun shone in Hell, and the skies above were forever darkened by warring thunderclouds, still the Mountain of Despair somehow managed to cast a shadow over everything, if only in the minds of those who were doomed, or damned, to exist there. It was so big that, no matter how far away you might stand, it never appeared any smaller. A lifetime might be spent trying to walk around it without success. A *short* lifetime might be spent trying to climb it, for some very disagreeable creatures lived among its cracks and crevasses, and they were always hungry.

Mind you, there were some inhabitants of Hell who had no objection whatsoever to the looming presence of the Mountain of Despair. It provided employment to those who were content to ensure that the business of running an empire based entirely on evil, misery and general demonic activity proceeded as smoothly as possible. A job, in their view, was a job, and, as with most jobs, you just had to find that perfect balance between doing as little as possible so you didn't get tired, and just enough so that you didn't get fired.

Two such beings were currently guarding the great carved entrance to the mountain. Their names were Brompton and Edgefast. Edgefast was, strictly speaking, simply a disembodied head,[20] and Brompton was about as much use at guarding as a toy dog on wheels, but they had somehow managed to continue to be employed as guards despite their general uselessness. This was because Brompton and Edgefast were members of the Union of Demonic Employees and Tormentors (Guards Branch), which fiercely protected the rights of its members to lean on their spears and nap any time their eyes got a bit heavy; to take tea breaks at unsuitable times, including during battles, invasions, and serious fires; and not to actually guard anything if they thought that it might place their personal safety at risk. All of

---

[20] In the first chapter of *Hell's Bells*, Edgefast was torn limb from limb for daring to question the right of Mrs Abernathy to enter the Mountain of Despair. Once again, if you'd read that book then you'd know all of this already. Look, why don't we just arrange for me to give you a telephone call and I can read the book down the line to you, or maybe I can act it out in your back garden for you and your friends? Or maybe, just maybe, you could go and read *Hell's Bells*, and maybe *The Gates* as well, and then when I mention a name like Edgefast you'll be able to say 'A-ha, that's the bloke who got torn apart by Mrs Abernathy in the last book!', and be very pleased with yourself, instead of forcing me to take time from the important task of telling the new story just so you don't feel left out. You've just kept everyone else waiting, you know. I hope you're happy. And I bet you didn't even buy this book: you probably received it as a gift, or stole it. Frankly, I don't know why I bother.

this made Brompton and Edgefast as hard to fire as a pair of chocolate cannons. The Mountain of Despair could have been stolen from under their noses and broken down to make garden gnomes and, thanks to the union, Brompton and Edgefast would still have been guarding the place where it once stood, in between taking essential naps and tea breaks.

'Quiet today,' said Edgefast.

'Too quiet for my liking,' said Brompton.

'Really?'

Edgefast couldn't help but sound surprised. Brompton was the laziest demon Edgefast had ever met. Brompton could fall over and make hitting the ground look like an effort.

'Nah, only joking,' said Brompton. 'Not quiet enough if you ask me, what with you piping up every few minutes about how quiet it is.'

'Sorry,' said Edgefast.

He'd only said that it was quiet *once*. It wasn't like he kept repeating the word 'quiet' over and over until nobody could remember what silence had been like.

Edgefast's nose was itchy. He'd have scratched it, but he didn't have any arms. It was one of the few problems with not having a body. Still, Brompton was very good about making sure that he had a straw through which to suck his tea, and he usually remembered to pick Edgefast up and take him home when they had finished guarding for the day.

'Would you mind scratching my nose for me?' Edgefast said.

'Oh, it's all about you, isn't it?' said Brompton. 'Me,

me, me, that's all I ever hear. Who made you king, that's what I'd like to know. Must have been when I wasn't looking. All right, your Majesty, I'll scratch your nose for you. There! Happy now?'

Edgefast wasn't, really. He couldn't be, not with the business end of Brompton's spear jammed up one nostril.

''Es bine,' he said. 'Mub bedder, dan gew.'

Brompton withdrew the spear and went back to leaning on it and staring glumly over the blasted landscape of Hell.

'Sorry,' he said. 'Trouble at home.'

'Mrs Brompton?' said Edgefast.

Brompton and Mrs Brompton had a difficult marriage. There were fatal diseases that had better relationships with their victims than Brompton had with Mrs Brompton.

'Yeah.'

'She move out again?'

'No, she moved back in.'

'Oh.'

There was silence for a time.

'I thought you were going to leave her,' said Edgefast.

'I did.'

'What happened?'

'She came with me.'

'Oh,' said Edgefast for a second time. There wasn't much else to say. Brompton always seemed to be unhappy with Mrs Brompton. The trouble was, he was even unhappier *without* Mrs Brompton.

'She'd be lost without you, you know,' said Edgefast.

'Nah, I tried that,' said Brompton. 'She found her way back.'

'Oh,' said Edgefast, for the third time, followed by 'Oh?' and then 'Oh-Oh!'

Crudford manifested himself directly in front of the two guards with a sound like a plate of jelly being dropped on a stone floor. He raised his hat with his left hand and said 'Evening, gentlemen.' Under his right arm he carried a jar, and in the jar a mass of blue atoms seethed and roiled, slowly forming something that became, as he drew closer to Edgefast, a single hostile eye surrounded by pale, bruised skin. The eye seemed to glare at Edgefast, who would have taken a step back if it hadn't been for his shortcomings in the leg department. Edgefast had clear memories of that eye. It had looked at him in a similar way just moments before some very sharp bits of the body to which it was then attached had ripped him apart.

Crudford put his hat back on his head, and patted the jar the way one might pat the comfortable carrying case of a beloved pet.

'Here we are, ma'am,' he said. 'It's nice to be back, isn't it?'

The Great Malevolence, the monstrous fount of all evil, sat in its lair of fire and stone at the heart of the Mountain of Despair, the flames reflected in its eyes so that it seemed almost to be burning from within. It had cast aside its armour for now, and set aside its shield of skulls and its burning spear. The great twisted crown of bone that grew from its head glowed red from the heat of the infernos that surrounded it. Its monstrous body, scarred and burned, lay slumped on its throne.

The throne was a massive construct of bones that twisted and tangled like pale branches and yellowed vines. There was no comfort to the throne, but that was as the Great Malevolence preferred: it never wanted to grow used to its banishment in Hell, and never wished to find a moment's peace there. It had come into existence milliseconds after the birth of the Multiverse, a force for destruction born out of the creation of worlds. It could, it supposed, have become an agent for good, but it was a jealous being, an angry being, and it had fought against all that was fine and noble in the Multiverse until at last a force greater than itself had grown tired of its evil. The Great Malevolence was cast down to Hell for eternity, and it had conspired to free itself ever since. It had almost succeeded too, but its plans had been spoiled by the boy named Samuel Johnson and his dog, Boswell.

The Great Malevolence had also lost its lieutenant, the demon Ba'al. It was Ba'al who had led the invasion of Earth, occupying the body of a woman named Mrs Abernathy and then, for reasons unclear, deciding that being a woman was altogether nicer than being a demon. When the invasion failed, the Great Malevolence chose to blame Mrs Abernathy, and she was banished from its presence. When she had tried to get back in its good books by opening another portal to Earth, Samuel Johnson had intervened again, and that was when all of the atoms in Mrs Abernathy's body had been separated from their neighbours and scattered throughout the Multiverse.

The Great Malevolence was a being filled with self-pity. It now regretted banishing Mrs Abernathy, not because of any hurt that it might have caused her, but because she had been useful and loyal, and the Great Malevolence's strength was reduced without her.[21] This was why it had ordered the creature named Crudford to find all of the pieces of her and bring them back to Hell so that she might be reassembled. Crudford wasn't much to look at but, like many creatures that appear humble and insignificant, Crudford had turned out to be far more important and gifted than he had first appeared.

Now Crudford oozed into the Great Malevolence's presence and added the eyeball in the jar to the other

---

[21] This is the curse of kings. While you or I might get annoyed with our friends on occasion, we tend not to order their execution simply because they've trodden on our toes or, if we do, people ignore us, which is usually for the best. The trouble with being a king is that, when you lose your temper with someone and order his head to be lopped off, a bloke appears with an axe and promptly does the deed, or someone drops a noose around his neck and – well, you get the picture. Then later, when the king announces that he misses old What's-His-Name and wonders where on earth he's got to because he was always good for a laugh, a courtier has to go through the awkward business of explaining that old What's-His-Name is unlikely to be cracking jokes any time in the near, or distant, future owing to his definite deadness. Henry VIII, for example, who was king of England from 1509 to 1547, ended his days surrounded by a great many young people for the simple reason that he'd had most of his old courtiers exiled or executed. Between the years 1532 and 1540 alone, Henry ordered 330 political executions, probably more than any other ruler in British history. If you worked for Henry VIII then you really didn't need to worry about putting money into your pension fund as you probably wouldn't live long enough to spend it.

body parts that were currently lined up on a stone platform in the throne room. Crudford had been summoned to the Great Malevolence's presence to detail his progress in tracking down the billions of atoms of Mrs Abernathy's being. Crudford was feeling nervous about this. He thought he'd done well in finding as many bits as he had so far. It was no easy business oozing between universes looking for tiny blue atoms. You needed a steady hand, and a good eye, and a lot of luck. On the other hand, the Great Malevolence wasn't very keen on listening to excuses, and it had a habit of tossing those who displeased it into bottomless pits, or leaving them to freeze in the great Lake of Cocytus.

'Afternoon, your Virulence,' said Crudford, lifting his hat in greeting. 'Nice day out there. Not too chilly.'

The Great Malevolence's voice boomed through the chamber. It made dust and pebbles and the occasional napping demon fall from the walls. Its voice really had a rumble to it.

'Show me what you have found,' it said.

It towered above Crudford, and the little gelatinous being felt himself grow cold in the Great Malevolence's shadow.

'Well,' said Crudford, 'we've made some progress, your Unpleasantness.'

He began to move down the line of jars, pointing a gloopy finger at each one in turn.

'This here's an eye, as you can see – and, I suppose, as it can see too, ho-ho. This one's half a pancreas. That looks like a bit of an ear. That one—'

Crudford paused and squinted. He tapped the jar, as if hoping that the atoms might rearrange themselves and give him a clue. They didn't.

'To be honest, I'm not sure what that is, so we'll just leave it for now and ooze along,' he said. 'That's a finger. This is three-quarters of a lung. In there we have part of a lip, and most of a lower jaw. This one here – actually, you don't even want to know what that is. Seriously, you don't. Over here we have . . .'

This went on for some time. When Crudford was finished, the Great Malevolence didn't exactly seem pleased, but the fact that Crudford was still in one piece meant that the Great Malevolence wasn't displeased either.

'How much longer before you find the rest of her?' it asked. 'I want my lieutenant restored to me.'

'Hard to say,' said Crudford.

'It will be harder to say if I freeze you, or feed you to the imps,' said the Great Malevolence.

'Good point,' said Crudford. 'I'll work doubly fast.'

Crudford was about to say something more, but decided against it. The Great Malevolence made a few more threats, and warned of the harm that would come to Crudford if he didn't find the rest of Mrs Abernathy soon. Crudford wasn't offended. The Great Malevolence was just letting off steam. Anyway, Crudford was the only one who could find Mrs Abernathy's atoms. The Great Malevolence couldn't do him any harm: if it did, then it would never get its lieutenant back.

But the search was harder than Crudford had anticipated, and each time he found some of Mrs

Abernathy's atoms he detected hatred in them. It was almost as if Mrs Abernathy didn't *want* to be found. That was what he had almost told the Great Malevolence before good sense made him stay silent. The Great Malevolence didn't need to hear that, just as it didn't want to hear about the beating, somewhere in the Multiverse, of what Crudford was certain was Mrs Abernathy's heart.

Because Mrs Abernathy wasn't supposed to *have* a heart.

CHAPTER XI

In Which We Learn Why People Should Just Call Their Children Simple Names like Jane or John – Especially John, Which is a Very Good Name. Manly. Heroic, Even.

The interior of Wreckit & Sons was still in the process of being redesigned, but Dan and the dwarfs could see that it was going to be pretty spectacular when it was finished. Already some of the displays had been set up: there was a giant teddy bear at least twenty feet high that dominated the cuddly toy section, and a train set that followed a circular track suspended from the ceiling of the second floor. There were dolls piled in corners, and toy soldiers, and cars and trucks and spaceships. There were board games, and a sports section, and books. What there didn't seem to be, Jolly noticed, were any computer games. Walking into Wreckit & Sons was like stepping back in time.

'It's not going to last a week, never mind until Christmas,' said Angry. 'Where are all the PlayStations and things?'

'Somebody should tell them that electricity has been invented,' said Dozy. 'It might come as a shock, but they'll be glad to know.'

In addition to the missing games consoles, Dan and the dwarfs could see no sign of any workers.

'I have a funny feeling that I'm being watched,' said Jolly. 'I was thinking of nicking something, just to keep my hand in, but I don't think I will after all.'

They all shared his uneasy sense of being under surveillance, although they could see no sign of cameras or security guards. There was no sign of anyone at all. They had arrived at the side entrance, just as a message had instructed them to do after Dan had called the number at the bottom of the advertisement. There they found the door unlocked and a handwritten note instructing them to proceed to the top floor via the main stairs.

It was Mumbles who caught a flash of movement in a corner as they neared the final flight of steps.

'Oberare!' he said.

He walked warily to the corner. There was a small hole at the base of the wall. He knelt and peered into it. He had the uncomfortable sensation that, from the darkness behind the wall, something was peering back at him.

'What is it?' said Angry.

'Umsall,' said Mumbles.

'Small?' said Angry. 'It was probably a rat. These old buildings are full of rats.'

But Mumbles didn't think it was a rat. He had only caught the slightest glimpse of it as it fled, but it had looked like a very small person.

If he hadn't known better, Mumbles might even have said it was an elf.

* * *

The dwarfs were stunned into silence when they reached the top floor. The entire space was in the process of being transformed into the most spectacular of Christmas grottoes. Frost glittered on the trunks and branches of the immense silver trees supporting the ceiling, and a pathway that felt like marble wound over the floor while snow fell from above.

'It melts,' whispered Dozy. 'When it touches your skin, it melts!'

And it did.

Somehow, the entire area had been lit so that it looked bigger than it was. It was like being in some great northern forest in the depths of winter. It even *felt* cold. As they progressed through it, the dwarfs saw the shapes of reindeer passing by. They appeared so real that the dwarfs could almost have reached out and touched them, running their fingers through the deer's fur.

At the heart of the forest was a cabin made not of logs but of old stones. Smoke poured from its chimney and was lost in the darkness above, which glimmered with stars. Looking up, Jolly had the sense of being just one small person on one small planet in a vast, icy universe. It made him vaguely depressed so he went back to looking at the cabin instead.

Angry was testing the stones with his hand.

'This cabin must weigh a ton,' he said. 'What's underneath it?'

Dozy tried to remember the floor plan of the store. 'I think it was more soft toys. I could go and check.'

'Well, I wouldn't hang about down there if I were you,' said Angry. 'If this thing falls through the floor it won't be just the toys that are soft. It'll reduce little kids to jelly.'

A man appeared from a doorway to their right. He wore a black three-piece suit with a grey tie and a slightly soiled white shirt. His face was blankly pleasant, like a greetings card without a personal message inside.

'Gentlemen,' he said. 'Can I help you?'

Jolly looked at the note in his hand.

'We're here to see Mr Cholmondeley,' said Jolly.

'Chumley,' said the gentleman, his expression unchanged.

Jolly examined the note again.

'No, it's definitely Cholmondeley.'

He handed it to Angry to check.

'That's it,' said Angry. 'Cholmondeley. It's here in black and white.'

'It's *Chumley*,' said the man. A small frown line had appeared on his forehead.

'Listen, mate,' said Angry, 'are you saying we can't read?'

'Not at all. The name is simply pronounced "Chumley".'

'Then why is it spelled "Cholmondeley"?' asked Jolly.

'It just is,' said the man.

'Well, that's nonsense,' said Angry. 'That's like spelling a name S-M-I-T-H and calling yourself Jones.'

'No,' said the man, with some force, 'it isn't.'

'Yes,' said Angry, with equal force, 'it is.'

It was left to Dan to intervene.

'It's a posh thing,' he explained to the dwarfs.

'Oooooh,' they said in unison, nodding in understanding. Posh people did things differently. Everybody knew that. Jolly had heard that posh people were born with silver spoons in their mouths, which probably explained why they all talked funny.

'Right you are then, guv,' said Jolly. 'We're here to see Mr *Chumley*. Mr Saint John Chumley.'

'Sinjin,' said the man.

'Bless you,' said Jolly.

'No, I didn't sneeze,' said the man. 'It's Sinjin.'

'Beg pardon?' said Jolly.

By now the man had started to look decidedly irritated.

'It's my name!' he said. 'It's Sinjin-Chumley. How hard can it be?'

The dwarfs crowded around Jolly, and all four of them examined the name on the note, running their fingers beneath it, pronouncing the syllables and occasionally glancing up at the gentleman standing before them as though trying to equate his name with the peculiar jumble of letters before them.

'Actually, pretty hard,' said Angry at last. 'You might need to have a think about that one. Don't take this the wrong way, mate, but you'll never get anywhere in life if you have a made-up name that doesn't sound the way it's spelled. You'd better hang on to this job. If you lose it, you'll never get another. It's always easier to hire someone whose name you can say without hurting your tongue.'

Mr St John-Cholmondeley gave Angry a hard stare.

'I take it that you're here about the job,' he said, in the tone of a man who is hoping that he might be mistaken.

'We were "invited to attend for an interview",' said Jolly.

'Indeed. Well, do come in. It shouldn't take long.'

Mr St John-Cholmondeley stepped aside to admit the dwarfs into his office. It was small, and contained only a desk and a chair. The shelves were entirely bare, and there was nothing on the desk except for a single sheet of white paper, a pen, and a small, sad-looking artificial Christmas tree with a red button on its base. Angry, who couldn't resist a red button when he saw one, pressed it. Immediately the tree began to bob from side to side and 'Jingle Bells' emerged from a hidden speaker.

'What language is that?' asked Angry.

'I'm not sure,' said Mr St John-Cholmondeley. 'I think it might be Urdu, or possibly Serbo-Croat. It's difficult to tell. We found a box of them in storage when we began fixing up the shop.'

'Do you think they're going to be big sellers?' asked Dozy doubtfully.

'Possibly if the shop was situated in a country that spoke Urdu or Serbo-Croat,' said Mr St John-Cholmondeley. 'Otherwise, probably not. I do wish you hadn't turned it on, though. It takes a while for it to finish the song.'

They all tried to ignore the tree as the interview began.

'Now, which job might you be applying for?' said Mr St John-Cholmondeley.

The dwarfs exchanged looks. They were in a toyshop. It was coming up to Christmas. The shop had a

Christmas grotto. They were hardly here to audition for roles as Easter bunnies.

'Elves,' said Jolly. 'We're here to be elves.'

'Not Father Christmas?' said Mr St John-Cholmondeley.

'No.'

'You're sure?'

'Are you trying to be clever?' asked Jolly.

'Not at all,' said Mr St John-Cholmondeley. 'I can't just assume that because you're gentlemen of, er, reduced stature you're only here to be elves. That would be wrong. It's all equal opportunities now, you know. I could get into terrible trouble for saying to you, "Oh, you must be here about the elf job, then." I could end up in court.'

'But we *are* here about the elf job,' said Angry.

'Wouldn't you at least like to think about being Father Christmas?' said Mr St John-Cholmondeley.

'No.'

'Why not?'

'Because we want to be elves. We're the right size for elves. It's not, if you'll forgive the pun, much of a stretch for us.'

'Well, I have to offer you the chance to apply for the job of Father Christmas. It's the rules.'

'We don't want to be Father Christmas.'

'You're sure?'

'Yes.'

'Wouldn't you like to try one little "Ho-Ho-Ho!", just a teeny one?'

'No!' said Jolly. 'We want to be elves.'

Mr St John-Cholmondeley scowled at him.

'What's wrong with being Father Christmas? Don't you like fat people?'

'What?' said Jolly.

He was confused. Beside him, the singing Christmas tree continued to sing. It seemed to know a lot more verses to 'Jingle Bells' than Jolly did.

'Are you saying you don't want to be Father Christmas because he's fat?' Mr St John-Cholmondeley persisted. 'Are you fattist? You know, we can't have people working here who are fattist. We won't put up with that kind of thing, do you hear? We won't put up with it at all. How dare you come into this store and say unpleasant things about fat people!'

'But—' said Jolly.

'Don't you dare go making excuses! You should be ashamed of yourselves. I've a good mind to call the police.'

Angry stared very intently at Mr St John-Cholmondeley. The singing Christmas tree continued to chirp away merrily. Angry was starting to hate it.

'Excuse me,' he said, 'but are you a mad bloke?'

'Oh, and I suppose you don't like them either!' said Mr St John-Cholmondeley. 'What if I was fat *and* mad, eh? What then? I suppose you'd come after me with pitchforks and flaming torches. You'd want me hidden away from sight, locked up in a cell somewhere with only bread and water!'

'Locked up might be a start,' muttered Angry.

'I heard that!' said Mr St John-Cholmondeley. 'Don't think I didn't!'

He opened a drawer in his desk, removed a hammer,

and brought it down hard on the Christmas tree. While the dwarfs watched, he continued hammering at the tree until it was reduced to little shards of green plastic. From somewhere in its workings, a final faint tinkle of bells could be heard before the tree expired. Mr St John-Cholmondeley moved a bin into place with his left foot and used his right hand to sweep the remains of the Christmas tree into it. They fell on the remains of lots of other Christmas trees. From what Angry could see, the bin contained nothing else.

Mr St John-Cholmondeley restored the hammer to its drawer, opened another drawer, and took a Christmas tree from it. He positioned it in precisely the same place occupied by the previous tree.

'Right,' said Mr St John-Cholmondeley. He smiled. 'Where were we?'

There was a long, careful silence.

'A job?' said Jolly. 'For us?'

'Of course! Elves, by any chance?'

'Er, if you like.'

'Oh, fine by me. You seem just the sorts. Very festive. Very *small*. We like our elves small. Doesn't work if they're big. Doesn't work at all. This week good for you to start? Nine until six on regular days, an hour for lunch, two tea breaks of not more than fifteen minutes each, although for the grand opening on Thursday you don't have to get here until sixish. Don't eat too many biscuits: they'll make you fat, and we don't want that, do we? Fine for Father Christmas, but bad for elves. Bad, bad, bad! Sign there.'

He pushed the pen and blank sheet of paper towards them.

'There's nothing on it,' said Dan.

'Doesn't matter,' said Mr St John-Cholmondeley. 'All friends here.'

'What about money?' said Jolly.

'Oh, I don't take bribes,' said Mr St John-Cholmondeley. 'That would be wrong.'

He leaned forward, placed a hand against his face, and whispered secretively.

'And you're supposed to offer me the bribe *before* you get the job,' he said. 'Doesn't work otherwise. Bear it in mind for next time, eh?'

'Er, no, I meant that we do get paid, don't we?'

'Oh! I *see*! Ha! Forget about the bribe stuff, then. Only joking. Our secret, eh? Yes, money. How much would you like? A lot? A little? How about something in between? What about ten pounds an hour?'

'That sounds—' Jolly began to say, when Mr St John-Cholmondeley interrupted him.

'OK, eleven.'

'What?'

'Twelve, but you drive a hard bargain.'

'I think—'

Mr St John-Cholmondeley puffed his cheeks and wiped his brow.

'Thirteen, then, but that's my final offer.'

'If you're—'

'Fourteen, but you're robbing me, ho, ho! You're stealing me blind!'

The dwarfs had no problem stealing anybody blind,

but on this occasion they weren't even trying. It bothered them. It didn't seem fair somehow.

'Listen,' said Angry, but Mr St John-Cholmondeley was too quick for him.

'Fifteen,' he said. 'That's it. I can't go any higher than sixteen. Seventeen's my last and final offer. Absolutely. Eighteen it is.'

Angry reached for the pen. Mr St John-Cholmondeley grabbed it before he could get to it.

'Nineteen!' he said. 'We need elves!'

'Give me the pen,' said Angry. 'Please.'

Mr St John-Cholmondeley burst into tears and buried his face in his hands.

'All right then, twenty,' he said, in a muffled voice. 'Twenty-one pounds an hour, but you'll be making more than I am.'

The dwarfs eventually managed to sign for twenty-five, but it was a struggle, and two of them had to hold on to Mr St John Cholmondeley's arms while the others wrestled the pen from him. They left him in his office, and closed the door behind them. From inside came the sound of 'Jingle Bells' in a foreign language, followed almost immediately by an intense burst of hammering.

Nobody came to show Dan and the dwarfs out of the store. They had to find their own way back to the street, and they were so troubled by their encounter with Mr St John-Cholmondeley that only later did they notice that, throughout the course of their meeting with him, he had not blinked once.

*　*　*

Mr St John-Cholmondeley sat back in his chair. He was very relieved that the dwarfs were gone.

'I think that went well,' he said to the Voice in the Wall. 'I don't believe they suspected a thing. I acted entirely normal.'

Twenty-five pounds an hour, said the Voice in the Wall. *Do you think I'm made of money?*

Mr St John-Cholmondeley shook his head. Whatever the Voice in the Wall was made of, it wasn't money. Money didn't smell that foul.

'They were tough little negotiators,' said Mr St John-Cholmondeley. 'Very tough indeed. They wore me down.'

They won't live long enough to collect a penny of it, said the Voice in the Wall. *Still, it's the principle.*

'I'll be more careful in future,' said Mr St John-Cholmondeley.

That's nice, said the Voice in the Wall, and Mr St John-Cholmondeley, who couldn't remember his past, failed to hear in its tones the sound of his very short future coming to an unhappy end.

CHAPTER XII

In Which Invitations are Received.

The invitations began to arrive in the days before the grand opening of Wreckit & Sons. Samuel received one, with a special note informing him that, as the hero who had saved Biddlecombe and the Earth from a demonic invasion, he would be a guest-of-honour. He was also warmly requested to bring the courageous Boswell along with him. The note was signed by Mr St John-Cholmondeley on behalf of the new owner, a mysterious Mr Grimly.

'That's very nice of him, isn't it?' said Samuel's mother as she examined the note. 'And look at that invitation! It's printed on ever such expensive card, and the handwriting is so lovely. It's odd that it's written in red ink, though, isn't it? You'd think they'd have used black, or blue. Maybe they thought it was festive in red.'

The invitation made Samuel uneasy for reasons he couldn't quite pin down. Perhaps it was the fact that Boswell took one sniff and decided he didn't care for it at all, or that the ink didn't look much like ink. It looked, to be honest, a bit like blood, and Samuel told his mother as much.

'Don't be silly,' said Mrs Johnson. 'You always see the worst in things.'

'Fighting demons and being dragged off to Hell will do that to a person, Mum,' said Samuel.

'Oh, hush,' said Mrs Johnson, who didn't like being reminded of the unpleasantnesses that had befallen her son, even if she did have two demons living in her spare room and making funny smells in the bathroom. She had decided to look upon Nurd and Wormwood as a pair of slightly eccentric lodgers, and leave it at that.

'Anyway,' Mrs Johnson continued, 'it's about time you got some recognition for all that you've done for this town. They should have put up a statue of you, if you ask me.'

In addition to the wandering statue of Hilary Mould, Biddlecombe only had one other such monument, and that was of Brigadier General Sir Charles MacCarthy, the hopeless nineteenth-century British commander, who, while on his way to be knighted in 1820, had stopped for tea in Biddlecombe and left a small tip.[22] It was often suggested that the town needed another statue or two, although this suggestion usually came from mayors or local politicians, who seemed to think

---

[22] Somebody should really have given Sir Charles himself a tip, namely, don't go into battle with only 500 men against 10,000 spear-wielding natives, which is what MacCarthy did in 1824 when he was governor of the Gold Coast in Africa. MacCarthy ordered his men to play 'God Save the King' in the hope that it might scare the natives away. It didn't. The natives attacked and MacCarthy's force was almost entirely wiped out, not helped by the fact that they had accidentally brought macaroni with them instead of spare ammunition. MacCarthy's heart was eaten by the victorious natives, and they kept his head as a souvenir, displaying it on special occasions and holidays.

it would be a good idea if the statue looked a bit like them, and maybe had their name carved underneath.

'I don't want a statue in my honour, thanks,' said Samuel. He could think of nothing worse than having a bronze version of himself providing a convenient head on which pigeons could poo. Life was hard enough as it was.

A thumping sound came from above, and moments later Nurd and Wormwood appeared in the kitchen. They were very excited. Samuel could tell because Wormwood had somehow set himself on fire and hadn't noticed, and the fire had spread to Nurd's coat but he hadn't noticed either. Samuel discreetly put out the flames with a damp tea towel and waited to find out what was going on.

'We've received an invitation,' said Nurd.

'To the opening of the new toyshop in the town,' said Wormwood.

He was positively glowing, which was probably how the fire had started. Wormwood had recently developed an unfortunate habit of bursting into flame when he got angry or embarrassed, or even if he coughed for too long. He would turn bright red, and the next minute you could toast bread on him.

Wormwood had never been invited anywhere before, unless you counted being invited outside for a fight, or to make a room smell better by his absence. Even Nurd had rarely received invitations to events, largely because he had spent billions of years going through a phase of wanting to rule worlds, and nobody wants to invite someone to a party only to find that he's declared himself king of their house and is now trying on their slippers for size.

'That's very peculiar,' said Samuel.

He examined the invitation that the demons had been sent. It was addressed to Mr Cushing and Mr Lee, the names under which Nurd and Wormwood were living in Biddlecombe. Only a handful of people knew that Nurd and Wormwood weren't exactly human: even most of their employers at the Biddlecombe Vehicle Testing Centre just regarded Nurd as unusually fire-proof, and quite bendy.[23]

'Why is it peculiar?' asked Wormwood. 'We're good company!'

He thought for a moment.

'Well, we might be, if there was nobody else in the room.'

'It's peculiar,' said Samuel, 'because, as far as most of Biddlecombe is concerned, you're just two odd-looking men who happen to be living with us. You haven't been drawing attention to yourselves, have you?'

'No,' said Nurd. 'Wormwood's been drawing flies, but that's nothing new.'

---

[23] Similarly, only old Mr Spiggit, the founder of Spiggit's Brewery, Chemical Weapons & Industrial Cleaning Products Ltd., knew that Shan and Gath, the chief brewers in his Dangerously Experimental Drinks Department (DEDD), were pig demons. Everybody else just thought they were two big blokes who had drunk too many of their own brews, since the list of side effects caused by sampling Spiggit's Old Peculiar on a regular basis included massive weight gain, hairy palms, moulting, and unusual beard growth.

And that was just what it did to women.

To the list could be added speech difficulties, tooth loss, tooth *growth*, and explosive wind. Basically, it was Shan and Gath in a nutshell.

'I like to think of them as pets,' said Wormwood. 'And, sometimes, as snacks.'

Mrs Johnson felt ill, but said nothing.

'So why would this Mr Grimly invite you two to the opening of his new shop?' asked Samuel.

It was only after he had asked the question that he realised how unkind it sounded. He hadn't meant it that way. He had been thinking aloud. But now he could see the hurt in Nurd's eyes, and even Wormwood, who was harder to offend than a dead person, looked a little pained. Nurd snatched the invitation back from Samuel.

'Why wouldn't he invite us?' said Nurd. 'We're nice.'

'No, you're not,' said Wormwood.

'And we work hard.'

'No, you don't.'

'And we— Whose side are you on, anyway?' he asked Wormwood.

'Sorry,' said Wormwood. 'Force of habit.'

'I didn't mean it that way,' said Samuel. 'It's just that Mr Grimly shouldn't have heard of you. We don't *want* people to hear about you, because if the wrong kind of people know about you then there'll be all sorts of trouble, and they might take you away. Don't you understand?'

Nurd's shoulders sagged. He wanted to argue, but he couldn't. Samuel was right.

'Yes,' he said, 'I understand.'

'I don't,' said Wormwood. 'But then, I never do.'

'I'll explain later,' said Nurd.

He placed a consoling hand on Wormwood's shoulder,

then looked for somewhere to wipe his fingers. Mrs Johnson gave him a cloth.

'It doesn't matter,' said Nurd. 'Honestly, it doesn't. But just for a while, it felt like we were part of something.'

'You are part of something,' said Samuel. 'You're part of our family. Right, Mum?'

Mrs Johnson didn't answer immediately.

'*Mum?*' urged Samuel.

'Yes, yes, of course they are,' said Mrs Johnson, under pressure. 'I'll just tell people they're from your dad's side.'

Nurd tried to smile, but couldn't quite manage it. He took one last look at the invitation, then tore it up and threw it in the bin.

'Let's go upstairs, Wormwood,' he said. 'You can entertain me by making unusual smells.'

They left the kitchen. When they were gone, Mrs Johnson turned to Samuel.

'He has a point, you know,' she said. 'We can't keep them cooped up in here forever when they're not working. If they're going to stay in this world, they have to find their place in it. I don't mean a physical place: they'll always have a home here, even if I do sometimes wonder what Wormwood does in the bathroom, because he certainly isn't washing, or if he is, then it isn't working. No, what I mean is that they need to be happy in it, and to be happy they have to discover what makes them happy. Maybe you should let them go with you to Wreckit's. They'll have a lovely time, and it will help them. I'm sure of it.'

Samuel nodded. 'I suppose you're right.'

'Go on,' said Mrs Johnson. 'Bring them back up their invitation, and tell them to think about what they're going to wear. Now, I'm late for bingo.'

She went into the hallway, grabbed her coat, and rushed out of the door. Samuel knelt by the bin and prepared to fish out the pieces of the torn invitation, but they weren't there.

The invitation had vanished.

CHAPTER XIII

**In Which We Learn That Hilary Mould May
Have Been Even Odder Than First Suspected.**

Samuel knocked on the door of the bedroom shared
by Nurd and Wormwood and waited until Nurd's voice
gave him permission to come in. Samuel was very
conscious of giving Nurd and Wormwood as much
privacy and space as he could. The little bedroom was
their home within the home, although they hadn't done
much to change it apart from putting up a few posters
on the walls. Nurd had opted for pictures of ancient
monuments in far-off countries: the pyramids of Egypt,
the temple complex of Angkor Wat in Cambodia,
and the Inca site of Machu Picchu in Peru. Wormwood,
by contrast, preferred pictures of terrible boy bands.
He even had a signed poster of BoyStarz, given to him
by Dan and the dwarfs. According to Dan, there were
plenty more posters where that came from. Hundreds.
Thousands.

Nurd was lying on the top bunk, flicking through the
travel supplement from one of the weekend newspapers.
Wormwood was listening to music on his headphones. It
was loud enough for Samuel to be able to hear some of
the words: something about how love was like a garden,

or a rosebush, or a snail. Whatever it was, it sounded dreadful, but Samuel said nothing. It made Wormwood happy, which was all that mattered. As if to confirm this, Wormwood gave Samuel a smile and a big thumbs-up. Samuel waved back and climbed the ladder on the bunks so that he could speak face to face with Nurd.

'Is everything all right?' asked Samuel.

'Everything's fine,' said Nurd, although his expression suggested the opposite was true.

'It's just that you don't seem to be yourself lately,' said Samuel. 'I'm worried about you.'

Faced with Samuel's obvious concern, Nurd put the travel section away.

'That's just it,' he said. 'I'm not sure what being myself means anymore. When I was in Hell, I was Nurd, the Scourge of Five Deities. I wasn't very important. I wasn't important at all, really, but I had a name, and I knew my place, even if it wasn't a very nice one. But here on Earth I live under a false name, and I have to hide my face. I crash cars for a living. Don't get me wrong, I like crashing cars, or I used to, but there's only so many times that you can crash a car and survive a fireball before it starts to get a bit samey.'[24]

'What can I do to help?' said Samuel.

'Nothing,' said Nurd. 'It's not your fault. It's just me, that's all. I'll figure something out.'

💀 [24] No matter how great your job is, there will be days when you might wish that you were doing something else. Everybody feels the need to have a bit of a moan once in a while. Your job could be knocking balls through the windows of buildings and every so often you'd still feel the urge to complain that your arm was tired.

Samuel wasn't convinced, but he didn't know how to make life better for Nurd. If he'd had money, he'd have given it to Nurd so that he could travel and see a bit more of the world, but Samuel and his mum were barely making ends meet as it was, even with the wages that Nurd and Wormwood earned from testing cars.

'Look,' said Samuel, 'maybe you should come along to the opening of the toy shop after all. It'll do you good.'

Nurd shook his head.

'No, what you said downstairs was right. We shouldn't attract any more attention to ourselves, and we wouldn't want to frighten anyone.'

He picked up his travel section again. On the cover, a young couple smiled in front of the Taj Mahal in India.

'I'm sorry,' said Samuel, as he climbed down from the bunk. 'I thought you'd be happy here.'

'I am happy,' said Nurd. 'I just wish I was . . . happier.'[25]

Maria, accompanied by Tom, came round to Samuel's house later that evening. Samuel showed the invitation to them, and they were both impressed.

'Maybe if we keep hanging around with you, some of your celebrity will rub off on us and we'll get invited to openings too,' said Tom.

'Well, can you keep rubbing, then,' said Samuel, 'because I don't want to be a celebrity at all.'

'Still, it's nice to be asked,' said Tom. 'I mean, if the only reward for being famous was being chased by

---

☠ [25] **Which is, in a nutshell, the story of life.**

demons and dragged off to Hell every so often, then it really wouldn't be worth being famous at all, would it? Are you going to bring someone along with you? I'd go, but my mum and dad are keeping me out of school that day so we can visit my gran in Liverpool.'

'I expect Lucy will want to go,' said Samuel.

Maria winced, but said nothing. The nature of her friendship with Samuel had changed a lot since Samuel had started seeing Lucy Highmore. Lucy didn't like Maria, and Maria certainly didn't like Lucy, so when Samuel was with Lucy he couldn't be with Maria, and even when he was with Maria without Lucy there was now a certain chill between them. Samuel wondered if it was always that way when a group of friends had to deal with the fact that one of them now had a girlfriend or boyfriend. He wished there was somebody he could ask about it, but the person he would usually have asked was Maria. There was no point in asking Tom: Tom was as close to being married to the rest of the rugby First Fifteen as it was possible to be without them all exchanging rings and sprinkling confetti on one another.

'Since we're all here,' said Maria, 'we may as well get some work done on our project.'

Tom groaned.

'I *hate* this project. I have to look at old buildings and try to find something to say about them other than that they're a bit gloomy and should probably have been demolished a long time ago. Yesterday I nearly got knocked out by a piece of brick that dropped off one of them. I'm lucky to be alive. Whose idea was it to write about Hilary Mould anyway?'

'It was *mine*,' said Maria icily. 'And you really will be lucky to stay alive if you don't stop complaining. We either studied the Mould buildings or spent our Saturdays wandering around shopping centres counting shoe shops. At least Mould is interesting.'

'Only if you're a depressed pigeon with no friends,' said Tom. 'And then there's that business with his statue.'

They all agreed that the statue was odd. Nobody ever saw it moving around. It would be in one place for an hour, or a day, or a week, and then it would be somewhere else. Some weeks earlier, Maria had suggested that their science class should do a study of the statue, but Mr Lugosi, the science teacher, didn't believe it was a good idea.

'Who knows what might happen if we start paying attention to it?' he said, a statement which led Maria to suspect that Mr Lugosi wasn't really cut out to teach science.

'Perhaps it's a quantum statue,' Tom had suggested, 'so that it's in every possible place in Biddlecombe until someone observes it.'

'Very clever, Hobbes,' said Mr Lugosi, 'except that the statue appears to have only six known preferred locations.'

'Sir?' called Mooch, who always sat at the back of the class and walked with a slight stoop, as though auditioning for the role of bellringer in an old cathedral.

'Yes, Mooch?'

'Seven, sir.'

'Seven what?'

'Seven places the statue seems to prefer.'

'Why do you say that, Mooch?'

'Sir, it's outside the window.'

And it was.

'Don't look at it,' said Mr Lugosi. 'Ignore it and it will go away.'

Everybody ignored Mr Lugosi instead and looked at the statue, but after a while it began to give them the creeps so they looked away again. Seconds later, the statue had gone.

'If anyone asks, that never happened,' said Mr Lugosi.

But Maria in particular continued to be intrigued, and when Mr Franklin, the geography teacher, had told them to form groups of three and come up with a project on buildings and public spaces in Biddlecombe, she had twisted the arms of Samuel and Tom until they'd agreed to look at the work of Hilary Mould. The subject was now quite topical due to the reopening of Wreckit & Sons.

'This bloke Grimly will have to do something pretty spectacular with Wreckit's if he doesn't want to send little kids home crying and wondering what the point of life is,' said Tom.

'It is a strange building to turn into a toystore,' said Samuel. 'I know it's right in the centre of town, but it still looks like it should be used for something else.'

'Storing dead bodies,' Tom suggested.

'Storing *undead* bodies,' Samuel offered.

'A rest home for retired vampires.'

'Kennels for werewolves.'

'Will you two shut up!' said Maria. 'Look, I've printed off a map of Biddlecombe. I thought we could use it as the centrepiece for the project, and mark the Mould buildings on it. Then we could add a picture of each building, and a little potted history of it. Now that Samuel is going to the grand opening, maybe he can find a way to interview Mr Grimly. He might have more luck than the local paper has had. How does that sound?'

It was certainly better than anything Samuel or Tom had come up with. There were six Mould buildings in total in Biddlecombe, and they had taken two each to study. Samuel and Tom hadn't done much more than walk by their buildings, which in Samuel's case included Wreckit's, and then move along as quickly as possible, but Maria had already completed her histories and taken her photos. Now, as they sat around the table, she placed dots on the map indicating the location of the six Mould buildings.

Maria sat back. She appeared troubled.

'What is it?' asked Samuel. 'Did you make a mistake?'

'She doesn't make mistakes,' said Tom, which was kind of true. What Maria did, she did well.

'Don't you see it?' said Maria.

Samuel and Tom didn't see anything at all, apart from the names of streets and buildings, and six black dots. Maria picked up her pen again, grabbed a ruler, and began drawing lines on the map, connecting the dots.

'*Now* do you see it?' she asked.

They did. It might have been a coincidence, but if it was, then it was a very large one. The dots, when joined by lines, made a very distinct pattern. It looked like this, with Wreckit & Sons at the centre:

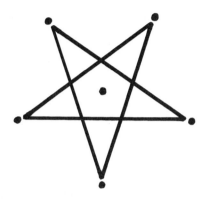

'I could be wrong,' said Maria, 'but that looks very like a pentagram.'[26]

Samuel, Maria and Tom talked for a long time about the pentagram. Maria was the most worried about it, and Tom the least. Samuel was stranded somewhere in the middle. It was unusual, he had to admit, but so what if weird Hilary Mould had set out to position his awful buildings in the shape of a pentagram? It just confirmed what everyone had always thought: he was as odd as two left shoes.

💀 [26] It was only in the nineteenth century that the pentagram – a five-pointed star – came to be regarded as a symbol for evil, and its use in old manuscripts of the supernatural is rare. Anyway, if it has one point at the top, then it's a symbol of good, and if there are two points at the top, like the one Maria found, it's a symbol for evil. Then again, like most things in life, it rather depends upon how one looks at it, doesn't it?

'Maybe you shouldn't go to the grand reopening,' said Maria, 'not until we know more. In fact, we should try to have the reopening postponed.'

'Are you mad?' said Tom. 'The reopening is tomorrow, and it's the biggest thing to have happened to Biddlecombe in years. Everybody is looking forward to it. Do you really think they're going to call it off just because you've made the shape of a star on a map?'

'Tom's right,' said Samuel. 'It doesn't mean anything, beyond the fact that Hilary Mould had an unusual sense of humour.'

'But what if it's more than that?' said Maria. 'What if it's dangerous?'

'How can it be?' said Samuel. 'Those buildings have been around for more than a century and they've done nothing worse than make the town look a bit uglier. Why should they start being dangerous now?'

And that was how things ended, because Maria had no answer to Samuel's question. She had only her instincts to go on, and they told her that something was very wrong here. She didn't want anything bad to happen to the people of Biddlecombe, and especially not to Samuel and Boswell. She didn't even want any harm to befall Lucy Highmore.

Or not much harm, anyway.

CHAPTER XIV

In Which the Worst Date in the History of Dating Begins.

Lucy Highmore looked lovely when she arrived at Samuel's house on the evening of the grand reopening. Her dress was lovely, her face was lovely, and her hair was lovely. Her dad had dropped her off at Samuel's house in a car that was so big it qualified as a boat, and he had glowed in the light of his daughter's sheer loveliness. If there had been a town called Lovely and its residents were looking for a statue of Loveliness to represent the town, they would have modelled it on Lucy Highmore. Samuel felt slightly awkward standing beside her, as though he were somehow dragging her down just by being around.

Lucy Highmore had agreed to go with Samuel to Wreckit & Sons because it was such a big event, even though she knew that, pretty soon, she and Samuel would not be going anywhere together; and Samuel had asked Lucy to go to the special event even though he knew that, pretty soon, he and Lucy would not be going anywhere together; and Boswell had gone with Samuel and Lucy to the special event because Samuel had put a leash on him and said, 'Come on, Boswell,' which was all that Boswell needed to hear.

'You two – um, three – have a lovely time,' said Mrs Johnson as they left the house. 'I just hope that it's a special evening for you.'

Even if the reopening of Wreckit & Sons had been the grandest event that Biddlecombe had ever seen, the evening would not have been destined to go well for these two young people and one small dachshund. As things happened, it was destined to be an opening unlike any other.

Dimensions were fragmenting.

Cracks were appearing in the Multiverse.

The Shadows were gathering.

Eternal Darkness was coming.

Not a good evening for a date then. Not a good evening at all.

CHAPTER XV

In Which Brian the Tea Boy Really Wishes That He Had Found Himself A Safer Job, like Hand-Feeding Great White Sharks, or Juggling Scorpions.

Brian the tea boy was still not used to the ghosts. Oh, he understood that they weren't really ghosts as such. Professor Stefan had sat him down shortly after the policemen had paid their visit, and explained to Brian in some detail his theory about why a former sweet factory seemed to be quite the hive of activity for people who had been dead for a long time.

'Think of the Multiverse as a series of bubbles, and each bubble is a universe,' said Professor Stefan. 'But they're not like the bubbles in a glass of fizzy pop. Instead, they're pressed very tightly together, so tightly that the "skin" of one universe almost, but not quite, shares the skin of another. And what is in these universes, you might ask?'

'Ghosts,' said Brian.

'No, Brian,' said Professor Stefan in the tone of a man who has just discovered a large hole in his bucket of patience, and is now considering hitting someone over the head with the bucket, 'not ghosts. Ghosts don't exist. Let's say it together on the count of three. One, two, three. Ghosts don't exist.'

'G – ghosts don't exist,' echoed Brian dully, casting an anxious glance over his shoulder in case one decided to pop up and prove him wrong. Brian felt that he had been reduced to a big jellied spine waiting for a shiver to run down it.

'Very good,' said Professor Stefan. 'If you could say it without stammering, that would be even better.'

'S – sorry,' s-said Brian.

'D – don't – Blast it, you have me at it now. Don't worry, just listen.'

'Right,' said Brian.

'What I think we are seeing in this sweet factory are quantum universes parallel to our own, but we're being given glimpses of different points in their time lines, which is why the people who keep popping up are wearing the clothing of Victorian servants, or Tudor courtiers or, in that slightly disturbing incident involving the elderly gentleman climbing into his bathtub, nothing at all. Similarly, it's entirely possible that somewhere on *their* time lines, people are glimpsing scientists in false beards who are pretending to run a sweet shop.

'Look, people think of time as a single straight line, like this,' said Professor Stefan. He drew a straight line for Brian, just to be helpful.

Past	Present	Future

'But suppose,' he continued, 'time isn't like that at all. Suppose time really looks like this.'

'Handy that you happened to have a picture of twigs with you, wasn't it?' said Brian.

'Yes,' said Professor Stefan. 'I have to explain this often. So, imagine that, every time you made a decision, like whether to come here to work with us—'

'So a bad decision?'

'Yes. No. Maybe. Anyway, suppose that every time you made a decision, the universe branched off, and another universe came into being. So there's this universe, the universe in which you work here, and there's another universe, in which—'

'In which I work somewhere there are no ghosts,' said Brian. 'Sorry, no not-ghosts.'

'Precisely. Now, if you think about all the decisions and actions that you take in a single day, suddenly time begins to seem a lot more complicated, doesn't it, with lots and lots of lines running alongside each other. And perhaps they're not straight lines either. Perhaps they tangle and cross over at points, just like those twigs. And sometimes, if the circumstances are right, we get a glimpse of one of those other universes, those alternative realities.'

'And you believe that's what's happening here?'

'It's a possibility,' said Professor Stefan. He decided not to mention that some of these universes might not contain just other, equally slow, versions of Brian, but potentially destructive beings. He was making some progress with Brian, and didn't want to spoil it all by introducing nameless horrors from the beyond.

'But how has this happened?' said Brian.

Professor Stefan shifted awkwardly on his seat.

'What may have occurred – and I stress "may", because we don't want people blaming us for things that we might not have done, and especially not for things that we might *actually* have done – is that, in the course of the Collider experiments, the skins separating some of the universes within the Multiverse might have been worn a little thin, thus enabling us to peer through them into other realms.'

'Weren't we talking about twigs a moment ago?'

'We were, but forget the twigs. We're back on skins.'

'So why can't the people in these other universes see us when we see them?'

Brian really was asking the most awkward questions, thought Professor Stefan. He began mentally weighing his empty patience bucket and practising his swing.

'Think of them as those windows in police stations that look like plain old mirrors on one side but, if you're sitting on the other side, allow you to watch suspects being questioned.' Professor Stefan had just thought of this explanation, and was quite pleased with it, even if it meant moving from twigs to skins to police stations. 'That would explain why we can see them, but they can't see us.'

'Oh,' said Brian.

It made a kind of sense, in a not very sensible way.

'So we're not going to talk about ghosts any more, OK?' said Professor Stefan.

'OK.'

'Because they're not ghosts, not in the way that you think, and they can't see you or hurt you.'

'Er, yes, right.'

'And we're not going to mention them to policemen, or anyone else, isn't that right?'

'Absolutely.'

'There's a good chap. Now, back to work you go. Milk, two sugars, and a Jammie Dodger, please.'

Brian did as he was told. He made a large pot of tea, put some mugs and a plate of Jammie Dodgers beside it on the tray, added a jug of milk and a bowl of sugar, and looked at his handiwork. It was all very neat and tidy. He picked up the tray, and instantly his hands began shaking so much that the Jammie Dodgers were awash with tea and milk before he even managed to get halfway to the kitchen door.

'Oh dear,' said Brian.

He turned round to return to the kitchen counter, and stopped dead.

There was a not-ghost in the room with him.

CHAPTER XVI

In Which a Scientist Tries to be Cleverer than Maria, and Fails.

The bell above the sweetshop door jangled. It was Professor Hilbert's turn to sell sweets for a couple of hours, but then it *always* seemed to be Professor Hilbert's turn. Professor Stefan didn't like dealing with children and, on the two occasions Dorothy had been left in charge, she had eaten so many caramel chews that her jaw had swollen on one side, making her look as though she was concealing a golf ball in her mouth. As for Brian, his hands continued to tremble so much that he inevitably poured more sweets on the floor than he managed to put into bags. If Brian and Dorothy had been left in charge, Mr Pennyfarthinge's would have gone out of business in a week.

Professor Hilbert was engaged in mapping reported sightings of strange phenomena in and around Biddlecombe, which was no simple task as *everything* about Biddlecombe seemed strange, even the stuff that people had begun to regard as comparatively normal. For example, it was widely accepted that something unusual was living at the bottom of Miggin's Pond, but attempts to discover precisely what it was had been hampered by the ducks, which were very protective of their new resident and tended to attack anyone who attempted anything more threatening than throwing bread for them. The long-dead, and very unpleasant, Bishop Bernard the Bad, who had popped back to life for a while with the sole intention of sticking hot pokers up people's bottoms, had been reduced to bits of broken bone and mummified flesh, but on quiet evenings his remains could still be heard rattling angrily in the crypt beneath the church. It had been suggested that someone should go down and examine them, but since the person who had made the suggestion was Professor Stefan, and the someone he had in mind was anyone but himself, that suggestion had been put on hold.

Nevertheless, Professor Hilbert had still managed to pinpoint at least five areas of Biddlecombe in which unusual numbers of residents had recently complained of seeing spectral figures. Professor Hilbert shared Professor Stefan's view that these were glimpses of parallel universes, although he also believed that there were other dimensions as yet unknown existing alongside these universes. From his interviews with the boy named Samuel Johnson, Professor Hilbert had come to some understanding of how beings from these other dimensions had entered our own, and had even managed to abduct humans from our world to theirs. Professor Hilbert suspected that Samuel Johnson wasn't telling the scientists everything he knew, but Professor Hilbert didn't mind. Like many adults, he believed that he was cleverer than any child and, quite possibly, most other adults. In this, of course, he was wrong. Being clever is not just about how much you know, but about knowing that you really don't know very much at all.

Professor Hilbert's model of the Multiverse looked something like Professor Stefan's, except that the bubbles[27] weren't all pressed quite so tightly together. There were little gaps between them here and there, and there was life in those gaps. Creatures, intelligent creatures existed in those spaces – and, yes, they were dangerous and evil and wanted to consume humanity, but that didn't make them any less interesting. Somehow, the little town of Biddlecombe had become a focal point for these creatures. Professor Hilbert was very curious to find out why.

But now he was about to be distracted from his important thoughts by a small child's need for a bag of bull's-eyes[28] or a quarter-pound of acid drops.[29] Putting in place his false beard, which itched something awful, Professor Hilbert walked from his desk to the sweet-shop. A young girl, who looked slightly familiar, was waiting at the counter. Professor Hilbert tried to recall where he had seen her before. He thought that she might be a friend of Samuel Johnson's.

'Can I help you?' he asked.

'My name is Maria Mayer and I'd like to talk to whoever is in charge, please,' said the girl.

---

[27] Or twigs. Or police stations.

[28] Formerly Uncle Dabney's Special Brand Bull's-Eyes, until it was discovered that the chewy centres were, in fact, actual bulls' eyes.

[29] Again, formerly Uncle Dabney's Unusually Fiery Acid Drops, until, well, you can work it out for yourself . . .

'Of the sweet factory?'

'No, of the scientists.'

Professor Hilbert coughed and straightened his false beard.

'No scientists here, young lady, not unless you count the science of making great sweeties!'

Maria stared hard at him.

'Seriously?' she said.

'Seriously what?'

'Seriously, is that the best you can do? I know you're scientists. The whole town knows you're scientists. I have a pet rabbit named Mr Fluffytail. Even Mr Fluffytail knows that you're scientists, and Mr Fluffytail eats his own poo.'

Professor Hilbert wasn't sure what poo had to do with anything, although he vaguely recalled that Mr Pennyfarthinge's basement had contained a number of boxes of Uncle Dabney's 'Rabbit Droppings'. They appeared to be pieces of chocolate-covered fondant but they'd smelled a bit funny and nobody had been in any hurry to try them out. They'd simply thrown them away, but now Professor Hilbert was wondering if they hadn't missed a trick by not selling them as Christmas treats to the Mr Fluffytails of the world.

'Um, if there were scientists here, which there aren't, what would you want to ask them?' said Professor Hilbert.

'I wouldn't want to "ask" them anything,' said Maria. 'I'd want to *tell* them something.'

'And what would that be?' said Professor Hilbert, only just resisting the urge to add 'little girl' to the end of the question. Even though he managed not to say it aloud, he did speak it in his head, and he got the impression that Maria had somehow heard him say it.

Maria's eyes narrowed. Her scowl deepened.

'Actually, now it's two things. The first thing I'd tell them is that at least one of them needs a lesson in not being a smartypants.'

'Yes, and the second?'

Maria placed a map of Biddlecombe on the desk, a map marked with an inverted pentagram.

'That he's a smartypants in a whole lot of trouble.'

Brian was watching the not-ghost carefully. Its back was to him, but he could tell that it was a woman. She wore a red robe that reminded Brian uncomfortably of a fountain of blood, its sleeves so wide that they concealed her hands, and her long black hair trailed down her back. It was moving slightly, as though buffeted by an unseen breeze, but as Brian continued to stare it began to fan out from her head, and her robes started to billow. Brian realised that, rather than glimpsing someone standing in a breeze, he was looking at a woman somehow suspended under water, an impression strengthened by the fact that the end of her robe was not touching the ground.

Brian's hands, which now tended to tremble at the best of times, began to shake harder. The mugs clinked together. The spoons jangled. The tea slopped. Together, they made what sounded to Brian's ears like the most awful racket.

The not-ghost's head twisted slightly. She seemed to be listening to the sounds coming from the tray, but that couldn't be right. Professor Stefan had said that it was all one-way traffic. We could see them, but they couldn't see us. On the other hand Professor Stefan had said nothing about hearing, but when Brian had seen his first not-ghost he'd dropped his tray in fright, and on that occasion the not-ghost hadn't reacted at all. Perhaps, Brian thought, the not-ghost was listening to something in her own universe. Yes, that was it. She wasn't listening to the noises coming from the tea tray. She couldn't be. Everything was fine. Happy thoughts, Brian, happy thoughts.

Still, just to reassure himself Brian decided to put the tray down on the small table in the kitchen. It was probably for the best. If he didn't he'd end up covered in tea and milk.

Carefully, Brian set the tray on the table to his right. He tried to do it as quietly as possible, but it still made a noticeable sound as it touched the wood.

The not-ghost's head inclined slightly to the right. This time, though, the rest of her body began to follow in the same direction.

Ooops, thought Brian. Oops, oops, oops.

The not-ghost slowly turned 180 degrees in the air until she was facing Brian, except that 'facing' was probably not the word Brian would have used. To face someone, the first thing you need is a face, and the not-ghost had no face at all. There was only darkness, and now Brian saw that what he had believed was hair was not hair at all but tendrils of shadow extending from the blackness where her face should have been.

Brian did what any sensible person would do.

Brian fled.

CHAPTER XVII

In Which BoyStarz Return to the Limelight, Thus Making a Bad Situation Worse.

A large crowd had gathered outside Wreckit & Sons to witness the grand reopening of the new store. There were lots of small children doing the things that small children do: talking, crying, complaining they wanted to go to the bathroom and, in the case of one little girl, asking Jolly where he thought he was going with her mother's purse. They were being entertained, if that was the right word, which it probably wasn't under the circumstances, by BoyStarz.

Dan had convinced Mr St John-Cholmondeley to allow BoyStarz to perform some songs at the grand opening. Mr St John-Cholmondeley had never heard of BoyStarz. More importantly, he had never heard them sing, which was why he had agreed to allow them near the store, and had also promised Dan some money, even if Dan was never going to live to collect it. Mr St John-Cholmondley started to regret his decision as soon as he heard the opening lines of 'Love is like a Toyshop', but by then it was too late.

Dan and the dwarfs walked to the rear of the store where Mr St John-Cholmondeley was waiting impatiently at the service entrance. He tapped his watch as the dwarfs approached.

'Your watch broken?' asked Jolly.

'No, it is not. You're late.'

Jolly looked at his own watch. At least, it was his own watch now, but about five minutes earlier it had belonged to someone else.

'I don't think so. I have us bang on time.'

'I'm telling you—' insisted Mr St John-Cholmondeley, but Angry interrupted him.

'Here, give me a look at that. I'm good with watches.'

Before Mr St John-Cholmondeley could object, the watch was off his wrist and in Angry's hand.

'Ah yes, I see what's wrong here,' said Angry. 'I'll have that fixed in no time.'

The watch vanished into Angry's pocket, never to be seen by Mr St John-Cholmondeley again.

'Now,' said Angry, steering the bewildered Mr St John-Cholmondeley into the store, 'best be getting along. Don't want to keep the little 'uns waiting, do we?'

'Er, no, of course not,' said Mr St John-Cholmondeley. 'By the way, do you think you could make BoyStarz stop singing?'

'What?' said Dan. 'Make them stop? But they've only just started. Listen to them. They're like nightingales, they are.'

'They're more like seagulls,' said Mr St John-Cholmondeley. 'And you can't hear them properly because your ears are stuffed with cotton wool. *All* of your ears are stuffed with cotton wool.'

'Ear infection,' said Dan.

'Very contagious,' confirmed Angry.

Outside the store, BoyStarz finished their first song. There was some applause, but only because people were relieved that they'd stopped.

'Quick, let's get inside before they start up again,' said Jolly, and Mr St John-Cholmondeley didn't try to argue.

He led the dwarfs down the back stairs of the store. They passed no one else along the way, and Wreckit & Sons seemed very quiet.

'Where are all the staff?' asked Dan.

'They're getting a last-minute pep talk from Mr Grimly,' said Mr St John-Cholmondeley.

'Will we get to meet Mr Grimly?' asked Jolly.

'Oh yes,' said Mr St John-Cholmondeley as they reached the dressing room. 'You'll be meeting him very soon, and he's very anxious to meet you too. Dying to meet you, you could say.'

He smiled at the dwarfs the way an anteater might smile at a line of ants, but the dwarfs were too distracted by their elf outfits to notice. In the past they'd worn suits that were either so loose that a bookmark was needed to find the wearer, or so tight around the neck and waist that the wearer resembled a Christmas cracker. Those same suits were often made of the kind of material capable of conducting near fatal levels of static electricity. Angry had stuck to a carpet on one job and had to be removed from it with wooden spoons; on another, Jolly had amused himself by building up a static charge and then poking Mumbles in the arm.

Mumbles had received such a shock that his eyeballs had lit up.

These suits, on the other hand, were made of what felt like velvet. They were red with green trim, and while they might have had too many bells on for Jolly's liking, they were still more than a step above normal.

'I'll leave you to get dressed,' said Mr St John-Cholmondeley. 'Please wait here when you're done, and I'll come and get you in—'

He tried to check his watch, then realised that it was no longer on his wrist.

'Excuse me, about the watch,' he said to Angry.

'What watch?'

'*My* watch.'

'Oh, that watch. I haven't had a chance to look at it yet.'

'Would there be – ? I mean, perhaps I should – ?'

'Out with it, man, out with it,' said Angry. 'We have elf work to do.'

'Well, I was wondering if I might perhaps have a receipt for it?'

When the dwarfs had finished laughing, which took a while, and Angry's sides had stopped hurting, which took even longer, he finally managed to speak.

'Friends don't need receipts,' said Angry.

'Are we friends?' asked Mr St John-Cholmondeley.

He sounded like he didn't believe that this was the case and, if it was, he was wondering if it might be a good idea to put as much distance as possible between himself and his new 'friend'.

'No, but we won't ever be if we start looking for

receipts from each other, will we?' asked Angry reasonably. 'Friendship is about trust. Without trust, what do we have? Nothing.'

Angry put his left hand on his heart. There were tears in his eyes, although they might have been left over from his laughing fit. He put his other hand over Mr St John-Cholmondeley's heart, and discreetly stole his pocket handkerchief.

'Well, since you put it like that,' said Mr St John-Cholmondeley, as he was hustled from the room by the rest of the dwarfs.

'I'd still quite like a receipt though,' he said, as the door closed on him. 'You can even sign it "Your Friend",' he shouted through the keyhole.

Eventually they heard his footsteps move away, but by then they were already changing into their outfits. They fitted almost perfectly, although Dozy's was a little more snug in certain places than he might have liked.

'I think something's being crushed down there,' he said. 'I'll do myself an injury.'

'You'll do someone else an injury if that button pops on your trousers,' said Angry. 'You could take an eye out with it.'

'I must have put on a pound or two since—'

Dozy stopped talking and began thinking.[30] 'Hang

---

[30] Dozy could do one or the other, but not both at the same time. This is not an uncommon flaw in those who tend to speak before they know what's going to come out of their mouths, and then look a bit surprised at what they hear. Before speaking, it's a very good idea to consider if what you're about to say is better than silence. If it isn't, then perhaps you shouldn't say anything at all.

on a minute, how did they know our sizes? I mean, these suits are very nicely cut. Very good quality, these suits. Not like the usual ones we're given.'

It was a good question. How did the suits fit so well?

'Nipsomash?' suggested Mumbles.

'Yeah, maybe Mr Singing-Chimney has a good eye for fashion,' agreed Jolly.

'If he does, then it's the only good thing about him,' said Angry. 'I wouldn't trust him an inch, and this is me speaking. I don't even trust me, but I trust me more than I'd trust him.'[31]

'It's the moustache,' said Jolly. 'You have to look out for blokes with moustaches. A bad lot, your moustache-growers.'[32]

'I wonder how they'll dress Father Christmas?' said

---

[31] Angry had once stolen one of his own shoes.

[32] The question of why men grow moustaches is one that has troubled philosophers for centuries. At best, a moustache looks like someone has decided to transport caterpillars on his upper lip; at worst, it looks like a bird has flown up his nose. It is also a fact that a great many bad sorts have been wearers of bad moustaches, as can be seen from the line-up below of Stalin of Russia, Hitler of Germany, and our old friend, Vlad the Impaler.

Dan. 'If you've got those threads, his suit must be fit for a king.'

'By the way, where is Father Christmas?' said Jolly. 'We should meet him before all this starts. We don't want any misunderstandings later.'

By 'misunderstandings', Jolly meant that he didn't want Father Christmas complaining when the dwarfs sneaked off for a nap, or took the occasional sip of Spiggit's Old Peculiar to keep their spirits up, or gave the odd annoying kid a clip on the ear.

'We should go and find him,' said Angry. 'Introduce ourselves. Let him know we're on his side, as long as he's on ours.'

'Hang on,' said Dan. 'Mr Snippy-Chinstrap told us to wait here. He seemed very keen that we didn't go wandering off.'

'Well, Mr Saggy-Chapstick isn't around, is he?' said Angry. 'And it's important that we say hello to Father Christmas: we're his elves. Without us he's nothing, and without him we're just small men with no excuse for going round a toyshop where there's lots of stuff that someone could steal if we don't get to it first.'

And so, with Dan in tow, the dwarfs set off to find Father Christmas and set him straight on the difference between 'stealing' and 'borrowing with no real intention of giving back'.

* * *

Now I am not trying to suggest that all those who grow moustaches are secretly demented dictators or bloodthirsty tyrants. That would just be silly. But, as our study shows, having a moustache is one of the signs that you might be one.

The stone house that served as Santa's Grotto sat silent and dark on the top floor of Wreckit & Sons. The trees of the forest seemed to stretch out their branches like arms towards the house. Ivy decorated their trunks, and frost sparkled on the bark. From a distance, it looked almost real. Up close, it became apparent that it *was* real. The trees had rooted themselves in the floor, breaking through the boards and anchoring themselves on the metal supports. A peculiar-smelling sap oozed from the bark, forming sticky yellow clumps that glowed with an inner light. The ivy was growing at a remarkable rate, twisting and coiling as it wound around the trunks of the trees, and extending itself across the floor to form a carpet of green.

And it was cold up there, so very cold. Had there been anyone in the vicinity to exhale, they would have seen their breath form thick white clouds that froze in the air and dropped to the ground with the faintest of tinkles as the crystals shattered. The walls began to disappear as the darkness nibbled away at them, and the little fairy lights in the ceiling blinked out one by one, and were replaced by strange constellations from another universe.

Slowly, a faint humming arose. It came from everywhere and nowhere, as though an unseen hand had set the strings of this universe vibrating. It was a foul, unsettling noise, a melody composed of pain sculpted into notes: if great evil had a theme tune, that is how it would have sounded.[33]

💀 [33] And it wasn't BoyStarz, who at that moment were being bribed to stop singing after the crowd had taken up a collection.

From inside the grotto, a white glow appeared. Tendrils of shadow forced themselves like smoke between the gaps in the stones. In one of the windows the shape of a man became visible and a voice that had, until now, spoken only from the walls found an almost human form.

'Bring them,' it said. 'Bring them to us.'

CHAPTER XVIII

In Which Maria Explains Things
to the Scientists.

Professors Stefan and Hilbert eyed Maria's map, then eyed each other. To their right, Dorothy was eyeing them both. She was still wearing her false beard. It struck Professor Stefan that she was growing disturbingly fond of it, and had taken to wearing it even when there was no danger of her being seen by strangers. She also seemed to be wearing a man's suit today, along with a shirt and tie. He made a mental note to have a serious conversation with her, while there was still a 'her' to have a conversation with.

Professor Hilbert, meanwhile, was regretting calling Maria 'little girl', even if he had done so only in his head. She had spotted something that he had missed entirely. It could have been a coincidence, but Professor Hilbert was a scientist and took the view that although coincidences were sometimes just that and nothing more, there were times when coincidences were actually patterns that you had previously failed to spot.

What they were looking at was clearly an inverted pentagram formed by five buildings, all of which had been designed by the mysterious Hilary Mould. It wasn't a perfect pentagram: the crematorium, which occupied the top left point of the star, was slightly too far to the right, but if you included the cemetery next to the Church of St Timidus then it was closer to the mark. Similarly, the Biddlecombe Visitor Centre and Battlefield Experience was slightly too far to the right but, again, if you allowed for the battlefield itself, it was spot on.[34] Throw in the old lunatic asylum, the abandoned prison, and Mr Pennyfarthinge's Sweete Factorye and, hey presto, there was your pentagram.

'Hilary Mould owned all of the land on which the buildings were constructed,' explained Maria. 'He came from a very wealthy family: at one point, the Moulds collected rent from half of Biddlecombe. Mould then offered to design the buildings and contributed half of the cost of construction himself. Biddlecombe didn't really need a prison or a lunatic asylum, or even a visitor centre – it didn't have very many prisoners, only a couple of people who qualified as even slightly odder than usual, and hardly anybody ever came to visit – but getting some nice buildings at a bargain price seemed like a good idea to everyone. And then, when the final stone was laid, Hilary Mould simply vanished.'

Professor Stefan shook his head in bemusement.

'But why bother?' he said. 'I mean, what's the point

---

[34] Biddlecombe had been the site of a famous encounter in 817 AD between Vikings led by Bolverk the Wary, and Saxons led by Oswald the Uncertain. It took quite some time for the battle to get started, and fighting was only believed to have commenced after both sides backed into each other in the dark.

of creating some kind of notional star in the town of Biddlecombe?'

Behind him, Dorothy coughed. It was a very deep cough. It sounded like a gorilla had just stepped into the room and politely wanted to be noticed.

'I might be wrong,' said Dorothy, 'but it looks like he was building a vast occult generator. You know, a kind of supernatural power station.'

'But powered by what?' asked Professor Hilbert, annoyed that he had been upstaged by a female for the second time that day.

'Death and suffering,' said Dorothy. 'You have a battle-field, a prison, an asylum, a crematorium, and Mr Pennyfarthinge's Sweete Factorye or, more particularly, Uncle Dabney's line in unpleasant eating experiences.'

'It would explain a lot,' said Maria, who was impressed by Dorothy's insights, and regarded them as another blow struck for feminism. 'Like how Biddlecombe became the focus for the invasion from Hell. It couldn't simply have been the Abernathys and their friends messing about in a cellar with things that they didn't understand.[35] They weren't powerful enough, and it made no sense that what was happening at CERN in Switzerland should have found an outlet in Biddlecombe.[36] It was because of Mould and his buildings.'

💀 [35] In *The Gates*, Samuel discovered the Abernathys and their friends trying to summon up demons in the cellar of a house. I really should be charging you extra for this.

💀 [36] Take that, critics. You thought I was just making all this stuff up as I went along, but there was a plan, I tell you, a plan! (Cue maniacal laughter, and a gibbering henchman calling me 'Master!' in an admiring way.)

'But Mould couldn't have known that, more than a century in the future, someone would construct the Large Hadron Collider and turn it on,' said Professor Stefan. 'He couldn't even have imagined people would own watches that didn't need winding, or shoes with wheels in the heels.'

'Perhaps he didn't, but something else did,' said Maria. 'Something much older, something that had been watching humanity for a long, long time, something with a lot of patience and a lot of anger. It guided Mould in the creation of the pentagram, and then added one more building for luck.'

She was about to place her finger at the heart of the pentagram, but Dorothy beat her to it.

'Wreckit & Sons,' said Dorothy.

They all remained silent for a few moments. They might have remained silent for a good deal longer had the quiet not been broken by the sound of a scream and a tea boy's feet running very, very fast.

'What is wrong with that boy now?' said Professor Stefan. 'Honestly, he'll be jumping at the sight of his own shadow next.'

Interestingly for Brian – although 'Terrifyingly for Brian' might have been more apt – he was in the process of doing just that as Professor Stefan spoke. To begin with, he'd been relieved to find that the not-ghost in the red robe wasn't chasing him. He'd taken a couple of glances over his shoulder as he ran, and there was no sign of pursuit. There was just his shadow extending behind him, the way a shadow should.

Unfortunately, his shadow quickly began catching up with him before passing him entirely and finally separating itself from his shoes and assuming a 'this far and no further' position in front of him. It stretched as he watched, growing both wider and taller, until it entirely blocked his way. It also had more substance than a shadow should. Brian thought that, if he poked it with his finger, it would feel like a big, dirty marshmallow, and his finger would be returned to him stained with black, if it was returned at all.

A crack opened in the shadow's head. It might have been mistaken for a smile, but only the kind of smile that a cannibal might wear before tucking into dinner. Teeth appeared in the mouth: they were sharp but wispy, as though the smoke from a series of recently blown-out candles had solidified. A clawed hand reached for Brian, and he ducked just in time to avoid having it close upon his skull. Since he was now heading in the direction of the floor, Brian decided simply to keep going. He dived through the shadow's legs, somersaulted to his feet behind it, surprising himself almost as much as the creature, and recommenced running and screaming. Meanwhile the creature, clearly deciding that two massive arms ending in jagged claws weren't enough for the job, began sprouting a third and a fourth, and grew another head while it was about it, since you never knew when a second head might come in useful. Then, seemingly content with these improvements, it returned to the task of trying to consume Brian.

It was at this point that Professor Stefan opened the door to the main laboratory with every intention of giving Brian a stern talking to about the importance of not mewling and squealing at the slightest sign of Multiversal activity. He got as far as saying 'Now look here—' before he took in the sight of a terrified Brian being pursued by a giant, multi-armed and dual-headed shadow monster.

'Never mind,' said Professor Stefan.

He held the door open for Brian and, as soon as the tea boy was safely inside, slammed it shut.

'Wibble,' said Brian. 'Wibble, wibble wibble.'

He then promptly fainted as wisps of dark matter began seeping through the keyhole.

CHAPTER XIX

In Which Wreckit & Sons Reopens,
and There Is Much Joy and Good Cheer.
(Part of This Chapter Heading May Be a Lie.)

At precisely 6.55 p.m., thousands of lights exploded into Christmas cheer on the front of Wreckit & Sons, bathing the crowd gathered below in green and white and gold. There was a collective 'Ooooh!' of appreciation which rose in volume as a grinning Father Christmas formed by red bulbs appeared at the heart of the display, the arrangement of the lights changing as the crowd watched so that Father Christmas's lips seemed to move, although no sound emerged from them, not yet. In truth, he didn't look like a very jolly Father Christmas. His face was a bit too pinched and thin for that, and his eyes were little more than narrow slits. As the lights continued to make his lips move, he looked as though he were threatening a child with something considerably worse than an absence of gifts on Christmas morning. He also, it had to be said, bore more than a passing resemblance to the statue of Hilary Mould.

But any doubts about Father Christmas were overwhelmed by the spectacle unfolding on Biddlecombe High Street. The dark cloths that had so far masked the windows fell away to reveal the most wondrous displays. Polar bears carried gifts on their backs across fields of pure white snow. There were scenes from fairy tales being enacted by mannequins: Snow White accepted a poisoned apple from her wicked stepmother disguised as an unspeakably ugly witch; a huge wolf in a nightdress towered above Red Riding Hood; a troll threatened three billy goats; and another wolf was proving that sixty-six per cent of little pigs were not very good at building houses. They weren't exactly cheerful moments from the history of fairy tales, and there was more blood and gore than was strictly necessary: it was clear that Red Riding Hood's grandmother had already met a nasty end, for the wolf was holding her severed head in one of its paws; the troll wore a necklace of billy goat skulls; and one of the three little pigs was missing most of its lower body, the rest having been reduced to a pile of bacon by a large, steam-powered bacon slicer. But they were very well done, even if it would have been nice had someone taken the time to give proper faces to the human characters. Instead, the dummies appeared to be made from a form of black material, some of which had been used to create the eyes for the other characters, for even the billy goats and the little pigs had eyes like deep, dark pools.

Hang on: weren't there *three* billy goats in the window just a moment ago? And why is that troll licking its lips? It looks very lifelike. Perhaps a bit too lifelike . . .

Meanwhile, what looked like hundreds of elves danced and sang as they laboured happily in Santa's workshop, although what they appeared to be producing were just more versions of themselves as more elves poured off the production line. Children pressed their noses against the windows, mouths agape. Even their parents were amazed. It was the greatest Christmas display anyone had ever seen. A bit graphic, admittedly, but very impressive.

The main doors of the store opened, and Mr St John-Cholmondeley appeared. Behind him, Wreckit & Sons remained dark. Clearly another surprise was planned, and people remarked aloud that if the windows were that good, imagine what the inside must be like!

'Welcome!' said Mr St John-Cholmondeley. 'Welcome all!'

His voice boomed, even though there was no microphone visible. A hush descended on the crowd.

'On behalf of Mr Grimly, I'd like to say how greatly pleased we are that you could join us on this very special evening. I can assure you it is one that will not easily be forgotten.'

A round of applause came from the crowd, although they weren't entirely sure what they were applauding. Most of them were hoping for some free stuff, just for entering into the spirit of the thing.

'I'm especially pleased to welcome our guest of honour for the evening: Mr Samuel Johnson and, of course, his dog, Boswell.'

There was another smattering of applause, but not much.

'Why him?' someone asked. 'What's he ever done?'

'Well, there was all that invasion from Hell business.'

'Oh, but that was ages ago. What's he done since

then, eh? I mean, yes, he saved the world and all that, but he can't expect us to go around bowing and scraping to him for the rest of our days just because of some demons. Anyway, I heard that they weren't real. It was all made up to promote a film, or a television show, or something.'

Samuel stepped forward, Lucy Highmore on his left arm, and Boswell's leash held tightly in his right hand. A photographer from the local paper popped up and took a couple of pictures, although Samuel noticed that he was pointing his lens at Lucy alone, and the only part of Samuel likely to end up in any photos was his left ear.

Mr St John-Cholmondeley placed a hand on Samuel's shoulder. It felt both hard and strangely light.

'So good of you to come,' said Mr St John-Cholmondeley. 'So very good.'

He looked around, as though expecting someone else to appear.

'And your, um, friends?' he inquired.

'What friends?' asked Samuel.

'Mr Cushing, and Mr Lee. Won't they be joining us?'

'I don't know who you mean,' lied Samuel.

Mr St John-Cholmondeley seemed about to differ, then changed his mind.

'Not to worry,' he said. 'Perhaps they're just a little delayed. They'll join us in time: I'm certain of it.'

He cleared his throat, and raised his hands to silence the crowd, who were getting restless.

'We have two other gentlemen whom we would like to honour this evening. They are the sleepless guardians of the law, the men who keep us all safe at night. May I please ask Sergeant Rowan and Constable Peel to step forward?'

Sergeant Rowan and Constable Peel looked shocked to be singled out in this way. They were simply supposed to be on crowd duty, and nobody had suggested that they would be honoured with anything other than overtime. Now their names were being called out, and the same voice that, moments earlier, had been complaining about Samuel was asking why they were so special, and commenting how, at the rate things were going, everybody in town would be special except him, and what kind of world were we living in, exactly?

The two policemen came and stood awkwardly beside Samuel and Lucy and Boswell. There was a third, generally polite burst of applause, as everybody liked to stay on the right side of the police.

'If all four of you – and, of course, the delightful Boswell – would come into the store for a moment, we have a small presentation we'd like to make,' said Mr St John-Cholmondeley.

'And when we're done,' he continued, addressing the crowd once more, 'the main festivities will begin, and you'll all get what's coming to you.'

Which was an odd way to put it, thought Sergeant Rowan, as he and the others moved towards the darkened interior of the store. He glanced again at the window displays and noted that, close up, the polar bears looked less like bears than some kind of abominable snowmen; and the reindeer had very vicious horns and spiked hooves; and the workshop elves had a mean, spiteful appearance about them; and those machines were producing an awful lot of them, so many, in fact, that pretty soon the window areas wouldn't be big enough to hold them all. They were already piling up, except that they weren't piling up so much as lining up. But the workshop machines were just tossing them on the floor of the store, and there was nobody around to set them on their feet, so how exactly were they ending up in neat rows before the windows?

And why would somebody design Christmas elves with such sharp teeth?

But by then the four humans, along with one small dog, had crossed the threshold of Wreckit & Sons. As soon as they were inside Mr St John-Cholmondeley vanished, and the darkness of the store closed so tightly around them that they could not see their own hands in front of their faces, and they were only vaguely aware of the sounds from outside of glass breaking and people screaming.

'Sarge?' said Constable Peel to the blackness.

'Yes, Constable.'

'Maybe we should have told the man that we didn't want to be special after all.'

'It's a little late for that, Constable, don't you think?'

But Constable Peel didn't get to reply, because the darkness swallowed his words, and then his breath.

And, finally, it swallowed him.

CHAPTER XX

In Which History Comes Alive.

Nurd was lying on the top bunk, staring at the ceiling. Mrs Johnson had gone out to bingo again. Nurd suspected that Mrs Johnson was a bingo addict. Whenever anyone mentioned a number in conversation, Mrs Johnson would instinctively try to cross it out.

Nurd was sulking, although it was hard to tell because Nurd's face naturally formed a kind of sulk, even when he was happy.

'I spy with my little eye—' said the voice of Wormwood from the lower bunk.

'I'm not playing any more,' said Nurd.

'Come on. It's fun.'

'No, it's not. "I-Spy" is only ever fun for the person doing the spying. I hate "I-Spy". Anyway, you're on the bottom bunk staring up at the top bunk. So far you've spied a mattress, some wood, and a sheet. You're unlikely to spot a camel, are you, or a spaceship? There's a limit to how interesting it can be.'

'I'll look somewhere else, then.'

'No.'

'Please, just one more? Oooh! Oooh! I've just spotted something. It's great. Seriously. Please? Oh, please?'

Nurd sulked even more. While he really did understood the reason why Samuel hadn't wanted him to go along to the grand reopening of Wreckit's store, he remained hurt. Once again, Nurd recalled that he had once been a demon with high hopes. He'd even had ambitions to take over the Earth. They hadn't worked out very well because Nurd was useless at being properly demonic, and a squirrel with a nut allergy had a better chance of ruling the world, but at least it had been something to aim for.

Now here he was, sharing a small room with Wormwood, and Wormwood wasn't meant for small rooms. Wormwood could have made a cathedral smell a bit funny. Nurd had grown fond of Wormwood in the way a dog might grow fond of a particularly friendly flea, but he really did wish that they could see a little less of each other.

A lot less of each other.

'Go on, then,' said Nurd. 'But this is absolutely, positively the last time, and I'm only taking three guesses.'

'Understood,' said Wormwood. 'You're the best demonic master I've ever had!'

'I'm the only demonic master you've ever had.'

'You have a point,' admitted Wormwood. 'Now, I spy with my little eye something beginning with "e".'

Nurd thought about it. He was very competitive and he didn't like to lose, not even at I-Spy. He had managed to guess mattress, wood and sheet easily enough. He wasn't about to be beaten on the final try by Wormwood.

'Eiderdown,' he said.

'Wrong!'

Nurd scratched his ear. It helped him to think. He poked at his earhole, and kept poking until the tip of his finger came out of the other ear. Nurd wasn't sure why it sometimes did that. Wormwood had once suggested a possible answer. Nurd had kicked him in the bum for his trouble, but not before putting on his pointiest boots.

'Electric blanket,' said Nurd.

'Wrong again!'

He heard Wormwood sniggering, and wondered where he might have left those pointy boots.

Nurd looked around the room, trying to see it from Wormwood's angle. Electricity? No, that couldn't be it. Samuel's exercise jotter? Possibly, although it was a bit of stretch.

Ah, he had it! On the floor by Samuel's bed was a small, stuffed elephant. It had once been Samuel's favourite stuffed toy, but was now beloved of Boswell, who liked to sleep with it for company.

Nurd made a trumpeting sound, and prepared for his final triumph.

'It is,' he said grandly, 'an elephant.'

'WRONG!' howled Wormwood. 'Wrongedy wrong wrong, Mr Wrongly Wrongington!'

'It has to be an elephant,' said Nurd. 'I've looked. There's nothing else around here beginning with the letter "e".'

'Ring-ring,' said Wormwood. 'Call for you. It has to be for you, because it's a WRONG number.'

'I'm warning you,' said Nurd, who now remembered where he had left those boots.

'You don't have a right hand,' continued Wormwood. 'You just have a left hand and a WRONG hand.'

'I shall inflict grave pain upon you with a pointy boot,' Nurd warned. 'I shall take a very long run-up to do it. It will be such a long run-up that you will have grown old by the time my boot finally reaches you, and I shall kick you so hard that, when you open your mouth, the tip of my boot will be visible at the back of your throat.'

'You lost, you lost . . .'

'Tell me what it was.'

'Don't have to if I don't want to.'

'TELL ᴔE!!!!!'

Flames shot out of Nurd's mouth and ears. His cloak billowed like the wings of a bat. His eyes turned red, and his eyebrows caught fire.

'It was an elf,' said Wormwood in a tiny voice.

'Excuse me?' said Nurd, as he regained control of himself.

'**An elf**,' said Wormwood, a little louder. 'I spied an elf.'

Nurd rubbed his finger along his forehead. He could just about feel where his eyebrows used to be.

'Elves don't exist,' he said. 'Dwarfs exist, not elves. You can't have seen an elf.'

'I did,' said Wormwood. 'And I still spy an elf. It's outside the bedroom window.'

Despite himself, Nurd leaned over the edge of his bed to take a look. Wormwood was right. Standing on the windowsill, wearing a jaunty green hat and a suit of red felt, was an elf. It had unusually sharp teeth, and red dots gave a kind of life to its cheeks. It had very dark eyes. They should have done something about the eyes, thought Nurd. Nobody likes an elf with scary eyes.

'How did that get there?' said Nurd.

'Maybe it climbed up,' said Wormwood.

'It's a Christmas elf,' said Nurd. 'It's made of wood. You might as well expect a clothes peg to climb up.'

Wormwood left his bunk bed and padded to the window. He peered at the elf. The elf peered back.

'It's very lifelike,' he said.

'It's. An. Elf,' said Nurd. 'It can't be lifelike. There's nothing *life* to be like.'

Wormwood began to open the window.

'What are you doing?' said Nurd.

'I want to take a closer look at it.'

Nurd suddenly had the sense that this might not be a good idea. He couldn't have said why except that they were on the second floor of a house and somehow there was an elf on their windowsill, which meant that either the elf had, as Wormwood suggested, managed to climb up, or, as seemed more likely, someone or something had put it there from above. Whatever the case, opening the window didn't strike Nurd as the wisest of moves.

'I wouldn't do that,' he said, 'not until—', but the rest of the sentence was drowned out by the creak of the window being opened. There was a blast of cold air. In the distance, Nurd could hear sirens and—

Were those screams?

At the Biddlecombe Visitor Centre and Battlefield Museum, the caretaker, Mr Karloff, was closing up for the evening. He wanted to get down to Wreckit's for the grand unveiling of the new store because very little that was exciting ever happened in Biddlecombe, or very little that didn't involve people claiming to have seen demons, or the dead coming to life. Mr Karloff wasn't sure that he believed all of that nonsense. During the supposed invasion of Biddlecombe by the forces of Hell, Mr Karloff had been visiting his sister Elsa in Skegness, and had missed the whole affair. Despite the fact that some very trustworthy people claimed it was all true – honest to goodness, would I lie to you? – Mr Karloff regarded it as evidence of some form of mass hysteria.

It had not been a busy day at the Visitor Centre, but then it was rarely a busy day there. For some reason, tourists didn't want to come to Biddlecombe to stare at a damp field in which, long ago, two small armies led by very cautious men had eventually got around to fighting each other by mistake. The sign above the museum's door read 'We Bring History to Life!', which was not true in any way, shape or form. There were stones with more life than the Biddlecombe Battlefield Museum.

Mr Karloff had tried to make the experience more interesting by constructing a reconstruction of the battle using small plastic soldiers which he had carefully painted with his own hands. There weren't enough Vikings and

Saxons to make it look impressive so he had bulked up the numbers with whatever he had lying around at home. If someone closely examined Mr Karloff's version of the Battle of Biddlecombe, they might have spotted some confused-looking German soldiers painted like Vikings, along with half-a-dozen cowboys and a couple of Indians who had been drafted into the Saxon ranks. The rest of the museum was filled out with some spearheads, broken axes, and the odd bone that had been found poking out of the field after spells of heavy rain.

The centre only opened on Saturdays, Sundays, and every second Thursday. During the summer, coach parties on very cheap tours would occasionally stop there. The money gained from their entry fees, along with what they spent on postcards, chocolate, and pictures of themselves dressed up in the Viking and Saxon costumes that Mr Karloff had put together for the purpose was just about enough to keep the centre open.

But it was now winter, and only seven people had shown up that day. One of them was lost, two of them just wanted to use the bathroom, and the others were visiting Americans who asked some awkward questions about the cowboys and Indians fighting on the Saxon side. Mr Karloff told them that they'd come over to help the Saxons when the Americans heard about their trouble with the Vikings, and they were happy enough with the answer, but it had been a hairy moment. Still, they had bought lots of postcards, and they got a kick out of dressing up as ancient warriors.

In his little office, Mr Karloff counted up the day's takings and put them in an envelope which he folded into his pocket. He would go to the bank with it on Monday once he had added whatever came in on Saturday and Sunday. He was about to turn off the lights when a loud knocking at the front door almost gave him a heart attack.

'We're closed,' he shouted. 'Come back on Saturday.'

He thought that he heard muttered words, and then the knocking came again.

'Oh, really!' said Mr Karloff. 'Some people have no manners.'

He popped his head round the door frame.

'I said we're closed. You'll have to come back at the weekend.'

There was a full moon that night. It shone on the two small glass panels of the door, or would have if most of its light hadn't been blocked by a huge shape holding a large stick. The figure's head was slightly misshapen by what appeared to be a thick feather sticking out of its hair.

The knocking started a third time. It was clear from the movements of the figure that whoever was outside was using the stick to bang on the door. It was probably some young rascal making mischief. No decent, self-respecting person would go round banging on museum doors with a stick.

'He'll have all the paint off, and I only gave it a new coat this summer!' said Mr Karloff aloud. He spent so much time alone at the museum that he had grown used to having conversations with himself.

'Well, I won't have it,' he continued, as he marched to the door. 'I simply won't. Young people these days.

There's nothing wrong with them that a spell in the army wouldn't cure.'

Mr Karloff yanked open the door. His first thought was that perhaps a spell in the army wouldn't solve this chap's problems at all because joining the army was probably what had caused his problems to begin with. Those problems included, but were not limited to, having:

1. No lower jaw in a face that was mostly bone and some apologetic grey skin.
2. One completely empty eye socket and one eye socket that was filled by the business end of an arrow, and last but most certainly not least . . .
3. Most of an axe buried in the top of his skull.

In his right hand the new arrival held not a stick, but a spear, a spear that still looked useful in a potentially fatal way despite having spent over a thousand years in the ground alongside its owner.

Mr Karloff had spent long enough at the museum to recognise a Viking when he saw one, especially a dead one. Under other circumstances, such as encountering the dead Viking laid out in a thick glass case, he might even have been pleased. He was slightly less pleased to find a dead Viking standing upright on his doorstep and apparently giving serious thought to abandoning the whole business of being dead and trying out being undead for a while.

The spearhead moved. Instead of pointing straight up in the air, it was now moving in a direction that suggested it fancied making friends with Mr Karloff's insides, although it wasn't planning on staying long because it would very soon pop out of his back, possibly with some of Mr Karloff's insides still attached to it.

'Oh dear,' said Mr Karloff.

Those might have been the last words that he ever said, and they wouldn't have been very memorable, as last words go. He was saved by a whistling sound from the embarrassment of dying without having something witty to say. The whistling sound was followed by a very solid *thunk*, and suddenly the Viking was relieved of the difficulties posed by the axe in his skull and the arrow in his eye by the removal of his head at the neck. His body remained vertical for a second or two, then appeared to think, Actually, what's the point?, and collapsed on the doorstep.

Mr Karloff was now staring into the undead face of a Saxon who was holding a sword almost as big as he was. Behind him, Mr Karloff could see more undead Vikings and Saxons digging themselves out of their graves. Those that were above ground were already fighting among themselves.

Mr Karloff gave the undead Saxon his biggest and best smile.

'I'm on your side,' he said. 'Keep up the good work.'

He closed the front door, grabbed his hat, and ran to the back door. That one he didn't bother closing after him. After all, as soon as he heard the front door explode behind him there really didn't seem to be much point.

CHAPTER XXI

In Which the Dwarfs Make
a New Friend. Sort of.

Dan and the dwarfs had discovered that getting out of the basement was harder than it looked. To begin with, the basement now seemed much bigger than it had when they arrived, which couldn't be right yet somehow was. They had been walking around for half an hour and still hadn't found the stairs. This development might have worried ordinary people, but the dwarfs were far from ordinary. They were seasoned drinkers of Spiggit's Old Peculiar, and so were well used to walking around small spaces for long periods of time without being able to find the door, often while singing loudly and seeing small multicoloured elephants flying around their heads.

On this occasion, though, the dwarfs were ninety-nine per cent sure that they hadn't been drinking. Dan had been very clear on that point: they needed this job. It was a steady earner until Christmas. Plus, if they made enough money, Dan would be able to have the van repainted, and they would no longer have go around advertising themselves as Dan's Sods.

'Maybe we should split up,' said Dan.

'Why?' said Jolly.

'Because we can cover more ground that way. Two groups: if one group finds the door, it keeps shouting until the other group arrives.'

The dwarfs thought about this.

'That sounds like a great suggestion,' said Jolly after a while. 'Nobody ever got into trouble by separating from his friends in a dark basement and hoping for the best.'

'Absolutely,' said Angry. 'It can't fail.'

So they split into groups, Dan, Jolly and Angry in one, and Mumbles and Dozy in the other.

'Lucky for us that Dan is in charge, eh?' said Dozy to Mumbles as the footsteps of the others faded away. 'We'd be lost without him.'

Which was literally true. Seconds after Dan had left them, Dozy and Mumbles were completely lost.

'Are we there yet?'

'No.'

Pause.

'Are we there yet now?'

'No.'

Pause.

'Are we there—'

'No!' said Dan. 'No, no, no! We're not there. We're here. I don't know where there is. I'm not even sure where *here* is.'

He stomped off to look around the next corner, leaving Jolly and Angry behind.

'I love doing that,' said Jolly. 'Never fails.'

'It's a classic,' admitted Angry. 'Still, I wish we were out of this basement. I'm getting a bit tired of looking at walls and boxes. And I could be wrong, but it does seem to be getting darker down here. I thought your eyes were supposed to get used to the darkness the longer you spent in it, but my eyesight is getting worse.'

He kicked at a scrap of crumpled newspaper. As it rolled away, the dim lightbulb above their heads caught the headline. It announced the defeat of Germany, and the end of the Second World War.

'I think it's been a while since anyone's been down here,' said Angry. 'That, or World War Two took a lot longer to win than I thought.'

There was a door to Jolly's right. They had been routinely opening every door they came to in the hope of finding a stairway, or a lift, or a beer. So far, they'd had no luck on any count. Jolly opened the door and wished silently for a little good luck.

Sometimes, if you squeeze your eyes shut, and you think about good things, happy things – snowflakes, and fairies, and bluebirds singing – and picture your wish coming true, picture it like it's happening in front of you right here and now, then the universe will find a way to make it come true.

This wasn't one of those times.

Reality was fragmenting, and when reality fragments strange things happen.

The tentacled entity inside the closet wasn't sure how it had got there, or how long it had been there, or even what a closet was. All it knew was that one minute it had been minding its own business in a quiet corner of the

Multiverse, idly wondering which tentacle to use to feed a smaller creature into one of its many gaping mouths, and the next it had been squashed into a very small space with spiders crawling across its face. Because the space was so small, the entity was entirely unable to move, and so it had been trying to blow the spiders away with whichever one of its mouths was nearest. It had tried eating one of the spiders by catching it on its tongue and pulling it into its mouth, but the spider's legs had caught in its teeth, which annoyed the entity greatly. The spider hadn't tasted very nice either. Now the entity's tentacles were starting to cramp, and it really needed to go to the toilet very badly, but it didn't want to go to the toilet in the closet because it already smelled bad. In addition, the piece of its bodily equipment that it needed to get to in order to go to the toilet was currently squashed against one of its legs and the entity wasn't sure what would happen if it just took a chance and decided to relieve itself. Frankly, it thought, that stuff could go anywhere.

Suddenly a light shone upon it. One of its heads peered from between a pair of crossed tentacles. Another peered from between its legs. A third popped out of the mouth of the first and squinted at the small figure before it.

Jolly stared at the entity for a couple of seconds, then closed the door. He scratched his chin. He nibbled a fingernail.

He called Angry over.

'What is it?' said Angry.

'Open that door,' said Jolly.

'Why?'

'Just open it.'

'No.'

'Come on, for me.'

'No! I know what's going to happen.'

'I bet you don't.'

'I bet I do.'

'Go on, then. Tell me what's going to happen.'

'I'll open that door, and a broom will fall out and hit me on the head.'

'I promise you that won't happen.'

'A mop, then.'

'No.'

'A bucket.'

'I guarantee,' said Jolly, 'that if you open that door, nothing will fall on your head.'

Angry raised a finger in warning.

'If anything falls on my head . . .'

'It won't.'

'Because if it does, we're going to have a disagreement.'

Jolly took a step back as Angry opened the door.

If the demon was surprised the first time that the door opened, it was better prepared on the second occasion. Jaws snapped. Tongues lolled. Tentacles squirmed ineffectually. It made a horrible sound somewhere between a gibbering howl and an echoing shriek.

Angry gave it a little nod and closed the door softly.

'Did you put that in there?' he asked Jolly.

'Yes,' said Jolly. 'I've been keeping it as a pet, but I didn't want to tell anyone because I thought they might make me hand it over to the zoo.'

'You can't keep that as a pet,' said Angry, on whom

sarcasm was sometimes lost. 'You need a bigger hutch, for a start. It's cruel keeping a – whatever that is – cooped up like that. I ought to report you.'

Jolly punched Angry on the arm.

'Of course I didn't put it in there,' said Jolly. 'I just opened the door and there it was.'

'Well, what's it doing in that closet, then?'

'I don't know!'

'I wonder how long it's been in there?' said Angry.

From behind the door came what sounded like a sigh of relief, and liquid began pouring from inside the closet. Jolly and Angry took some quick steps back.

'Quite a while, I think,' said Jolly.

'We can't just leave it there,' said Angry.

'We can't take it with us,' said Jolly. 'Did you see those teeth? Nasty, those teeth. Not the teeth of a vege-tarian. Never met a bone they didn't like, those teeth.'

On the wall nearby was an ancient blackboard. Fragments of dusty chalk lay on a shelf beside it. Angry picked up one of the pieces of chalk and wrote on the door. The writing was slightly uneven because Angry had to lean at an awkward angle to avoid the liquid that was still spilling from inside the closet.

'What's it been drinking?' said Jolly. 'If he doesn't finish soon, we'll drown.'

'There,' said Angry. He looked admiringly at his handiwork. On the door were now written the words

DO NOT OPEN!

'That should do it,' said Angry.

'Can I have that chalk?' said Jolly.

Angry handed it to him, and Jolly added one more word.

MONSTER!

'Better,' said Angry. 'Much better.'

He slipped the chalk into his pocket.

'Now let's find Dan, just in case we need any more doors opened.'

CHAPTER XXII

In Which All Threats Begin
with the Letter 'E'.

Meanwhile, in another part of the basement that should not have been very far away but, because of the strange things happening in the Multiverse, was now much further away than before, Mumbles and Dozy had stumbled upon old Mr Wreckit's selection of unsold Nosferatu photographs. They came in all shapes and sizes, and while most simply lounged against the walls as though recovering from a heavy meal of blood and a long flight home on bat wings, others had been nailed to the walls, creating a gallery of vampiric figures.

Just in case you'd forgotten, or were not having trouble sleeping, some of them looked like this:

Dozy tapped Mumbles on the shoulder and pointed to the nearest picture.

'Your mum's looking well,' he said.

Mumbles kicked him in the shin.

A lightbulb flickered above their heads, casting an unpleasantly sickly light on the faces that surrounded them. It also made them look distinctly alive. The depictions started to seem less like pictures and more like windows through which far too many vampires were peering. It made the dwarfs feel like walking blood banks, and toothy creatures were queueing up to make a withdrawal.

'It's like the eyes follow you round the room,' said Dozy.

It was true. No matter where they stood, the gathered vampires kept a close watch on them.

'Unkebyem?' said Mumbles.

Dozy shrugged.

'I've no idea who'd buy one of those pictures and put it on his wall,' he said. 'Except maybe your dad, to remind him of your mum.'

Dozy kicked him in the shin again. The bulb above their head flickered one last time, then died.

'This isn't doing us any good,' said Dozy. 'Come on, let's get out of here. I feel like we've been walking in this basement for hours. We must be under the sea by now.'

They trooped on, Dozy limping slightly from the repeated kicks to his shin, and Mumbles sulking in front of him.

'I like your mum,' said Dozy. 'Seriously. You're just lucky you got your looks from your dad.'

Mumbles turned to aim another boot in Dozy's general direction, but he paused mid-kick.

'Erat?'

'Hear what?' said Dozy.

'Er*at*!'

Dozy listened. From the shadows behind came the sound of something landing on the floor. It didn't sound like a big something, which was good. On the other hand, it was definitely *a* something, which was bad. The sound came again, and again, and again. Not a something, then, but lots of somethings.

Which was very bad.

'Rats?' said Dozy. They hadn't seen any rats or mice yet, which he found odd. There were usually rodents in old basements.

Dozy listened harder.

'No,' he said. 'That's not the sound of claws. It's more like soft fruit dropping on a floor. Maybe someone's making jam.'

The two dwarfs faced the darkness. The sounds had stopped, but now there was movement in the gloom

A small object rolled towards them and came to a halt a couple of inches from Dozy's right foot. It looked up at him. It couldn't do much else, since it was a just an eyeball.

'Somebody will be missing that,' said Dozy.

Another eyeball rolled into view, and a third. Very soon, Mumbles and Dozy were looking down on a field of eyeballs. They were all slightly yellowed, and all very familiar, since the last time the dwarfs had seen them they had been lodged in the skulls of the vampiric pictures in the previous room.

I had to say it, thought Dozy. I had to say that the eyes seemed to follow you around the room. Mumbles had just the same reaction.

'Adzaeyfollroo!'

'I didn't mean it literally,' said Dan. 'It's not like I was hoping it would happen. All right, here's what we're going to do. We're going to ignore them. After all, they're eyeballs. What can they do, stare us to death? We're going to turn around, continue our search, and pretend that they're not there, agreed?'

Mumbles nodded. 'Ooly.'

They each took a deep breath, spun on their heels, and started walking.

It turned out to be a lot harder than they had expected to ignore the eyeballs. Most of us, at some time or another, will have had the sensation that someone is staring at us. Our instinct is to find out who, and why, and make them stop doing it. If lots of people stare at us, we start wondering what might be wrong with us. Has our face turned a funny colour? Do we have a bird on our head? Have we left something unzipped that shouldn't be unzipped in public? Being stared at for any length of time is very unpleasant.

As Dozy was bringing up the rear he was more aware of the eyeballs than Mumbles. He felt hundreds of eyes boring into his back. He could hear them rolling along the dusty floor behind him. It was slowly driving him mad. Occasionally he would cast a glance over his shoulder and the eyeballs would stop moving. They would even stop staring at him for a while and suddenly find something interesting to look at on the ceiling or the walls. If they could, he was sure that they would have started whistling innocently, as if to say, 'Don't mind us, we're not really following you, we just happen to be heading in the same direction.'

'Look—' Dozy began to say, then realised that a) the eyeballs couldn't do anything else and b) what he actually wanted was for them to stop looking, so telling them to look wasn't helpful.

'Listen—' he tried, but that wasn't right either.

'Oh, just go away!' he said. 'We don't want any eyeballs. We have enough of our own. We only need two each. We've nowhere to put any more. We can't keep you in our pockets. It would defeat the purpose.'

The eyeballs looked hurt, or as hurt as it was possible for disembodied eyeballs to look. The eyeballs peered at one another questioningly, then back at Dozy in a vaguely pleading manner.

'No, don't try that with me,' said Dozy. 'I mean it. You've had your fun, now go back to your pictures.'

He began walking again, but had taken only a few steps when he heard the wet rustling of eyeballs rolling, and felt them staring at his back again.

Dozy turned round in a fury.

'That's it!' he said. 'I've had it! For the last time, go back to your pictures!'

Just to be sure that they understood how angry he was, he stamped his foot hard on the floor. Something popped wetly under his heel, and there was the kind of squishing noise that only comes from standing on a round object that is mainly liquid and jelly held together by a thin membrane.

An eyeball, for example.

'Oops,' said Dozy.

He didn't want to look down, but he didn't have much choice. He lifted his foot and winced. He was no expert, but he was pretty certain that this particular eyeball's days of staring at strangers had come to an end.

Mumbles came back to find out why he had stopped walking, and told Dozy not to worry: the bits of eyeball would clean off easily enough.

There was no way that the eyeballs could have heard him, thought Dozy. After all, they were just eyeballs. Even if they had, they probably couldn't have understood him. Nevertheless, Mumbles's words coincided with a burst of activity among the eyeballs. They began to vibrate. The red veins running across them expanded until the eyeballs were no longer big enough to contain them. They burst through the membrane of the eyes to form what to Dozy's mind looked disturbingly like little legs. Each eyeball split beneath its retina to reveal a mouth filled with teeth. The two upper canines were longer than the rest, and needle-sharp.

'Vampire eyeballs!' said Dozy. 'Or eyeball vampires!'

Mumbles said nothing. He was too busy running away.

Meanwhile in the Johnson house, Nurd and Wormwood were about to have problems of their own.

The window was now open, but so far the elf on the

windowsill had not moved. Wormwood poked his head through the gap and peered down.

'Well, look at that,' he said.

'Look at what?' said Nurd.

He was still keeping a close eye on the elf. It was making Nurd very nervous.

'Elves,' said Wormwood. 'Lots of 'em. It's a pyramid of elves.'

Nurd climbed from his bunk and went to the window. He stuck his head out. Wormwood was right: there was a pyramid of elves under the window, each layer supporting the next until the topmost elf would be on the same level as the windowsill. But who would bother to build a pyramid of elves? Nurd twisted his head and tried to see if there was any sign of activity on the roof, but there was none.

'That's quite unusual,' he said.

Wormwood poked the elf on the windowsill.

'You know what else is unusual?' he said.

'What?'

'This elf. It's made of wood, but it feels warm.'

Wormwood leaned back so that Nurd could test it for himself. Nurd reached out a clawed finger and jabbed at the elf's nose.

'Now that you come to mention it—' he said, just as the elf's mouth opened and bit Nurd's finger. Nurd lifted his hand up to examine it more closely. The elf remained dangling from it.

'Er, Wormwood?' said Nurd.

Wormwood had poked his head out of the window again, and was admiring the elves.

'Aren't they pretty?' he said.

'Wormwood, if you have a moment . . .'

Wormwood waved a stubby hand at the elf pyramid. 'Hello, elves!'

All of the elves grinned at Wormwood. One or two even waved back.

Wormwood scratched his chin. He hadn't expected that.

'You know,' he said, quickly pulling his head back in and turning to Nurd, 'I could be wrong, but those elves may be alive.'

Nurd coughed and showed Wormwood his finger, now with added elf. He shook his hand in the hope of dislodging the elf, but the elf wasn't going anywhere. The bell on the end of its hat tinkled.

'Does it hurt?' asked Wormwood.

'A bit.'

'Would you like me to try to get it off?'

'That would be nice.'

Wormwood grabbed the elf by the legs and gave an experimental tug.

'It's holding on very tight.'

'I know that, Wormwood. It is my finger that is involved.'

Wormwood pulled harder.

'Ow!' said Nurd. 'Stop! That's no good.'

'Try knocking it against the wall.'

Nurd did. On the third attempt, the elf released its grip on Nurd's finger and fell to the floor, where it stumbled about holding its head and looking dazed. Nurd examined his finger. There was a ring of small teeth marks around the tip.

'Nasty,' said Wormwood.

Nurd picked up the elf by one leg and stared at it. The elf struggled a bit, and tried to twist its body in order to bite Nurd again.

'Not very Christmassy, is it?' said Wormwood.

'No,' said Nurd. 'I suspect that if you found one of these in your Christmas stocking, you'd write a strongly worded letter to Santa.'

There were noises from outside. The pyramid of elves, seemingly aware that the elf in the bedroom was now a captive, was trying to rearrange itself. One of the two elves who now formed the tip of the pyramid was trying to climb on to the windowsill with the aid of its colleague. The pyramid wobbled uncertainly.

'Wormwood,' said Nurd, 'could you get the football from under your bunk, please?'

Wormwood did as he was asked. He handed the football to Nurd, who exchanged it for the elf. Nurd leaned out of the window.

'Oh elves!' he called.

The elves looked up. Nurd raised his arms, and threw the football with as much force as he could muster.

The pyramid disintegrated, scattering elves and bits of elves over the front garden of the house.

'What about this one?' asked Wormwood, holding up the captive elf.

'Unless you're planning to adopt it, I'd suggest you get rid of it.'

'I can't throw it out the window! It doesn't seem right.'

Wormwood had let the elf get a little too close to his face. It snapped at him, and missed the end of his nose by a finger's width.

'Oh, all right then,' said Wormwood. ''Bye, elf.'

Out of the window it went. They watched it land in a thornbush. It managed to free itself with the help of some of its friends, and shook its little elf fist at Nurd and Wormwood. It then went into a huddle with some of the other elves. Nurd and Wormwood could hear them giggling. As they watched, more elves were trying the windows and the doors on the ground floor of the house. One of the brighter ones found a stone and threw it at the living-room window, but the elf couldn't send it high enough to hit the glass. Still, it had the right idea. Soon the elves would find a way inside, and then Nurd and Wormwood would be trapped.

'We have to get out before they get in,' said Nurd.

'But what do they want?' asked Wormwood.

'You know,' said Nurd, 'I think they want us.'

CHAPTER XXIII

In Which the Cracks in the Relationship Between Samuel and Lucy Become Greater.

All was still and silent on the ground floor of Wreckit & Sons. The darkness had cleared to reveal the store; it was as if they had passed through a tunnel in order to enter. Samuel, Lucy and the two policemen could now see out of the windows perfectly well, and so could take in the unusual sight of the people of Biddlecombe fleeing from elves, abominable snowmen, and various fairy-tale villains who seemed more smoke than substance, but they could hear nothing. When they tried to leave through the door they met only resistance from the air, and ripples like waves on water ran through it from floor to ceiling. Of Mr St John-Cholmondeley there was no sign.

'Well, this isn't much fun,' said Lucy. 'What kind of date is this?'

She glared at Samuel accusingly.

'It's not my fault,' said Samuel.

'Oh, really? And who invited me to this rotten opening in the first place?' said Lucy.

'I didn't invite you,' said Samuel. 'You saw the invitation and invited yourself!'

'So it's all *my* fault, is it? That's typical, just typical!'

There then followed a long speech blaming Samuel for every unfortunate event that had blighted Lucy Highmore's young life so far, most of which Samuel was fairly certain were not his fault, along with a lot of others that he was absolutely certain weren't his fault because he hadn't been born when any of them happened or, if he had been, then they were out of his control, including a number of wars, world hunger, global warming, and the business with the apple in the Garden of Eden. When she had finished, Lucy folded her arms and looked away. Her bottom lip trembled. After a great deal of effort, she managed to force a single small tear from one eye. It hung on her cheek for a second, decided that it wasn't about to have company any time soon, and promptly dried up somewhere around her chin.

Sergeant Rowan and Constable Peel, who had been doing their best not to get involved, or to attract Lucy's attention for fear that they might catch an earful as well, watched her from a distance. When it became apparent that the storm had calmed itself for now, Constable Peel sidled up to Samuel.

'Are you going out with her?'

'I am,' said Samuel. 'Or I was.'

Constable Peel gaped at him.

'Why?' he asked.

'It seemed like a good idea at the time to ask, and she said yes,' said Samuel.

'You live and learn,' said Constable Peel. 'Now you know why some people become monks.'

Sergeant Rowan coughed deliberately.

'None of this is helping,' he said. 'There's some bad

business going on here, and it's up to us to get to the bottom of it. Come along now, Constable. You too, Samuel. And you, young lady, suck in your bottom lip. It looks like someone has built a shelf over your chin.'

Lucy gave Sergeant Rowan her best glare of rage.

'I shall tell my father what you said. He'll have your job!'

'He can have it if he wants it, miss, although why he would, I don't know. Constable Peel, are you crying?'

'No, Sarge. Why do you ask?'

'Because I heard crying and simply assumed it was you.'

'Not me, Sarge. I can't say that I'm not tempted, but I'm holding it in.'

'Very brave of you, Constable.'

'Thank you, Sarge.'

'That said, I can still hear someone crying for mummy. I think there may be a child in here with us.'

Constable Peel listened.

'More than one, Sarge. I can hear lots of them.'

'Oh, for goodness' sake!' said Lucy. 'They're dolls! We're in a toyshop. They're probably demonstration models left out for children to play with.'

To their left was the entrance to the doll section of the store. It was clear that the sounds were coming from there.

'That's a relief,' said Constable Peel, just as a doll waddled into view and blinked at them. It was about eighteen inches tall, with dark hair. It wore a blue dress and blue shoes. Its eyes were entirely black.

'Mummy,' said the doll, its lips moving to form the word.

'That's very impressive,' said Constable Peel. 'In a creepy way. And it has quite big teeth for a doll.'

'It has quite big teeth for a *shark*,' said Sergeant Rowan. 'Constable, I'd take a step or two back from it if I were you.'

Constable Peel didn't need to be told twice. More dolls were joining the first. Some walked and some crawled. One doll pushed another doll in a pram. A number of them were armed with knives. The ones that couldn't talk just cried, but the ones that could talk said things like 'Mummy', and 'Bottle', and 'Change me'.

And 'Kill!'

Mr Karloff had managed to stop running for long enough to call the police. PC Wayne and WPC Hay, who were out in a patrol car, were now aware that Biddlecombe was in trouble again. There were rumours of eerie noises from the old prison, and strange lights in the abandoned asylum. They had tried to contact Sergeant Rowan and Constable Peel, with no result, so they had locked up the police station and headed out to investigate.

As it happened, their route back to the centre of town took them by the battlefield. They paused for a moment and took in the sight of dozens of undead Vikings and Saxons merrily attempting to kill one another and, when that didn't work due to the fact that they were already dead, contenting themselves with lopping off limbs and heads.

'Let's just leave them to it, shall we?' said WPC Hay.

'That seems like the best thing,' said PC Wayne.

They drove away, and did not look back.

CHAPTER XXIV

In Which Nurd and Wormwood
Plan a Great Escape.

Nurd and Wormwood crouched in the darkness of Samuel's bedroom, watching the activity below. Nurd turned to Wormwood and examined him critically, which wasn't difficult where Wormwood was involved. He straightened Wormwood's costume, and adjusted his hat.

'This plan will never work,' said Wormwood.

'It might,' said Nurd.

'I look ridiculous.'

'Wormwood, you always look ridiculous. Admittedly, you now look slightly more ridiculous, if such a thing were possible. I did not believe it was, but it seems you have just proved me wrong. How do I look?'

'You look ridiculous too. And it still won't work.'

'Do you have a better plan?' asked Nurd.

'I have never had a plan in my life,' admitted Wormwood, although he was tempted to add that he was currently trying to come up with his first, because whatever he thought of, it couldn't be worse than this one.

They were under a state of siege. The elves had surrounded the house, but so far had failed to enter it.

They had found the double-glazing on Mrs Johnson's windows harder to break than expected, mostly because their little arms weren't strong enough to hurl stones at the glass with sufficient force to do any damage, while attempts to squeeze through the spring-loaded letter box had resulted only in severe injury to the elves involved.

In desperation, the elves had resorted to fire.

Nurd and Wormwood had looked on as a gang of elves struggled under the weight of a can of petrol, along with some matches and various rags, all stolen from the shed of Mr Jarvis, who lived next door to the Johnsons and was currently away on business.[37]

'Mr Jarvis won't like that,' said Nurd. 'He doesn't even allow people to borrow his lawnmower.'

This was true. Mr Jarvis was very mean. If Mr Jarvis had been a ghost, he would have charged people for frights.

'What are they going to do with that petrol?' said Wormwood.

'I'm not certain, but I suspect that they're going to try to burn us out.'

'They do know that we're demons, right?' said Wormwood. 'Demons don't burn.'

'No,' said Nurd, 'but this house will burn nicely, whether we're in it or not. What do you think Samuel's mum will say if she comes home from bingo and finds her house on fire?'

'She won't be happy,' said Wormwood.

☠ [37] You should not play with fire. You are about to discover why.

'She won't be happy at all.'

'Will she blame us?'

'She might, unless we can show her some elves with matches in their hands, but I'd prefer it if the house didn't burn to begin with.'

'I'll start filling buckets,' said Wormwood.

'That would be helpful,' said Nurd.

He continued to watch the elves. Even by the standards of not-very-bright creatures, the elves were spectacularly unintelligent. Perhaps it was because they were made from supernaturally animated wood. Say what you like about wood, but if you're on a quiz team and one of your team members is made from birch, or if you and your fellow prisoners are trying to come up with a cunning plan to escape from prison and one of you is carved out of oak, there's a limit to how much help the wooden representatives are going to be. Animated entities made from wood are usually not clever. So it was that the elves were splashing petrol around, and failing to light matches, and getting themselves wrapped up in bits of rag like small wooden mummies. More and more elves arrived to help, adding a second can of petrol to the first, and more matches, and even more confusion. They began carrying everything to the front door, spilling more petrol as they went.

'Tut-tut,' said Nurd.

'What?' said Wormwood, who had arrived with a bucket of water.

'Very dangerous, mucking about with fire. Someone could do himself an injury, and I think a lot of wooden someones are about to do just that.'

It's a funny thing about fire, but it burns very well when there is wood involved. It burns even better when there is wood and petrol involved, and better still if a little paint is added to the mix for good measure. Basically, Mrs Johnson's garden was now full of small, painted, petrol-soaked pieces of wood.

Suddenly, one of the elves finally managed to get a match lit.

'Weeeee!' it said, with delight, holding the match above its head like a small, and not very impressive, Olympic torch

'Weeeee!' said the other elves.

'Weeeee!' said the first elf again. It watched as the flame neared its fingers.

'Oh-oh!' it said, and dropped the match.

There was a loud *whoosh*, and a burst of flame. Mrs Johnson's garden was immediately turned into an elf bonfire. Somewhere in the middle of it, small figures could be seen running around trying to put themselves out. Bells tinkled hotly before melting.

'Can I make a joke about elf and safety?' said Wormwood.

'No, you can't,' said Nurd.

They waited until the flames began to die down. Some of the elves, now slightly charred, had made it to safety, although they were still stunned by what had happened. In a very short time, though, it was likely that they would overcome their shock and get angry, and then they'd start looking for revenge.

'Now is our chance,' said Nurd. 'If we don't make it, I'd like to say that it's been an honour to have you as a friend, Wormwood. I'd *like* to say that, but I can't, because it wouldn't be true.'

'Thank you,' said Wormwood. He was getting quite tearful. 'That's the nicest thing you've ever said to me.'

'It is, Wormwood. In return, do you have anything you'd like to say to me?'

Wormwood thought for a moment. Nurd picked up a faint smell of burning. He thought it was coming from the elves until he realised that it was the smell of Wormwood thinking.

'I couldn't have asked for a better demonic master,' said Wormwood finally.

'Really?'

'Really. I couldn't have asked, because nobody would have paid any attention.'

'How true, Wormwood, how true.'

Nurd and Wormwood went down the stairs and paused at the front door. They each took a deep breath and crossed their fingers. Wormwood had an extra one on each hand, which made it more complicated for him.

'Ready?' said Nurd.

'Ready,' said Wormwood.

Nurd opened the door, and together they stepped into the garden.

The elves, as we have already established, were not the sharpest tools in the box. They had, until recently, been perfectly anonymous bits of wood before unexpectedly finding themselves infused with supernatural energy. They had only two purposes: to cause as much mayhem as possible in Biddlecombe, and to capture the demons known as Nurd and Wormwood and bring them to Wreckit & Sons. So far they'd been doing reasonably well on the mayhem front, but the attempts to capture Nurd and Wormwood had been less successful. Various elves had lost limbs and heads due to collapsing pyramids and letterbox-related injuries. Half a dozen more had been crushed when stones and rocks thrown optimistically at windows had fallen tragically short of their targets. Finally, fire had taken care of most of the ones that were still standing, leaving only a handful in any condition to resume the mission.

The elves had pictures of Nurd and Wormwood implanted in their minds. They were sure of what the wanted demons looked like. What they did not look like was elves, which was why the remaining elves were slightly puzzled to see two more elves step out of a house previously occupied only by two demons. They were very large elves, and one of them smelled odd, even from a distance, but there was definitely something elfish about them. They had pointy ears, their cheeks were painted a rosy red, and they were wearing hats with bells on the end. They even had white beards, which made them very senior elves, and probably explained why they were so large.

Wormwood tried to keep from scratching at his cotton-wool beard, and from adjusting the Father Christmas hat that Mrs Johnson had bought to be worn on Christmas Day, and which was making his head sweat. He had also borrowed Mrs Johnson's red bathrobe. Nurd, meanwhile, was looking radiant in the green shower curtain from the bathroom, belted at the waist.

The elves stared at them. Anybody would have, really.

'We're going to die,' whispered Wormwood.

'We can't die,' said Nurd. 'We're demons.'

'Then we're going to nearly die, and we're going to keep nearly dying for a very long time.'

'Keep smiling,' said Nurd, while keeping smiling, so that it came out as 'Keek smigink.'

'Keek what?' said Wormwood.

'Keek *smigink*.'

'Oh. Right.'

Wormwood still had no idea what Nurd was saying, so he decided just to keep smiling and hope for the best. Together, he and Nurd walked down the garden path, their gaze fixed on a point somewhere over the heads of the elves, their smiles never wavering. As they passed, the elves fell to their knees in awe.

'It's working!' said Wormwood.

'Keek quige!'

But it *was* working, and it would have kept on working had Nurd's tail not poked out from beneath the folds of the shower curtain. The tail had been growing shorter of late, and Nurd was certain that eventually it would disappear altogether, but it still liked to make an appearance when Nurd was in stressful situations. One of the elves spotted it as it threw itself to the ground.

'Weeee?' it said.

It nudged the elf beside it, and pointed at the tail.

'Weeee!'

The word was passed among the elves. By now, Nurd and Wormwood were at the garden gate. Another step or two and they'd be on the street, and Nurd had Mrs Johnson's car keys in his pocket. He had promised her never, ever to drive again without permission, or unless he was being paid to crash the car in question, but Nurd looked at promises as things you said just to make other people feel better. You never knew what might happen in the future, and you didn't want to go pinning yourself down.

Nurd reached for the keys. The car was in sight. He took one more step towards it and stopped: not because he wanted to, but because his feet wouldn't carry him forward. He looked over his shoulder to find a dozen elves hanging on grimly to his tail. One of them was even gnawing at it. Nurd wished him luck. His tail was tougher than leather, and tasted like it, too.

Nurd sighed. There was a discarded match on the ground beside him. He picked it up and flicked at it with a curved fingernail, causing it to ignite.

'Wormwood?' he said. 'Will you do the honours?'

He held the match out by his side. Wormwood leaned in close, took a deep breath, and blew hard.

The match disappeared in a torrent of flame that continued in the direction of the elves. If they thought the petrol was bad, the effect of Wormwood's lit breath on them was a thousand times worse. Nurd wasn't sure what Wormwood's digestive system was like, but he decided that whatever was happening inside Wormwood must be very horrible, and certainly explained where a lot of those smells were coming from. The elves didn't even burn. They just went straight from wood to black ash without any stops in between.

'Thank you, Wormwood,' said Nurd. 'Well done. Indeed, they're probably very well done now, come to think of it.'

Wormwood stopped blowing. Nurd dislodged the remaining pieces of charred elf from his tail, and lifted the tip to examine it. It, too, was on fire. He gave a little puff of breath, and the fire went out.

'What now?' said Wormwood.

'We go to Wreckit & Sons,' said Nurd.

'Why there?'

Nurd picked up an elf foot that had survived the blaze and pointed to the sole of its little painted boot. On it were written the words *Property of Wreckit & Sons*.

CHAPTER XXV

In Which Battle Commences.

Dozy and Mumbles collided with Angry, Jolly and Dan, who had just been reunited. They came together next to a pile of old yellow boxes marked, peculiarly enough, 'Odd Shoes', although nothing could have been odder than what they'd already encountered in that basement.

'You won't believe what happened to us!' said Jolly, then remembered that, not too long before, they'd all been trapped in Hell together. 'Hang on, you probably will believe it.'

'You won't believe what's *still* happening to us,' Dozy managed to gasp, as the first of the running eyeballs rounded the corner and pulled up short. It had been expecting to encounter two dwarfs, but was now facing four, and a human. If it had been gifted with hands, it would have rubbed itself just to be sure that it wasn't seeing things.

'Is that an eyeball on legs?' said Angry.

'One of many,' said Dozy. 'The rest are on their way. Oh look, here they are.'

More eyeballs appeared, and paused to consider Dan and the dwarfs.

'They've got teeth,' said Jolly. 'That can't be right. Why are they chasing you?'

'Because I stood on one of them,' said Dozy. 'I stamped on it hard, to be honest, but it was an accident.'

'Messy,' said Jolly.

'I think I still have some of it stuck to my heel,' said Dozy.

'Nasty,' said Angry. 'Just so we're clear, you stood on one, and then the others got angry, so you ran away from them?'

'That's right.'

'Why didn't you just stamp on the rest of them?'

'Well, they have teeth.'

'Not much they can do with them though, really, is there?' said Angry. 'Bite your feet, maybe, but then you are wearing big boots, which is where the trouble started to begin with, if I'm not mistaken.'

Dozy looked at his boots, and back at the eyeballs.

'Are you suggesting – ?'

'I am.'

'They squish,' said Dozy. 'It made my tummy feel funny.'

'You'll get over it.'

'I suppose you're right. I think I'm almost over it already.'

'There you are, then,' said Angry.

Slowly, deliberately, meaningfully, the dwarfs and Dan advanced on the eyeballs. The eyeballs eyeballed each other. They may not have had ears, but they could see perfectly well, and what they saw was trouble advancing on them in big boots. As one, the eyeballs turned tail and headed back in the direction from which they'd come. Dan and the dwarfs watched them as they scarpered into the shadows.

'See?' said Angry. 'How hard was that?'

'Not very,' said Dozy.

'Bet you feel a bit silly now, don't you?'

'A bit,' Dozy admitted.

'Where did all those eyeballs come from anyway?' asked Jolly.

'Well,' said Dozy, 'there were all these pictures of a bloke with big ears and teeth – a bit vampirish he was – and I said that the eyes seemed to follow you around the room, and next minute the eyes *were* following us around the room. Very unsettling it was, so—'

'Uh,' said Mumbles. He tapped Dozy on the arm.

'Not now,' said Dozy. 'I'm explaining. Anyway—'

Mumbles tapped him on the arm again.

'Really,' said Dozy, turning to give Mumbles a piece of his mind, 'you have to learn some . . .'

What Mumbles had to learn was destined to remain undiscovered. Music was coming from somewhere nearby, the sound of an organ being played in a very dramatic manner, and a shape was emerging from the murk. It was hunched, and wore a long dark coat. The parts of it that were not covered by the coat were very pale. They included its hands, which had long fingers ending in even longer nails. Its head was entirely bald, and its ears were big and pointed like those of a bat. Its two front teeth, to reference the famous song,[38] were not the kind that anyone would want for Christmas. They extended over its lower lip and resembled the fangs of a snake. As for its eyes, when last Dan and the dwarfs had seen them they'd been running along on two little feet and brandishing teeth of their own. They looked more at home in that awful face, and considerably more threatening.

'Oh,' said Dozy.

He had seen many horrible things in this time. He had seen demons. He had seen Hell itself. He had even, due to an unlocked bathroom door, seen Jolly without any pants on. But he believed that he had never seen, and never would see, anything more terrifying than the figure standing before him.

Until he saw the one that appeared next to it, because, unlike its nearly identical twin, it had only one eye. The remains of the other, Dozy guessed, were still stuck in the treads of one of his boots.

'Eh, Dozy,' said Jolly. 'I think there's a bloke here who'd like a word with you.'

'Should we start running again?' said Dozy.

'I believe,' said Jolly, 'that would be a very good idea.'

*   *   *

---

38 'All I Want for Christmas is My Two Front Teeth' was written in 1944, although why anyone would want to wake up in the early hours of Christmas Day to find Santa Claus performing some makeshift implant dentistry on them remains to be seen, and would be likely to result in long-term trauma. What next? 'All I Want for Christmas is My Appendix Removed' or '. . . My Nose Broken and Reset'? What's wrong with a train set, or a doll? Some people are very complicated.

Above the dwarfs, in the store itself, Samuel, Lucy and the policemen were fighting a rearguard action against ranks of dolls that had been reinforced by assorted cuddly toys. The humans had retreated to the first floor where Samuel had equipped them with guns capable of firing plastic darts and foam bullets. They were having some effect on the demented dolls and threatening teddy bears and yapping demon dogs with large jaws, most of whom struggled to get back on their feet once they'd been knocked over. Some, though, were made of sterner stuff, so Samuel and Lucy, their relationship problems temporarily set aside in the fight for survival, had begun to collect footballs, basketballs, toy cars, and various heavy objects instead. Now, like soldiers in a castle raining down boulders on the besieging forces, they tossed their ammunition with maximum force at their attackers, and watched with satisfaction as dolls lost heads and teddy bears lost limbs.

'I never liked dolls anyway,' said Lucy, as a particularly well-aimed rugby ball fragmented a Sally Salty Tears. 'They represent the imposition of outdated gender roles on girls too young to know better.'

Samuel looked at Constable Peel, who shrugged. Samuel thought that Constable Peel might have been almost as frightened of Lucy as he was of the attacking dolls.

'Have you noticed anything funny about those dolls?' asked Sergeant Rowan.

Constable Peel goggled at him. He looked like a goose trying to cough up a feather.

'Funny, Sarge? Funny? You mean, apart from the

fact that they've come alive and seem intent upon killing us, or isn't that funny enough for you?'

'Now, now, son,' said Sergeant Rowan, 'panicking won't do us any good. No, what I mean is that they seem to have stopped trying to get up the stairs. It's as if they're happy enough just to have forced us up here.'

The sergeant was right. The initial assault had petered out, helped in part by the fact that so many dolls and soft toys were no longer in a position to do much assaulting because of a lack of legs, arms, and heads. Reinforcements continued to arrive, but instead of attempting to scale the stairs they were retreating to positions of cover, from which they were happy just to bare teeth or wave sharp items of cutlery. There had been a worrying moment when the giant twenty-foot teddy on the ground floor had begun moving and seemed about to join in the conflict, but it turned out to be too big and heavy to get to its feet. It had instead remained slumped in a corner growling, like a fat man who had eaten too many pies.

Samuel took a moment to get his bearings. They were in the games department, and it didn't look like any of the board games, tennis rackets or cricket bats were about to come to murderous life. The walls, he saw, were decorated with lifesize cardboard models of characters from nursery rhymes. He recognised Miss Muffet sitting on her tuffet, Humpty Dumpty on his wall, and Little Bo Peep along with assorted sheep. At the very rear of the floor was another flight of stairs. A thin figure watched them from halfway up it.

'Look!' said Samuel. 'It's that Mr St John-Cholmondeley.'

'He doesn't look very happy,' said Constable Peel. 'Then again, half of his doll department is in pieces on the ground floor.'

Sergeant Rowan stood up. He unbuttoned the top left hand pocket of his jacket and from it removed his notebook.

'Oh, he's in trouble now,' said Constable Peel to Samuel. 'Once that notebook comes out it's not going back in the pocket without someone's name being written down.'

Sergeant Rowan coughed and licked his pencil. It hung poised over the notebook like the Sword of Damocles.[39]

'Right you are, Mr St John-Cholmondley,' said Sergeant Rowan. 'I'd appreciate it if you'd join me here for a moment and explain just what's going on.'

'I'm afraid I can't do that,' said Mr St John-Cholmondeley. 'The answer you seek can only be found by moving higher into the store. The truth lies on the top floor.'

---

[39] Damocles was reputed to have been a courtier in the court of Dionysius II, a tyrant ruler of Syracuse in the fourth century. Perhaps unwisely, Damocles suggested that Dionysius was quite the lucky fellow to have such a nice throne, and lots of gold, and all of that power, so Dionysius invited Damocles to take a turn on the throne, just to try it out for size. Unfortunately, as with most tyrants, there was a catch, for Dionysius arranged for a big sword to be hung over the throne, held in place by a single hair from the tail of a horse. Not surprisingly, Damocles didn't care much for sitting in a throne under a sharp blade that might, at any moment, drop on his head with unpleasant consequences, and after a while he politely asked Dionysius if he might be allowed to sit somewhere else instead. Dionysius, having had his fun, agreed. The moral is that those in power are always in peril too, especially if they're tyrants whom nobody likes. The Sword of Damocles is thus very famous, much more so than the lesser known Onion of Unhappiness and the Custard Tart of Doom.

'Well, sir, we don't have time to be running around chasing answers and truth. We're policemen, not philosophers. I think you should come down with us to the station and we'll have a chat about it all over a nice cup of tea in one of the cells. Why don't you just open the doors and stop all of this nonsense, there's a good gentleman. In the meantime, I'm going to write your name in my notebook as a "person of interest".'

Sergeant Rowan was just about to do that when he noticed that his pencil was gone.

'Here, who's made off with my pencil?' he asked, as his notebook was yanked from his hand and disappeared into the shadows on the ceiling, leaving only a sticky residue on Sergeant Rowan's fingers. He pulled at it, and saw that it was spider web. He looked again at the ceiling, and noticed that the shadows on it appeared to be moving.

'Ah,' he said. 'Right.'

Mr St John-Cholmondeley smiled at them from the stairs, then skipped up to the next floor. Samuel barely noticed him go because another figure was moving towards them. It was coming from where the cardboard model of Miss Muffet used to be, except the model was no longer on the wall.

What appeared before them was not Miss Muffet, the beloved figure of nursery rhyme fame.[40] Either this one

---

💀 [40] You know the one:

Little Miss Muffet sat on a tuffet
Eating her curds and whey,
Along came a spider,
Who sat down beside her

loved spiders an awful lot or she hadn't run away fast enough when the first one appeared, and it had brought plenty of friends along with it for company. She was dressed entirely in black, and wore a veil over her face, a veil that, as she drew closer, was revealed to be made, not from fabric, but from spider silk. The little black spiders that crawled across it, and the dead flies trapped in it, gave the game away on that front. More spiders poured from her sleeves and from beneath her skirts: brown ones, black ones, red ones, yellow ones. There were webs between her fingers, and webs under her arms. Beneath her veil of black spider silk her features were almost entirely concealed by sticky white strands, with only the vaguest of holes torn in them for her eyes and her mouth.

A small black spider descended from the ceiling and dropped on to Sergeant Rowan's shoulder. He quickly brushed it away, but another fell, and another. He got rid of them too. One of them scuttled towards Lucy. She stamped on it. When she lifted her foot, it was still there. It looked unhappy but was otherwise unharmed. Lucy tried again, but was still unsuccessful in killing it. This was clearly no ordinary spider.

'Eugh!' said Lucy loudly. 'How horrid!'

And frightened Miss Muffet away.

Or alternatively:

Little Miss Muffet sat on a tuffet
Eating her curds and whey,
Along came a spider,
Who sat down beside her
We lose lots of Miss Muffets that way.

Little Miss Muffet's head turned in her direction. It was one thing trying to crush her pets, but obviously quite another entirely to describe them as horrid.

'*Not horrid,*' said a soft voice from somewhere behind the silk. '*Beautiful.*'

Miss Muffet was having trouble speaking properly. She sounded like she had hairballs caught in her throat. The spider strands around her mouth trembled, and a fat brown spider emerged from between what might have been her lips. It was quickly followed by another, and another, and another.[41]

Sergeant Rowan backed away. Above them, ranks of spiders moved across the ceiling, forcing the humans and Boswell to retreat further to avoid having the spiders drop on them. More of the nasty creatures were spreading across the floor. There was a sense of purpose to their approach. The spiders were herding Samuel and the others, moving them closer and closer to the stairs.

In case they needed any more convincing, a massive shape disengaged itself from the darkest corner of the

---

☠ [41] If swallowing a spider sounds unpleasant, it should be noted that most of us consume bits of spiders and insects every day. In the United States, the Food & Drug Administration has even published a guide to the level of insect fragments permitted in food. Frozen spinach is allowed fifty aphids or mites per one hundred grams, peanut butter can have thirty insect fragments per one hundred grams, and chocolate is allowed to have sixty. Don't worry, though: insects are an excellent source of protein. So eat up, they're good for you.

Incidentally, in 1911 a scientist named C.F. Hodge calculated that if a pair of houseflies started breeding in April and continued until August, their offspring, if they all survived, would cover the earth forty-seven feet deep by August. So by accidentally eating the odd fly here and there, you're saving the earth from being buried by them. Well done, you! Try them with ketchup. They're tasty. (Warning: may not actually be tasty.)

room and moved steadily towards them. A beam of moonlight caught it, causing the eight black eyes in its head to gleam. It was the size of a small car, except small cars didn't have eight legs and long poisonous fangs that dripped venom as the enormous spider detected the presence of prey.

'*My pretty*,' said Miss Muffet, stroking the dense hairs on the spider's head. '*Pretty is hungry*.'

'You know,' said Sergeant Rowan, 'perhaps we should see what's upstairs after all.'

So they ascended to the next floor, and the spiders, thankfully, did not follow.

CHAPTER XXVI

In Which Constable Peel is Reduced to Tears of Unhappiness.

Nurd decided that the scenes of Christmas chaos in Biddlecombe were very inventive, even for someone who had previously witnessed an invasion by the forces of Hell itself. It was one thing to encounter people being attacked by, and fighting against, assorted demons, ghouls and chthonic[42] forces, which were, by and large, simply terrifying, and therefore capable of being understood on those terms. It was quite another to witness a running battle in August Derleth Park between the Biddlecombe Ladies' Football Team and a half-dozen very rough-looking fairies that had climbed down from the tops of various Christmas trees with murder on their minds. So far, the Biddlecombe Ladies seemed to have the upper hand, mainly because the Biddlecombe Ladies were bigger than some of the Biddlecombe Gentlemen,

---

[42] *Chthonic* (pronounced *thonic* to rhyme with *sonic*) is a great word of Greek origin, and means of, or relating to, the Underworld. Feel free to drop it into conversations at home, where it has many amusing uses. For example: 'Mum, this broccoli is positively *chthonic*.' Or: 'I'm not sure about that tie, Dad. It looks kind of *chthonic*.' And, of course, the ever popular: 'I'd give that bathroom a minute or two. It smells a bit *chthonic*.'

and had a such a reputation for violence on the pitch that opposing teams had been known to injure themselves at first sight of them, just to save the ladies the effort. The fairies were doing some damage with their wands, though, which had been weaponised by the addition of chains and spiked metal balls.

'Those fairies are walking a bit funny,' said Wormwood.

'You'd walk a bit funny too if someone stuck a Christmas tree up you,' said Nurd.

A large troop of elves crossed their path, struggling beneath the weight of a tree trunk that they were hoping to use to break down the door of the post office. It was quite clear to Nurd and Wormwood that the tree trunk, while heavy enough to use as a battering ram, was too heavy for even a great many elves to carry for any distance.

'Weeeee!' urged one of the lead elves. 'Weeeee!'

Nurd and Wormwood watched as first one set of legs buckled, and then another. By the time the third set went there was only time for a single, worried 'Oh-oh' before the competition between the elves and the tree trunk was won by the trunk with a crushing victory, leaving various elf limbs sticking out from beneath it.

'Ow,' said a small voice.

A lead elf, who had managed to escape being trapped through some nifty footwork, looked pleadingly at Nurd and Wormwood for help.

'Weeeee?' it said. 'Weeeee?'

Nurd trod on it.

Further along the way, they saw a giant ferocious

reindeer with sharp horns and black eyes standing before a herd of local deer as it tried to incite them to rebellion.

'Rise up!' cried the demon reindeer. 'Rise up against the puny humans who know you only as Bambi, the oppressors who think you're cute but occasionally eat you in stews, or with parsnips and a reduction of juniper berries.'

The local deer did what local deer do, which was to glance nervously from the demon reindeer to one another before returning to eating grass in the hope that the demon reindeer would go away and stop bothering them.

'Oh, have it your way, then,' said the demon reindeer. It looked at the grass. It nibbled a bit. Actually, it thought, the grass was rather good. It ate some more. It continued to graze happily until it was joined by a couple of other demon reindeer who'd had no more luck starting the deer revolution than it had.

'What do you think you're doing?' asked the leader of the demon reindeer.

The lone demon reindeer did some quick thinking. 'Trying to win their trust?' it suggested.

'No, you're just eating grass. Stop it and come with us. We must sow fear and chaos. The Shadows are about to fall.'

The demon reindeer nibbled one last piece of grass and joined the rest of the demon reindeer herd. It paused only to look back at the local deer and whisper, 'Don't eat it all, right? Save some for me. Seriously. Please. You're really lovely deer, and very handsome. Sorry I shouted at you.'

The deer ignored it. After all, it wasn't fawning season.[43]

Fires had broken out in houses and gardens. On Wells Street, a large wolf was trying to blow down a house made of bricks while the lady inside threw pots at it from an upstairs window. A troll had hidden under a canal bridge, hoping to spring out and trap unwary travellers, but that was Bill the Tramp's bridge, and he wasn't about to share it with anyone. Bill had tied the unconscious troll to a shopping trolley and left it outside the police station with a note attached that read 'Possibly from abroad'. Meanwhile Mr Thompson the greengrocer, who did not like competition, had found a wicked stepmother going around with a basket of apples for sale and had forced her to hide in a dustbin to escape his wrath, and his rotten fruit and vegetables.

A water main had burst and was already starting to freeze. It was growing colder. Nurd hadn't noticed before. He looked at Wormwoood. The tip of Wormwood's nose had turned blue.

'Your nose has turned blue,' Nurd told him.

'Has it? It was feeling a bit funny.'

Wormwood scratched at his nose. It fell off in his hand. He peered at it, then shrugged. These things happened, or they happened to Wormwood. He excavated a disturbingly filthy handkerchief from somewhere on

---

[43] A very clever joke that plays upon the fact that the word 'fawn', meaning to gain favour through flattery, and 'fawn', meaning a young deer, are spelt the same. See? Oh, please yourself. It's like casting pearls before swine . . .

his person, carefully wrapped his nose in it, then stuck it in his pocket for safekeeping.

'Why did you wrap it in a handkerchief?' asked Nurd.

'In case I sneeze,' said Wormwood. 'I don't want to make a mess.'

'Ah,' said Nurd. 'Very sensible.'

They walked on, offering Nurd time to think about what Wormwood had just said. Nurd stopped walking, gave Wormwood a hard flick on the ear, and they continued on their way.

Snow fell on them. Nurd looked up, but there wasn't a cloud in sight. The night was so clear that the sky was filled with stars, like millions of gemstones scattered across a great swatch of dark cloth. Nurd had never seen so many. They took his breath away, but there was something wrong about this sky. It seemed blacker than he remembered, which made the stars shine brighter. The problem was that they weren't the right stars. The constellations had changed. No, that wasn't quite true. Nurd thought that he could still pick out Gemini, and Draco, and Ursa Major and Ursa Minor, the Great Bear and the Little Bear, but other stars were overlaid upon them. They were dimmer, but growing in intensity. It was as though one solar system was somehow being introduced over another.

Nurd found Polaris, the North Star, the centre of the night sky, which had guided travellers on land and sea ever since the earliest days of exploration. Once Polaris was visible it was hard to be lost, for it marked the way due north. There was consolation in its presence.

As Nurd watched, the great star blinked once, and disappeared.

Dan and the dwarfs were still being pursued, although not very quickly. The Nosferati, as Dan had dubbed them, were addicted to sneaking along, their long fingers grasping, their shadows stretching ahead of them, almost touching the heels of Dozy, who was bringing up the rear. But they did so very, very slowly, and had a fondness for stopping occasionally and making scary faces.

And while there was no doubt that they were horrible, and nasty, and smelled of the grave, they might have been more troubling had their every move not been accompanied by music played on an unseen organ. Every footstep, every raised hand, every arch of the eyebrows came with a tune. They were monsters from a silent movie, and in the days of silent movies each cinema would pay an organist to play along with the film. It was part of the deal, and even these Nosferati, liberated from picture frames, had to play by the rules.

'I wish that music would stop,' said Dan. 'It sounds like the ice-cream van from Hell.'

The music was bothering the Nosferati as well. Some of them snatched at the air, as though trying to pull the notes from the ether and grind them into musical dust. It was no good. The unseen organ kept on playing.

It was Jolly who wondered aloud if the Nosferati had ever even heard the organ music before. By now, Dan and the dwarfs had slowed from a run to a stroll, as it was clear that the Nosferati, though a nuisance, weren't likely to catch up with them any time soon.

'I mean, they were in a silent film,' said Jolly, 'which was, you know, silent. It was only in the real world, our world, that the music played. Imagine if, every time you took a step, there was some bloke banging away on an organ behind you. It'd drive you mental. They'd have to put you away before you killed him.'

The Nosferati had stopped making any progress at all. They were now curled up in little balls with their coats over their heads, or were trying to jam their fingers in their ears, which didn't work because their fingernails were too long. One of them was banging his forehead repeatedly against a wall.

'See?' said Jolly. 'There's only so much of it you can take before—'

The one-eyed Nosferatu, the one who had had his eye (singular) on Dozy, started to shake. He raised a questioning finger as if to say, 'Hang on a minute, this doesn't feel right,' and then his head exploded. As he had been undead for a very long time, there wasn't much blood or brain to contend with. His head simply disappeared in a puff of grey dust, and his body quickly followed.

This began a chain reaction of exploding heads and bodies collapsing like old pillars, filling the basement with the dust of the undead. When it finally settled, Dan and the dwarfs were all that remained standing, although now covered from head to toe in grey bits of vampire. The few surviving Nosferati who had managed to plug their ears beat a hasty retreat.

Angry coughed up ash.

'I think I swallowed some,' he said. 'That can't be good for me.'

'Look,' said Dozy. 'It's a lift.'

And it was. It was rickety and old and bore an unhappy resemblance to a cage, but it was definitely a lift of sorts. Its floor was made of wood, and its walls were lined with velvet. Instead of a door, it had a metal gate that could be pulled across and secured.

Dozy poked his head inside.

'I don't see any buttons,' he said. 'There's a control lever, though.'

He stepped into the lift and gave the lever an experimental tug, but nothing happened.

'You have to close the gate first, I think,' said Dan.

'Hang on,' said Jolly. 'Don't do anything until we're all inside.'

Dan, Jolly, Angry and Mumbles joined Dozy in the lift.

'All aboard?' said Dozy. 'Right. Up we go!'

He pulled the lever. There came the groaning of ancient machinery. The lift vibrated, and slowly began to rise.

Samuel, Lucy and the policemen had just reached the next floor when they heard a rumbling in the basement.

'What's that?' said Sergeant Rowan.

'Sorry,' said Constable Peel. 'That's me. I haven't been feeling very well.'

'No, not that,' said Sergeant Rowan, although he took a couple of cautious steps back from Constable Peel. '*That!*'

They all heard it now. It was the sound of a lift ascending.

'Over there,' said Samuel.

To their right was a dark, gated shaft, and above it a panel displaying floor numbers had just lit up.

'Something's coming up from the basement!' said Lucy.

'It has to be something nasty,' said Constable Peel. 'There are only nasty things in this shop, present company excepted.'

The number '1' lit up.

'It'll be here in a couple of seconds,' said Constable Peel.

'Be brave, lad,' said Sergeant Rowan.

He gripped his cricket bat tightly. He'd had the foresight to grab a weapon as they ran from the spiders. Samuel and Lucy hefted their pool cues threateningly, for they had been wise enough to do the same.

Constable Peel took his place beside them.

'What are you holding?' said Sergeant Rowan.

'Ping-pong bat,' said Constable Peel. 'It was all I could find.'

'Constable, we need to have a long talk when this is all over.'

'Yes, Sarge.'

The lift came into view. The light on the second floor was poor, and the lift itself remained dark, but as it stopped Samuel and the others could pick out five grey shapes.

'Ghouls!' whispered Lucy.

'Wraiths!' said Constable Peel.

The lift's gate opened. The five figures emerged and stepped into a small pool of moonlight cast through the murky glass of one of the windows. It was Constable Peel who reacted first.

'It's Dan and the dwarfs,' he said. 'Look at them! They're all grey and spooky and sickly. They're dead, but somehow they're still upright. Only the shells of them remain! Oh! Oh!'

He fell to his knees, buried his face in his hands, and began to weep. Jolly raised a hand and opened his mouth.

'Look,' said Sergeant Rowan. 'One of them is trying to speak.'

Constable Peel peered over the tips of his fingers. It was true. He waited to hear the hollow, undead rattle of what had once been Mr Jolly Smallpants.

Jolly didn't speak. He sneezed. The sneeze was so massive that it caused most of the ash to lift from him, and Jolly used the opportunity to step to one side and avoid the dust as it came down again.

'It's all right,' he said. 'It's just bits of dead vampire.'

Constable Peel stared at him for a time, then burst into tears again, crying even harder than before.

'Oh no!' he wailed. 'They're alive. They're *still* alive . . .'

CHAPTER XXVII

In Which Dorothy Seems Slightly Confused.

Maria and the scientists, trapped in the sweet factory with a hostile figure apparently made entirely from darkness, had considered their options and done the sensible thing, which was to leave as quickly as possible. They were now in Professor Hilbert's car, heading in the direction of Wreckit & Sons by taking the shortcut through August Derleth Park. Professor Hilbert was driving, Professor Stefan was in the passenger seat, and Maria, Brian, and Dorothy were crammed in the back. Brian was beginning to recover from his encounter with the dark woman, although his entire body continued to tremble involuntarily, and he would occasionally emit a startled squeak.

Dorothy, meanwhile, was still wearing her beard. Maria had tried not to notice, but it was difficult as it was quite a big beard.

Dorothy caught Maria looking at it.

'It's the beard, isn't it?' she said, in her new deep voice.

Maria nodded.

'I was just wondering why you were still wearing it.'

'I like it. It's warm.'

'Right,' said Maria. She would have moved over a little to put some space between herself and Dorothy, but there wasn't room because of the human jelly that was Brian.

'And I don't want to be called Dorothy any more.'

Professor Hilbert, who had been listening, gave Dorothy a worried look in the rear-view mirror. Professor Stefan turned round in his seat. His face wore the confused expression of a builder who has just been handed a glass hammer.

'What do you mean, you don't want to be called Dorothy?' he said. 'It's your name, and it's a perfectly lovely one.'

'I want to be called Reginald,' said Dorothy – er, Reginald. 'Inside, I feel like a Reginald.'

Professor Stefan frowned.

'But why Reginald?' he said. 'Nobody is called "Reginald" these days. It would be like me announcing that I wanted to be called Elsie, or Boadicea.'[44]

'I like the name Reginald,' said Dorothy, or Reginald. 'It was my mother's name.'

Even Brian stopped shaking for long enough to look bewildered, then went back to trembling again.

💀 [44] Boadicea was the queen of the Iceni tribe in Britain who led a rebellion against the Roman Empire in A.D. 60 or 61. Three settlements were destroyed during her war, including the young city of Londinium, or London. She was finally defeated in a battle in the West Midlands, but died without being captured. The Roman historian Dio said of her that she was 'possessed of greater intelligence than often belongs to women'. Mind you, he said that after she was safely dead and gone, otherwise she'd have cut his head off and stuck it on a spike for saying stupid things about women.

'Right,' said Professor Hilbert. 'I'm glad we cleared that one up.'

Any further discussion of the matter was postponed by the appearance of a Viking on the road. He wore a metal helmet, but was otherwise entirely naked. This might have been more disturbing had he not been little more than leathery skin and yellowed bone. In his right hand he held a rusty sword, and a shield hung from his left arm.

'You know, you really don't see that very often,' said Professor Hilbert.

Even though he was a physicist, he had a scientist's general fascination with anything new and unusual in the world, and a naked undead Viking counted as unusual in any world. Issues of personal safety took second place to things that were just plain interesting.

'How splendid!' said Professor Stefan. 'Slow down, Hilbert, so we can take a good look at him.'

Professor Hilbert slowed the car to a crawl, and rolled down his window.

'Hello!' he said to the Viking.

'You look a bit lost,' said Professor Stefan.

The Viking glared at them. Darkness seethed and roiled in its eyes.

'Garrrgghhhh,' it said. 'Urrurh.'

'Ah, yes, of course,' said Professor Hilbert. 'How true, how true.'

He looked at Professor Stefan and shrugged. Professor Stefan rolled his eyes.

'Where are you from?' said Professor Hilbert. He spoke very slowly and very loudly, which is how

English people who don't speak foreign languages try to communicate with those who do.

'Harruraruh,' said the Viking.

'Where is that?' said Professor Stefan. 'Could he show us on a map?'

'Map?' said Professor Hilbert to the Viking.

He drew squiggles in the air, in the faint hope that the Viking might make the connection. Instead the Viking simply waved his sword and said, 'Rarh!'

'I don't think we're going to get much out of him, I'm afraid,' said Professor Hilbert. 'His English leaves a lot to be desired.'

'What a shame,' said Professor Stefan. 'You'd think the chap might have brought a phrasebook with him so he could communicate a little better. You know, "Hello, I come from Norway." "Where is Buckingham Palace?" That kind of thing. Hardly seems worth making the trip if you can't speak the language. Never mind.'

He waved at the Viking.

''Bye, now!' he said. 'Thanks for visiting.'

'Warrghhh,' said the Viking.

'Ha-ha!' said Professor Stefan. 'Absolutely, yes.'

He puffed out his cheeks as Professor Hilbert prepared to drive off.

'No idea what the chap was saying.'

He gave the Viking a final wave, just in time to witness a Saxon with one leg dragging brokenly behind him hit the Viking repeatedly on the top of the head with an axe.

'And they wonder why tourists don't come here very often,' said Professor Hilbert.

'It's the battlefield,' said Maria.

'What?'

'We're close to the site of the Battle of Biddlecombe. Hilary Mould designed and built the visitor centre there. It's one of the points on the pentagram. I'll bet there's supernatural activity at the old asylum too, and the crematorium, and the prison. Which makes me more certain than ever that the centre of the activity is here.'

She tapped her finger on the map, right on the location of Wreckit & Sons.

A small troop of Christmas elves crossed their path, forcing Professor Hilbert to brake suddenly.

'You don't want to try talking to them as well, do you?' said Maria.

'Don't be silly,' said Professor Stefan. 'They're elves.'

'Of course,' said Maria. 'Duh.'

The elves paid them no notice. They were too busy running from something. Seconds later, one of the groundskeepers appeared. He was carrying a heavy rake, but was still making good progress. He caught up with the elves just as they reached the other side of the road, and began beating them to splinters.

'The sign said,' he screamed, '"KEEP OFF THE GRASS". What part of keeping off the grass did you' – *Bang!* – 'not' – *Smash!* – 'understand?' –*Thud!*'

When the elves were no more, the groundskeeper looked up to see five people watching him. He tipped his hat at them.

'Evening,' he said.

'Evening,' replied Professor Hilbert.

The groundskeeper indicated with a thumb the stack of firewood and splinters that had once been elves.

'Elves,' he said. 'They trampled on the grass.'

'So we gathered.'

'And the flowerbeds,' added the groundskeeper. His tone suggested that, while some might feel reducing elves to kindling for trespassing on the grass was a bit of an overreaction, no sane person could take issue with pummelling them for stepping on the flowerbeds.

He wiped his sweating brow.

'I quite enjoyed that,' he said. 'I think I'll go and look for some more of them.'

And off he went, whistling what sounded like 'Heigh-Ho, Heigh-Ho.'

It struck Professor Hilbert that, if the groundskeeper was anything to go by, the citizens of Biddlecombe were taking the evening's events in their stride. This view was confirmed when they came across the Biddlecombe Ladies' Football Team standing by half a dozen large and very bruised Christmas tree fairies who had been tied to tree trunks with stout rope in order to prevent them from doing any further harm.

Professor Hilbert stopped the car.

'What are you doing?' said Professor Stefan.

'Look!' said Professor Hilbert, pointing to the west.

There was a faint shimmer to the air. Beyond it Maria could see more trees and, some way in the distance, the spire of the church in the nearest village, Rathford, but it was as though a mist had descended upon the landscape, blurring the image. It struck Maria that they shouldn't even have been able to see Rathford. It was night-time, and yet the spire of the Church of St Roger the Inflammable was plainly visible, although there was a touch of shiny grey to it, like an old photographic negative.

Professor Hilbert stepped from the car and walked toward the location of the shimmering. The others followed, even Brian, although he was not so much curious as frightened to be left alone. As they drew closer, they saw that the ground came to a kind of end at the fence surrounding August Derleth Park. Beyond the boundary it was less actual firm ground than the memory of it, and its level didn't quite match the grass on their side of the fence. Worse, the other ground was transparent, and beneath it Maria could see a terrible blackness spotted with the odd lonely star. It felt to her as though Biddlecombe had somehow been set adrift in the Multiverse while still bringing with it the memory of the planet of which it had once been a part. The dividing line was the shimmering, like the heat haze that rises from the earth on sunny summer days, except this one brought with it no warmth.

Reginald/Dorothy reached out to touch it, and only Professor Hilbert's sudden grip on his/her wrist prevented him/her from doing so.[45]

💀 [45] Look, this is going to get very confusing. Unless someone decides otherwise, let's call Dorothy 'Reginald', but stick with the use of the feminine pronoun. That way, she'll be Reginald, and we can still refer to her as 'her', if you see what I mean.

It's very troubling when characters take a funny unplanned turn in a book. They really should do what their creators tell them to do, but that brings us to the whole thorny subject of the problem of free will. If I knew what was going to happen at the end of this book – which, at this point, I don't – then characters

'I wouldn't,' he said.

Reginald withdrew her hand. Professor Hilbert's fingers tingled after touching her. It must be the power of the boundary, he thought.

'How can we see Rathford?' asked Maria. 'We shouldn't be able to. It's night, and anyway Rathford

---

like Reginald/Dorothy would have to do whatever I told them to do, because that would be what was needed to make the plot work.

But right now I'm not sure what's going to happen, and I'm discovering the plot of the book as I write it. This makes me a bit like a god, in that I created these characters, but not the type of god who knows everything in advance. The thing is, if I was that kind of god, and characters like Reginald/Dorothy were, in fact, real, would the fact that I knew what was going to happen to them mean that they had no free will of their own?

Some philosophers have argued that, if there is a god, and he knows everything that will happen in the future, then free will doesn't really exist. I'm not sure that's the case because, if it is, then we are all like characters in a book being written by a writer who knows the ending. Maybe it's truer to say that, if there is a god, then he just happens to know how our story ends, and the choices we make are the ones that will lead to that particular ending.

So can we ever really predict what people will do? Perhaps on one level we can: we are biological machines, each of us made up of – remember? – atoms, and those atoms are made up of – yes, that's right – quarks and gluons. If we can predict how each of these particles will behave in a given situation then we can predict how lots of them packed together into a single human body will behave, right?

Yes, theoretically. In practice, it's a bit harder. We like to think that we're something more than just a collection of atoms. We use the term 'I' to describe ourselves. We have a consciousnesss. (Philosophers call this experience of mental states – seeing colours, smelling food, feeling pain – the 'qualia'.) But what if even consciousness is just an illusion, another product of the actions of all those quarks and gluons in our brains? 'I' may not even exist, and if I start having doubts about that, then where does it leave you? You may not exist either. My brain may just have invented you. In that case, you're as real as Reginald/Dorothy, and I can make you do what I want. Right, I want you all to club together to buy me a yacht. You can send it care of my publishers. Thank you. Even an imaginary yacht is better than no yacht at all . . .

is quite far from Biddlecombe. We can't even see the church spire during the day.'

'You can see *a* Rathford,' said Professor Hilbert. 'It's one of an infinite number of Rathfords, or it may be the point at which all of those potential Rathfords are bound together until a decision is made on which one should come into being.'

'We've become unmoored from reality,' said Professor Stefan. 'I believe that a dimensional shift has occurred, and we're just fractionally off-kilter with the rest of the Multiverse.'

'But what's on the other side of that boundary?' said Brian.

'Perhaps a version of Rathford, once you bring it into being by its observation, or nothing at all,' said Professor Hilbert. 'Then again, you might thrust your fingers into another dimension, and who knows what could be waiting on the other side? Or your fingers might end up between dimensions, which could be just as bad. It might be like wearing fingerless gloves in space, which would be very unwise.'[46]

☠ [46] Deepest, darkest space is very cold, so cold that all molecules stop moving. This is called 'absolute zero' and is calculated as − 273 degrees Celsius, although the temperature in space is probably closer to − 270 degrees Celsius because of three degrees of background microwave radiation.

So how long could you survive in space if you weren't wearing a suit? First of all, you shouldn't try to hold your breath, as that will cause the air in your lungs to expand and burst things that shouldn't burst, so you'd die painfully but quickly. If you didn't hold your breath, you'd probably have about fifteen seconds before you passed out. You wouldn't get frostbite at first, as you would in cold temperatures on Earth, because there's no air in space, and frostbite is a result of heat transfer accelerated by air. But your skin would start to burn because of ultraviolet radiation, and your skin tissue would swell.

'Did we do this?' asked Brian. 'I mean, all that fiddling around with particle accelerations and the nature of reality: could it have caused this?'

Professor Hilbert found something interesting to look at beside his right foot. Professor Stefan whistled and peered at the fathomless depths of space.

Eventually Professor Hilbert said, 'This is not the time to go around blaming people for what may or may not have happened, Brian.'

'When would be a good time, Professor Hilbert?' said Brian.

'When I'm not here,' said Professor Hilbert, 'but preferably when I'm dead and can't get into any trouble. I'd advise you to think very hard about your part in all of this as well, young Brian. You're an important part of our team, which means that you can be blamed too.'

'But I only made the tea!' said Brian.

'Yes, but it was very good tea,' said Professor Hilbert. 'If it had been bad tea then we might not have been so productive, and none of this might have happened or, if it did, then it might have happened much more slowly.'

'Don't forget the biscuits,' Professor Stefan chimed in.

'Oh yes, the biscuits,' said Professor Hilbert. 'Don't

Overall, then, you'd probably have a good thirty seconds before serious, permanent injury occurred, and a minute or two before you'd begin to die. In 1965, a spacesuit leaked in a vacuum chamber at NASA's Manned Spacecraft Center. The gentleman involved, who was rescued and recovered, remained conscious for about fourteen seconds. His last memory was of the saliva on his tongue beginning to boil. I just thought you'd like to know that.

get me started on the biscuits. All I can say is that you're up to your neck in this, Brian, mark my words. If the world comes to an end because of our experiments, you'll be in big trouble. They'll throw the book at you, or they will if there's anyone still around to throw books, or anything else, which there probably won't be. You know, now that I come to think about it, everything is fine at our end. If the world doesn't get destroyed, we're free and clear, and if it does end then there's not much anybody can do to make us feel bad about it.'

Professor Hilbert smiled happily.

'There, glad that's sorted out. Still, all things considered, it would be nice if we could prevent the end of the world from happening. With that in mind, onwards we go.'

He began to lead them back to the car. Brian didn't move. He just stood where he was, looking confused.

'But I only made the tea,' he said.

Professor Stefan steered him towards the car.

'Never mind,' he said. 'Try looking on the bright side.'

'Is there one?'

'Not really.'

'Oh.'

'But if you come up with one, do let us know, won't you?'

And high above their heads the stars were swallowed, one by one.

CHAPTER XXVIII

In Which Crudford Proves to be the Smartest Gelatinous Blob in the Room.

The Great Malevolence, the Watcher by his side, had been spending a very long time staring at the bits and pieces of what had once been Ba'al, the most fearsome of its allies, its second-in-command, its left-hand demon, and considering the problem presented by them.

It had seemed like such a good idea to allow Ba'al to travel to Earth, exploiting the gap in space and time created by the experiments with the Large Hadron Collider. Ba'al was an entity of pure awfulness, but Ba'al was also completely loyal to the Great Malevolence, and there weren't many beings in Hell who could be trusted entirely. This was one of the problems with running a business based entirely around evil, destructiveness, and rage. It attracted bad sorts.

Unfortunately, the successful planning of the invasion of Earth had required Ba'al to take on human form, and the particular human form that Ba'al had chosen to inhabit was that of Mrs Abernathy. But Mrs Abernathy had turned out a) to have a strong personality of her own; and b) to be horrible even before she became possessed by a demon. And so the personalities of Ba'al and Mrs Abernathy had become mixed up in one body, and much of Mrs Abernathy had come out on top. This had left the Great Malevolence with a demonic lieutenant who liked to dress up in a lady's skin and clothing. Ba'al didn't even like being called Ba'al any more. It was Mrs Abernathy or nothing. Not that this was a huge problem, but it was unusual.

The Great Malevolence missed Ba'al – sorry, Mrs Abernathy. It wasn't as though they had ever played draughts or tiddlywinks or Twister together, or gone for long walks with a picnic at the end. No, it was simply that, without her, the whole business of trying to take over the Multiverse was a great deal harder, and the Great Malevolence, in addition to being great and malevolent, was also more than a little lazy. It came with being in charge: if you can find someone else to do the hard work, then why would you do it yourself?

But now all that was left of Mrs Abernathy were various body parts in jars, and those body parts weren't doing much at all. Quite often, when it came to the residents of Hell, you could disassemble them into all kinds of small pieces, and each bit would do its best to continue being evil. Fingers would crawl across floors and try to poke the nearest eye; jawbones would try to bite; and intestines would slither like snakes and coil themselves around the nearest neck. Really, there was never a dull moment in Hell when it came to tearing things apart.

'Why does she not react more strongly?' asked the Great Malevolence. 'Why does this chamber not vibrate with the force of her evil?'

If Crudford could have shrugged, then he would have. Instead, he lifted his hat and scratched his head in puzzlement. He scratched slightly too hard though, and his fingers appeared inside his head somewhere behind his eyeballs. He pulled them out, thought about wiping them clean, and decided, well, why bother? Slowly, he examined each jar in turn, taking note of its contents on a small notepad that he kept in his hat. When he had finished, he went to work on his notepad. He scribbled and drew. He crossed things out, and did a lot of sucking on his pencil. The Watcher tried to peer over his shoulder to see what was being produced, but Crudford shielded the notepad from view like a small boy worried that his homework was about to be copied by the student next to him.

Eventually, after an hour had gone by, and two pencils had been worn down to almost nothing, Crudford was finished.

'I think I may have the answer,' he said.

'We are waiting,' said the Great Malevolence. It came with the unspoken warning: *This had better be good.*

Crudford turned the notepad to face the Great Malevolence. This is what it contained:

The Great Malevolence looked at the drawing. It then looked at the Watcher. The Watcher shrugged because, unlike Crudford, it could. The Great Malevolence, having nowhere else left to look, looked at Crudford and thought about the many ways in which it could reduce a gelatinous mass to lots of much smaller pieces of jelly.

'It is,' said the Great Malevolence, 'a picture of a lady. It is not even a very good picture of a lady.'

Everyone, thought Crudford, is a critic.

'It's not just a lady,' said Crudford. 'It's Mrs Abernathy. But see here—'

Crudford pointed at the question mark beside the heart shape.

'The heart is missing.'

The Great Malevolence considered this.

'Ba'al does not have a heart,' it said. 'No creature in Hell has a heart. Hearts are not needed.'

'But Ba'al isn't Ba'al any longer, not really,' said Crudford. 'Ba'al is Mrs Abernathy, and Mrs Abernathy is Ba'al, and Mrs Abernathy has a heart because Mrs Abernathy is, or was, human. Those jars contain bits of every organ in the human body except the heart. The heart is missing. All of it.'

'But what is the heart pumping?' said the Great Malevolence. 'Not blood, for Mrs Abernathy's body died the moment that Ba'al took it over.'

'I'm just guessing,' said Crudford, 'but I'd say that it's pumping pure evil. What we're looking for is a big, black, rotten heart-shaped thingy filled with nastiness.'

'Then where is it?' asked the Great Malevolence.

'That,' said Crudford, 'is a very good question.'

Crudford wandered the halls of the Mountain of Despair, alone with his thoughts. 'Wandered' probably wasn't the right word, strictly speaking: 'slimed', 'oozed' or 'smeared' might be closer to the mark, but if Crudford had said that he was just off to slime around the halls for a while then he would probably have been advised to take his gelatinous self elsewhere, or someone would have been following him with a mop and a bucket.

His search of the Multiverse for bits of Mrs Abernathy had not been entirely random. He had been able to narrow it down to specific universes, or corners of them, either because he could smell Mrs Abernathy, or his keen eyesight had been able to pick out the blue atoms in the darkness. There were only two places he had not explored: the Kingdom of Shadows, and Earth.

He had not entered the Kingdom of Shadows because to do so would have been the end of him: the Shadows had no loyalty to the Great Malevolence, and would have snuffed out Hell itself if they could. He had stayed away from Earth simply because he had detected no sign of Mrs Abernathy there, but now he began to wonder if he might not have been mistaken. Just because he could pick up no trace of her did not mean that she was not there, and it was only recently that he had begun to detect the tell-tale beating of her heart. Mrs Abernathy was cunning and wicked. Her dark heart, he realised, must be filled with hatred. And what or, more correctly, who did she hate more than anything else in the Multiverse?

Samuel Johnson.

Crudford snapped his fingers. A small blob of gloop was flicked away by the action and landed on something in the darkness.

'Hey!' said the something.

'Sorry,' said Crudford.

Could it be true? There was only one way to find out.

CHAPTER XXIX

In Which Efforts Are Made to Console Constable Peel.

A question that is sometimes asked by human beings is why bad things happen to good people. It doesn't seem entirely fair that folk who try to make the world a better, nicer place, who don't go around scowling at puppies or frightening kittens, or trying to set someone's shoes on fire when he's asleep, should suddenly find themselves having a run of bad luck including, but not limited to, feeling a bit poorly, running out of money, having heavy objects fall on their heads, or stumbling off cliffs in the dark.

Equally, one might ask why bad things don't happen to bad people, which was just what Constable Peel was asking himself at that precise moment. Somehow, against all the odds, the dwarfs had survived in a basement filled with carnivorous eyeballs, bald vampires, and at least one monster with bladder control issues. If Constable Peel had been stuck in that basement he'd have been dinner for something within seconds, but Jolly, Angry, Dozy and Mumbles had waltzed safely through it all as if it were nothing more dangerous than a field of daisies.

'We appear to have upset him,' said Angry, as Constable Peel continued to weep and curse the gods from his position on the floor.

'He's very sensitive for a policeman,' said Jolly. 'I think he's just relieved that nothing bad happened to us.'

'He's swearing a lot for someone who's relieved,' said Angry. 'He seems to be doing a lot of fist-shaking as well.'

'He's getting rid of tension, that's all,' said Jolly. 'It can be a very emotional experience when you find out that someone you care about has been in danger. Imagine how much worse he must feel knowing that the four of us – and Dan – were almost killed.'

Constable Peel's wailing grew louder.

'I mean, think about it: just one little bit of bad luck and we might not have been here at all.'

Constable Peel began banging his head on the ground.

'Constable Peel,' Jolly concluded solemnly, 'would never have seen us again.'

Jolly shed a tear at the near-tragedy of it all. It fell on Constable Peel's neck. As it trickled down his back Constable Peel reached for his truncheon, and he might have done to Jolly what the eyeballs and vampires and monster had failed to do had not Sergeant Rowan stepped in and ushered Dan and the dwarfs away.

'Give him a little space, lads,' he said. 'Poor old Constable Peel has had a bit of a shock.'

He knelt by his fellow policeman, who was taking deep breaths to try to calm himself.

'Are you going to be OK?' asked Sergeant Rowan.

'It's not right, Sarge,' said Constable Peel. 'Even Hell

couldn't get rid of them fast enough. Every time it looks like we might be about to see the last of them, something terrible happens and they survive.'

'I know, son, I know, but we can't have you beating them to death with your truncheon; we'd have to find somewhere to hide the bodies, and right now we're stuck in a toystore with all kinds of nasties so we don't have the time to go stuffing the bodies of dwarfs into closets or under floorboards.'

He handed Constable Peel a handkerchief. Constable Peel blew his nose loudly and wetly on it and tried to hand it back to the sergeant.

'No, you keep it,' said Sergeant Rowan.

'Very kind of you, Sarge.'

'Not really,' said Sergeant Rowan.

Constable Peel folded the handkerchief, stuffed it in his pocket, and got to his feet.

'When all this is finished . . .' said Constable Peel.

'Yes?'

'And if we survive . . .'

'It's a big "if".'

'But if we do . . .'

'Yes?'

'Can I kill them then?'

Sergeant Peel handed Constable Peel his hat.

'We'll see, Constable, we'll see . . .'

High above the Earth, within sneezing distance of the moon, a small hole appeared in the fabric of space and time, and Crudford squeezed through it. He gazed down at the small blue planet below. It was, as planets went, nothing to write home about. It didn't have spectacular rings. It wasn't made of diamond. It did not, unlike the planet Cerberus IV in the Dragon Dimensions, have jaws and teeth, and move around the galaxy chewing up smaller worlds. It was just kind of pretty in a blue, watery way.

Crudford floated closer to the Earth. He hovered over England. He narrowed his focus, concentrating on the area around Biddlecombe. He saw that it was there but not there, as if he were seeing the town in a dream. Black smoke swirled around it, great columns of it like tornadoes.

No, not smoke: shadows.

And not shadows, but *Shadows*.

'Oh, the Great Malevolence is not going to like that,' said Crudford. 'It's not going to like that at all.'

CHAPTER XXX

In Which Help Arrives,
Wearing a Very Fetching Hat.

The streets of Biddlecombe's town centre were largely deserted as Maria and the scientists drew closer to Wreckit & Sons. Most of Biddlecombe's citizens had barricaded themselves in their homes and businesses, or were off battling elves and reindeer elsewhere. A small crowd had taken refuge inside the Town Hall, where the forces of darkness were being kept at bay by the singing of BoyStarz, as it turned out that even demonic elves and reindeer had a limited tolerance for infinite variations on 'Love is Like . . .' Some of those trapped inside with BoyStarz had tried to make a break for freedom to take their chances with the forces of darkness, but common sense had prevailed, helped by earplugs and the contents of the mayor's drinks cabinet.

Professor Hilbert parked the car outside Mr Tuppenny's Ice Cream Parlour, where a quartet of abominable snowmen had made the mistake of breaking in and eating some of the stock. Mr Tuppenny's ice cream had a reputation for being heavy on the ice and light on the cream. It was said of his Lemon Surprise that the only surprising thing about it was the fact that it eventually melted at all, and lumps of coal had more lemon in them. There were people who swore that they had eaten one of Mr Tuppenny's Special Ice Cream Sundaes in May and still had an icy ball moving slowly and painfully through their lower intestine come September. Mr Tuppenny had only stayed in business because of tourists and mad people. The abominable snowmen had eaten so much Strawberry Swirl that it had made them very unwell, and were now unable to do anything more threatening than wave their claws in frail 'Kill me now and make the icy pain go away' gestures.

It was Professor Stefan who spotted the two figures picking their way through the broken glass and ruined Christmas decorations.

'They're a bit tall for elves, aren't they?' he said. 'Seems to defeat the purpose, having tall elves.'

'They're not elves,' said Maria 'They're demons! Unlock the car doors, please. I want to get out.'

Professor Hilbert did as he was told, even though it didn't seem like a good idea to go after two large demonic elves. The small ones were bad enough.

Maria leaned over Reginald, opened the door, and clambered out.

'Nurd! Wormwood! It's me!'

Nurd and Wormwood were just as pleased to see Maria as she was to see them. They hugged, and were soon joined by Professors Stefan and Hilbert, and Brian and Reginald, who kept a cautious distance from them.

'When you say "demons", that usually implies a degree of badness,' said Professor Hilbert to Maria.

Maria tried to explain.

'Look, not all demons are demonic,' she said.

'I did try for a while,' said Nurd. 'I just wasn't very good at it.'

'He was useless,' Wormwood added unhelpfully.

'I wasn't useless, I was just . . .'

Nurd tried to find the right word.

'Rotten?' Wormwood suggested. 'Incompetent? Gormless?'

Nurd settled for 'different'.

'Differently useless,' muttered Wormwood.

The scientists were examining Nurd and Wormwood with some curiosity. Professor Stefan poked Wormwood with a pen, which came back with something unpleasant stuck to its tip. As Professor Stefan watched, his pen began to dissolve.

'That does happen if you're not careful,' said Nurd. 'It's best to avoid touching him without gloves, or even with them if you fancy wearing them a second time.'

'You'd better explain how you got here,' said Maria. 'After all that's happened, I don't think it matters much if they know the truth about you now.'

So Nurd did. He covered his banishment in the wilderness, the way he'd been pulled from Hell to Earth, and how he had managed to foil the invasion of Biddlecombe by the forces of Hell using only a borrowed/stolen car. He then explained how Samuel had ended up in Hell, along with two policemen, some dwarfs, and an ice cream salesman,[47] and the manner in which they had all returned to Earth together. [48]

There was a chorus of questions from the scientists when he had finished. They wanted to know about other dimensions, and reverse wormholes, and what the weather was like in Hell. Nurd tried to answer, but each answer seemed to invite ten more questions. Eventually it was left to Maria to call a halt.

'We don't have time for this now,' she said. 'We need to find Samuel. If there are demons, and problems with reality, he has to be involved somehow. And, if I'm right, he's probably trapped somewhere in there.'

They all took in the great mass of Wreckit & Sons. There was a field of energy surrounding the store, but it was different from the one separating Biddlecombe from the rest of the country. When Maria threw a stone at it, the stone simply bounced off, although it was hot to the touch afterwards.

'Do you know what's happening?' she asked Nurd.

'The stars are going out,' he said. 'There's a darkness approaching. Don't you feel it? It's as though the shadows are becoming deeper.'

'Not just that,' said Brian. 'They've developed a life of their own. I should know. I was chased by one.'

'Who is that, and why is he shaking?' said Nurd.

---

[47] Although unfortunately not Mr Tuppenny the ice cream man.

[48] He did all that in a paragraph. It took me two books. I'm in the wrong business.

'His name is Brian,' said Maria. 'He made the tea, so according to Professor Hilbert this is all his fault.'

'Hello, Brian,' said Nurd. 'Perhaps you should stop making tea. You should probably stop drinking it too. You might not shake so much.'

He returned his attention to Maria.

'Where were we?'

'The darkness, and the shadows. Is it the Great Malevolence?'

'No, I don't think so. It doesn't feel like his work. It's *blacker*.'

'Whatever is causing it, it lives in the shop,' said Maria. 'Wreckit & Sons is at the heart of some kind of supernatural engine designed by the architect Hilary Mould.'

'It's also a trap,' said Nurd. 'It drew in Samuel, and I know that Dan and the dwarfs were given jobs there. It would have taken Wormwood and me as well, but Samuel told us not to go. He didn't think it would be safe for us.'

'So it wanted Samuel, and Dan and the dwarfs,' said Maria. 'It also wanted you and Wormwood, and I wouldn't be surprised if Sergeant Rowan and Constable Peel are in there too. Someone springs to mind.'

'Mrs Abernathy,' said Nurd. 'But I saw her being torn apart. I *felt* it happen. We all did. She's just atoms scattered throughout the Multiverse now. And even if she was involved, she doesn't have this kind of power. She can't darken universes.'

From somewhere at the level of Nurd's knee, something went *glop*.

'Evening, all,' said a small gelatinous being, raising

his hat in greeting. 'My name is Crudford, Esq., and I think I may be able to answer some questions for you.

"And by the way, is it just me, or can everyone else hear what sounds like a big heart beating?"

Crudford had not headed directly to Earth. Upon glimpsing the Shadows above Biddlecombe, his first act had been to take a closer look at them from above. What he saw confirmed his worst fears: there were faces in the gloom, faces that had never been glimpsed before because the place from which the Shadows came was a kingdom of utter darkness. The Shadows were blind – what good were eyes when there was nothing to see? – but like so many other creatures that lived without light, their hearing was very, very sensitive. They had been listening to the sounds of the Multiverse for almost as long as it had been in existence. They believed that they were the true owners of the Multiverse, for before the Multiverse there was nothing, and they were as close to nothing as one could find. They hated the light, and all that dwelt in it. They even hated the Great Malevolence, and all who resided in Hell, for in Hell too there was light, even if it was the light of red fires. The only thing that had saved the Multiverse from the Shadows was the fact that their realm was sealed off from every other: they were prisoners inside their own Kingdom, for the Multiverse had ways of protecting itself.[49]

☠ [49] So how big is the Multiverse, exactly? According to quantum theory, particles can pop into and out of existence, and there are scientists who believe that our universe was the result of just such a quantum 'pop'. So if one universe

The Great Malevolence had once thought about trying to recruit the Shadows as its allies, but the messengers it sent to their kingdom had never returned. They had been absorbed into the blackness, their eyes taken from them, and eventually they had become Shadows themselves. The Great Malevolence had learned that the Shadows could not be used, and it was better if they were not allowed to pollute the Multiverse or interfere with Hell's efforts to dominate it.

---

can pop into being, why not many universes? This would require extra dimensions, which is where very complicated string theory comes into play. String theory proposes that our universe is made up of very, very small vibrating strings, and when the strings vibrate in different ways they produce different particles. Think of the strings of a guitar producing different notes, and so the universe can be imagined as a great symphony of particles being produced by an unseen orchestra. Pluck one string and you get a proton; pluck another and you get an electron.

One of the difficulties in understanding string theory lies in the fact that it doesn't work in our four-dimensional world (the three space dimensions of up/down, left/right, and forwards/backwards, and the fourth dimension of time). String theory requires eleven dimensions, ten of space – which are buried within our existing three dimensions – and one of time. One of the tasks of the Large Hadron Collider was to find proof of these extra dimensions: if, during the Collider's proton collisions, some of the bits of shattered particles were found to have gone missing from the sealed vacuum, then that would suggest the possibility that they had disappeared into other dimensions.

Anyway, to get back to our original question of how many universes there may be in the Multiverse, some string theorists suggest the number is 10^{500}, or one for every possible model of physics that string theory offers. (See, I told you it was complicated. It's so complicated that this latest version of string theory, the eleven-dimension one, is known as M-theory, and even Edward Whitten, the man who came up with it, isn't sure what the 'M' stands for.) Mind you, there are some scientists who say that the number of universes in the Multiverse could be far more than 10^{500}, and that the only way you can get it down to 10^{500} is by fiddling about with the (coarse) Moduli Space of Kähler and Ricci-Flat (or Calabi-Yau) metrics and then enforcing extra supersymmetry conditions, which is just cheating, obviously. I mean, everybody knows that.

But then the balance of the Multiverse had been disturbed by the actions of men. Humans were endlessly curious, and their curiosity led them to take risks. They had built the Large Hadron Collider to try to recreate the beginnings of their universe, and in the process they had opened a gateway between Earth and Hell that had almost caused the end of their world. They had also begun to investigate the nature of reality, and reality was a delicate business. What was unreal only stayed that way as long as reality and unreality kept to their own sides of the fence. If you opened a gate between the two, then all kinds of confusion reigned. That was how dwarfs ended up being chased by eyeballs, and tentacled entities got trapped in closets, and little girls with a fondness for spiders, and web for skin, climbed down from walls to bother people.

But even all of the messing about with reality might not have come back to bite the humans had they not gone poking their noses into dark matter. It was all very well deciding that, yes, what they saw when they looked through their telescopes was only four per cent of the stuff of the universe, and the other ninety-six per cent had to be made up of something else. They called that something else 'dark matter' and 'dark energy'. Dark matter was the universe's hidden skeleton, giving structure to universes and galaxies, while dark energy was the force changing universes, forcing galaxies farther and farther apart. Humanity decided that the universe was about seventy per cent dark energy and twenty-five to twenty-six per cent dark matter. Heigh-ho, problem solved, who fancies a cup of tea and a biscuit before we clock off early for the afternoon?

But that wasn't right. They should have paid more attention to one important word: 'dark'. The dark was where things hid. The dark was the place where unpleasant creatures that didn't want to be seen waited until the time was right.

The dark was the place in which the Shadows were imprisoned.

By engaging in dark matter detection experiments – including projects such as Multidark, the Dark Matter Time Projection Chamber, and the Cryogenic Dark Matter search – the humans had alerted the Shadows to their existence. Even in their isolated realm, they had been able to hear the humans: voices, music, rockets, wars, the Shadows had listened to them all. When the detection experiments had begun, it was the equivalent of someone tapping on the outside of a prison wall with a pickaxe – *tap-tap-tap* – except that the person doing the tapping didn't know that there were entities imprisoned inside, entities that were very anxious to escape and smother every light in the Multiverse.

Professor Stefan was right: the Large Hadron Collider had worn thin the walls between dimensions, and the pickaxe jabs of the detection experiments had done the rest. A hole had been opened, and now the Shadows were about to pour through.

The Great Malevolence might have wanted to destroy humanity and burn worlds. It might have wanted misery and ruin. But it also wanted the Multiverse to remain in existence. It wanted to transform universes into branch offices of Hell, and to do that required the continued survival of the Multiverse.

The Shadows wanted only darkness. They were as much a danger to the Great Malevolence as they were to humanity. This was why Crudford, after a quick return visit to Hell, had come down to Earth. He now believed that he knew why Biddlecombe was the place to which the Shadows had come. Mrs Abernathy's heart had hidden itself on Earth, and its blackness had found an echo in the Kingdom of Shadows. She had called out to the Shadows, and an alliance had been formed. She would give the Earth, and then the Multiverse, to the Shadows.

And in return, they would give Samuel Johnson to her.

CHAPTER XXXI

In Which the Funniness of Clowns is Doubted.

Things were going from bad to worse inside Wreckit & Sons, which was surprising given how bad things were to begin with. It seemed that, as Samuel and the others drew closer to the highest floor of the store, the nature of reality was becoming more and more distorted. In fact, as far as Samuel was concerned, reality had pretty much given up on Biddlecombe and gone to live somewhere slightly more down to earth.

First off, there were the clowns. Everyone trapped in the store was beginning to realise that Wreckit & Sons had been designed with one purpose in mind: to provide a series of threats that would gradually force the humans to the top floor. While they had made the best use that they could of whatever weapons they could find – bats, balls, bows and arrows, and foam blasters, for the most part – it wasn't as if the store had been littered with rocket launchers or heavy artillery. The dangers on each floor were simply meant to force them upwards, not kill them, or so Samuel believed, although Dan and the dwarfs were pretty convinced that, had the Nosferati managed to get their fangs into them, they would soon have been singing in some heavenly choir, assuming heaven was willing to let them in.

They saw that the next-to-last floor had been given a circus theme. There was a Ferris wheel in one corner, large enough for very small children to ride, and the wooden façade of a big top. There were signs that read 'Hoop Toss' and, slightly worryingly, 'Ghost Train'. Over them all hovered the head of a ringmaster in a top hat, his black moustache curling almost to his eyebrows, and his smile wide enough to swallow a person.

The ringmaster was Hilary Mould.

Beneath the ringmaster stood three dummies dressed as clowns. One was bald and entirely covered in white-face make up. He wore a suit of broad yellow check, and a little red hat was positioned on the side of his head. Samuel wondered how it stayed in place: glue, perhaps, or a very thin rubber band. It was only as he drew closer to the clown that he saw the hat had been nailed to his skull.

The second clown wore a huge pink wig that looked like the aftermath of an explosion in a candyfloss machine. Only the areas around his eyes and mouth were painted white: the rest of his face was a sickly yellow. He wore a long green coat with tails, and purple trousers decorated with pink polka dots. A huge plastic flower was pinned to the buttonhole of his jacket.

The third clown was female. She was wearing white one-piece overalls decorated with big red fluffy buttons, and her wig was black. So, too, was the make-up around her mouth and her eyes, while the rest of her face was very pale. Strangely, her mouth had been painted into a frown instead of a smile. Her fingernails were long and pointed, and varnished a deep, dark red, as though she had recently been tearing apart raw meat.

Samuel had never seen a female clown before, [50] but then he had only been to the circus once in his life. Samuel didn't care much for the circus, or clowns. He wasn't scared of clowns; he just didn't think they were amusing.[51]

The dwarfs wandered over to join him.

[50] The history of clowning does not record the appearance of female clowns until 1858, which is quite amazing as clowns have been around since at least the time of the Pharoah Dadkeri-Assi in 2500 BC. The first female clown was said to have been Amelia Butler who was part of Nixon's Great American Circus, but the next female clown, Lulu, was not mentioned until 1939. Now, though, lots of clowns are female, and can be found alongside the various trapeze artists, tightrope walkers, and lion tamers of the circus. Interesting fact: no clown has ever been eaten by a circus animal. This is because clowns taste funny.

[51] Coulrophobia is the word for a fear, or phobia, of clowns, which is not uncommon. Some fears are strangely specific, though, and unlikely to be a real problem unless you actively try to scare yourself. For example, Zemmiphobia is a fear of the great mole rat, which is, despite its name, a small, almost hairless, slow-moving rat with protruding teeth that it uses to carve out tunnels for itself. It tends to avoid people and live underground, so it's not like it's knocking on doors and shouting 'Boo!' Similarly, arachibutyrophobia, the fear of peanut butter sticking to the roof of your mouth, can probably be dealt with by not eating peanut butter, or just eating it carefully. Unfortunately, there's not much that can be done about geniophobia, the fear of chins, since you do rather bring that one with you wherever you go. Phobophobia, meanwhile, is the fear of phobias, or the fear of being afraid. Unfortunately, if you have phobophobia then you're already afraid, so the very fact that you're a phobophobe means that you're in trouble from the start.

'They're not going to get many laughs looking like that,' said Dozy.

'Never liked clowns,' said Angry. 'They always seem to be trying too hard.'

'What do you call the gooey red stuff between a circus elephant's toes?' asked Jolly.

'I don't know,' said Samuel.

'A slow clown,' said Jolly. 'Get it? A *slow clown*.'

The female clown turned her head slowly in Jolly's direction. Her fingers tested the air. The bald clown opened his mouth and licked his lips, and the clown with the fuzzy wig put his hand inside his jacket and squeezed the bulb on his plastic flower. A jet of liquid shot from it, which just missed Angry. It sizzled when it hit the floor, and began burning a hole in the carpet. The others immediately stepped out of range, but instead of joining them Angry began shouting at the clowns.

'Losers!' he said. 'I've seen funnier dead people.'

The flower-wearing dwarf tried again, firing a stream of acid in Angry's direction. Again it landed on the carpet and began eating its way through.

'How do you get a clown off your porch?' called Angry. 'You pay him for the pizza.'

By now the bewigged clown was growling and spraying a constant stream of acid at Angry as he circled the trio. The others tried to snatch at him with their fingers, but he was too fast.

'What are you doing?' cried Samuel. 'You're going to get hurt!'

The smell of burning carpet and wood was very

strong now, and a near perfect acid-drenched circle was sizzling at the feet of the clowns. The liquid stopped pumping. The clown's supply of acid was exhausted. He looked at the flower in disgust before deciding to take care of Angry and the others personally. He took one step forward. The other clowns did the same.

The ceiling collapsed, taking the three clowns with it and leaving only a hole where they had previously stood. Carefully, Samuel and the dwarfs peered over the edge at the floor below. The clowns had shattered on impact, like china dolls. The ceiling had also landed on Miss Muffet's giant spider: they could see the tips of eight legs sticking out from under the mass of wood and plaster, and its insides were leaking out. Lucy's boot might not have been strong enough to crush one of the smaller spiders, but three clowns and a heavy ceiling seemed to have done the trick for the big one.

'Like I told you,' said Angry, 'I never liked clowns. Never had much time for spiders either.'

Miss Muffet appeared beside the remains of her spider. She glared up at them.

'*Bad!*' she said, pointing a web-covered finger at them. '*Very bad!*'

'Oh-oh,' said Jolly. 'We've done it now.'

As they watched, Miss Muffet started to make her way to the stairs. She had obviously decided that someone had to pay for the destruction of her spider, but they were distracted from her approach by the ringmaster. His wooden face had contorted into a mask of rage. Thin streams of black smoke poured from his nostrils. Beside him, the Ferris wheel rattled on its foundations. Bolts popped, and its supports collapsed. The Ferris wheel dropped to the floor and headed towards them.

'Incoming!' shouted Jolly.

Samuel and the dwarfs dived out of the way of the rolling wheel. Samuel was relieved to see Lucy and the policemen do the same. They reacted fast, certainly faster than Miss Muffet, who reached the top of the stairs just in time to be hit by the wheel. It rolled halfway down the stairs before striking a wall at speed, tearing through the brickwork and taking Miss Muffet with it. All that was left to show she had ever been there at all was a trail of crushed black spiders.

And that was when the Polite Monster appeared.

To start with, Samuel and the others didn't know that he was polite. When monsters appear, the general approach is to assume that they don't mean anyone any good and set about getting rid of them. If that doesn't work, it's a good idea to make your apologies and leave while you still can. The Polite Monster had a lot of horns, and a great many teeth in its jaws, and four eyes, two on each side of its head. It was about twelve feet tall, and almost as wide, and was covered entirely in coarse red fur. It popped into existence in a puff of purple and yellow smoke, accompanied by the most horrendous smell combining the worst aspects of rotting fish, dog poo, and very old eggs that had been scrambled and fed to someone with bad digestion and worse wind.

The Polite Monster sniffed the air, made a face, and said, 'That wasn't me.'

It had a very cultured voice. It sounded like a monster that liked light opera, and perhaps acted in plays for the local dramatic society, the kind in which chaps called Gussy popped up dressed in tennis whites, and people laughed like this: 'I say, ah-ha-ha-ha!'

By that point, everyone who wasn't a monster had found somewhere to hide. This floor of the shop was devoted entirely to books and some more board games, which had been a relief to everyone until the Polite Monster appeared. There was a limit to how much damage a game of Scrabble could inflict: at worst, it could probably arrange some of its tiles into a rude name.

'Hello?' said the Polite Monster. 'Anybody home?'

Samuel poked his head up from behind a pile of boxes of Risk. The boxes were rattling alarmingly, suggesting to Samuel that some games might be more dangerous than others. This was confirmed when he heard a muffled shot from the topmost box, and a tiny cannon-ball pierced the lid and flew past his ear. A very small voice, muffled by cardboard, shouted, 'Reload!'

'Oh, hello,' said Samuel.

'Ah,' said the Polite Monster. 'I'm terribly sorry for intruding – nine letters, "to force oneself in without invitation" – but I was hoping that you could tell me where I am?'

Samuel was still wary.

'Where do you think you are?'

'I can tell you where I was a moment ago,' said the Polite Monster. 'I was doing a crossword puzzle in my cave. Tricky one. Two down, eight letters: "Insecure now that the horse has bolted".'

'Unstable,' said Constable Peel, who did a lot of crosswords.

'Unstable!' said the Polite Monster. 'Oh that's very good, very good. Let me just—'

It patted its person looking for something with which to write and then it blushed, or blushed as much as a large hairy monster could blush, which wasn't a lot.

'Oh dear,' it said. 'This is most embarrassing – twelve letters, "to be ill at ease". I appear to be completely naked.'

Another cannonball popped from the Risk box. This time it nicked Samuel's left ear, and drew a little blood.

'Hey!' said Samuel. 'That's enough!'

He gave the box a thorough shake.

'Earthquake!' shouted the same small voice.

The Polite Monster was now attempting to cover itself with its arms. Samuel wasn't sure why it was bothering. It really was just one big ball of fur. If it had any bits that it didn't want seen, the fur was already doing a very good job of hiding them.

'Sorry?' said Samuel.

'Naked,' said the Polite Monster. 'Five letters, "to be bare, or without clothes".'

The dwarfs appeared, hauling behind them a large, paint-spattered sheet that had been left behind by the decorators.

'Will this do?' said Angry.

'Oh, yes,' said the Polite Monster. 'Anything would be better than my current situation – nine letters, "a state of affairs".'

It arranged the sheet as best it could over its shoulders

and around its hips. Jolly found a piece of rope, and the Polite Monster used it to secure the sheet. It now looked like a monster that had been cast in the role of Julius Caesar.

'Thank you, that's much better,' said the Polite Monster.

Dan and the policemen joined Sam, Lucy and the dwarfs. It was clear that they were in little danger from the Polite Monster. The Polite Monster looked curiously at the dwarfs.

'I say: little chaps,' it said. 'Did you have an accident to make you that way – eight letters, "an unforeseen event or mishap"?'

'We're dwarfs,' said Jolly. 'Six letters – "to thump someone who suggests that we're small because something fell on our heads".'

'Oh dear,' said the Polite Monster. 'I seem to have offended you – eight letters – "to cause to feel upset or annoyed". I really am most dreadfully sorry.'

'Apology accepted,' said Jolly.

He hadn't wanted to beat up the Polite Monster anyway. Even if he'd been able to, it wouldn't have been, well, polite somehow.

'And in answer to your question,' Jolly continued, 'you're on Earth, in Biddlecombe, in Wreckit & Sons' toyshop. And it's not a good place to be right now.'

'Oh, isn't it?' said the Polite Monster. 'You all seem very nice, I must say – four letters, "pleasant or agreeable" – and it makes a change from the cave, but I really should be getting back. I was baking scones, you see. Mother is coming to visit.'

'We're all trying to get out of here,' said Samuel, 'but there are vampires in the basement, killer dolls on the ground floor, and spiders just below us. We're being forced higher and higher in the store because I think that whatever is causing this is waiting for us on the topmost floor.'

The Polite Monster adjusted its tarpaulin toga.

'I'm sure there's a perfectly reasonable explanation,' it said. 'We'll just ask politely to be sent on our way, and that will be the end of it. I find that politeness – ten letters, "tact, or consideration for others" – goes a long way. Shall we?'

It extended a hairy, clawed hand, inviting them to take the lead.

'After you,' said Jolly.

'Such manners,' said the Polite Monster, as it stepped past Jolly. 'Wonderful, just wonderful.'

'Four letters to describe that bloke,' whispered Jolly to Angry, once the Polite Monster was out of earshot. 'Here's a clue: hazel-, wal-, or pea- . . .'

CHAPTER XXXII

In Which We Learn That if
One Can't Go Through Something,
and One Can't Go Over It, or Around It,
then There's Only One Way Left to Go.

Maria was finding it difficult to keep the minds of the scientists on the problem in hand. As if suddenly finding themselves in the company of two demons from another realm – the scientists seemed reluctant to call it 'Hell', preferring instead to use the term 'climatically challenged dimension' – wasn't enough, they now had the bonus of Crudford, who was a gelatinous demon from the same place with a great fondness for hats. But the answers that Crudford was giving to their questions seemed to be causing them even more problems than the ones they had been receiving from Nurd and Wormwood.

'So,' said Professor Stefan, 'have you always been a gelatinous mass?'

'Indeed I have,' said Crudford proudly. 'I've been a billion years before the ooze. It trails behind me, you see.'

'Yes, I do see,' said Professor Stefan, who had slipped in some of Crudford's ooze and almost landed on his head as a consequence. 'And you say you work for a being called the "Great Malevolence"?'

'That's right,' said Crudford, 'the most evil being that the Multiverse has ever known. It is the fount of all badness, the well from which the darkest thoughts and deeds spring. No single entity has ever contained so much sheer nastiness as the Great Malevolence. On the other hand, I work regular hours, get weekends off, and the canteen's not bad.'

'And what does this Great Malevolence want?' said Professor Hilbert.

'Well, it would really like to see the Earth reduced to a burning plain, with all life on it either wiped out or left screaming in agony. That aside, it would probably settle for Samuel Johnson's head on a plate.'

'Is that what you want?' asked Maria, who was quite shocked to hear Crudford speak of her friend in that way. Once you got over the fact that he was largely transparent, and clearly demonic,[52] Crudford appeared very good-natured.

💀 [52] A small joke playing on the words 'transparent' and 'clear', which mean the same thing, pretty much. It troubles me that I have to explain some of these jokes – not to you, obviously: I know that you're hugely intelligent, and you got that joke straight off, but not everyone is as bright as you. Maybe there should be a test before we allow people to read this book. We could pay people to wait in bookstores and libraries, and when someone picks the book up with the intention of reading it, the tester could then step in with a list of simple questions. You know:

1. If you see a door marked 'Push', should you a) Pull; b) Push?
2. If you see a sign on the street that reads 'Caution: Do Not Cross Here', do you a) cross; b) look for somewhere else to cross.
3. If you are at the zoo, and see a notice on the lions' cage that says 'Dangerous Animals: Do Not Put Hand Through Bars', do you
   a) put your hand through the bars, and waggle your fingers invitingly;
   b) keep a safe distance and, therefore, keep your hand too.

If you have answered a) to any of these questions, then you are not bright enough to read this book, and we also have another question for you: namely, how come you're still alive?

'I don't know Samuel Johnson personally,' said Crudford, 'and he's never done anything to hurt me. I wouldn't like it if my head was lopped off, although I'm pretty sure that it would grow back again. But life is a lot easier when the Great Malevolence is happy, which isn't very often. If you're worried about me trying to cut Samuel Johnson's head off, though, then don't be. I'm not the head-cutting kind. Also, I'm here to help, because right now you have bigger problems than the Great Malevolence. In case you haven't noticed, your town has been dimensionally shifted. It's now stuck in the space between dimensions, and that's somewhere you don't want to be.

'In a way, it's a bit like the Multiverse's equivalent of the back of the sofa: all sorts of stuff gets lost down there, some of it sticky and unpleasant. But it's also a place where things hide, things that aren't supposed to be hanging around between dimensions but should be locked up nice and safe in dimensions of their own. The problem is that there are weak points in the Multiverse, and your experiments with Colliders and dark matter and dark energy have turned those weaknesses into actual holes. That was how the Great Malevolence nearly got through the first time, and it's how the Shadows are trying to get in this time.'

'Shadows?' said Professor Hilbert.

Crudford pointed a stubby finger at the sky.

They looked up. More and more stars were vanishing, and darkness swirled in their place. To Maria it felt like they were trapped inside one of those glass domes that are usually filled with water and imitation snow and a village scene, and beyond the glass the world was filled with smoke. As they watched, the darkness assumed a face. It was a face unlike any they could have imagined, a face constructed by a presence that had only heard stories of faces, but never actually seen one. The mouth was askew, and the chin too long, and one pointed ear set lower than the other. Only the eyes were missing.

'The Shadows,' said Crudford. 'A little of their essence has already managed to get through, otherwise none of this would be happening, but it's the difference between smelling the monster's breath and feeling its teeth ripping into your flesh. They won't be kept out for long, and once they get in here the whole Multiverse will be at risk. Biddlecombe has been turned into a gateway, a bridge between the Kingdom of Shadows and your universe. But all universes are connected, if only by threads, and once the Shadows infect one universe then the Multiverse is doomed. They'll turn it black, and everything in it will suffocate and die, or be turned to Shadow.'

'And the Great Malevolence doesn't want this to happen,' said Maria, 'because it doesn't want the Shadows to have the Earth, or the Multiverse. If anyone is going to destroy all life, it's going to be your master, right?'

'Absolutely,' said Crudford. 'It's the whole point of its existence. Without it, it'd just be bored.'

'But why is this happening now?' said Maria.

'Someone built the engine that allowed Biddlecombe to be shifted,' said Crudford. 'But it had to be powered up, and that power came from elsewhere, from outside.

It came from Hell and, if I'm not mistaken, it took the form of a beating heart. Furthermore, the Shadows are blind. They had to be led to Biddlecombe, and the only way that could happen was with sound. They followed the heartbeats. Can't you hear them? The heart is close, very close.'

But try as they might, they could hear nothing.

'That shop is the core of the engine,' said Crudford. 'We have to get in there and switch it off before it's too late, and move that beating heart out of this universe.'

'But whose heart is it?' asked Maria. 'Whose heart could be capable of powering an occult engine, and leading a legion of Shadows to Biddlecombe?'

'Mrs Abernathy's,' said Crudford, and he sounded almost apologetic. 'The heart of Ba'al.'

In the Mountain of Despair, the Great Malevolence brooded.

Before he had travelled to Biddlecombe, Crudford had popped back to Hell for long enough to let his master know what appeared to be happening on Earth. The Great Malevolence had not been happy to hear about it. In its anger it threw a couple of demons at walls, and tossed a passing imp on the fire. The imp didn't mind too much about the flames as it had fireproof skin, but it had been on its way to do something very important and had now completely forgotten what the important thing was.[53] With nothing else to do, it

___

[53] You will know that you are getting old when you go upstairs to do something and, by the time you get there, you've forgotten what it is that you

found a nice patch of hot ash and settled down for a nap.

'She has betrayed us,' said the Great Malevolence to the Watcher. 'She has betrayed *me*.'

The Watcher, as was its way, said nothing, but there was something like sorrow in its eight black eyes. It had once served Mrs Abernathy, and had even admired her, but its loyalty ultimately lay with the Great Malevolence. Being loyal to the Great Malevolence was better for your health, and ensured that all of your limbs remained attached to your body.

The Great Malevolence felt powerless to act. Had there been a way, it might have sent an army of demons to fight the Shadows, but what good would that have done? They might as well have hacked at smoke with their swords, or tried to run mist through with spears. In the end, the Shadows would simply have swallowed the Great Malevolence's forces, and those whom the Shadows did not destroy would be condemned to an eternity of utter blackness. But the option of battle was not even available to the Great Malevolence: there was no way to move its troops from Hell to Earth, not since the first portal had been closed by the boy named Samuel Johnson and his friends. Only the little demon named Crudford was able to move from realm to realm without difficulty, and now the future of the Multiverse lay in his small, slimy hands.

---

went upstairs to do. You will know that you are *very* old when you get upstairs and can't remember where you are. And you will know that you are very, *very* old when you get upstairs and can't get downstairs again. You may laugh now, but the old age bus has a seat for everyone.

How strange, thought the Great Malevolence, that so much power should reside in such an unthreatening, and curiously contented, little body. Had Crudford been larger, or more vicious, or more cunning, he might even have been a threat to the Great Malevolence itself. Instead, Crudford just seemed happy to help. The Great Malevolence was baffled. It couldn't figure out what Crudford was doing in Hell to begin with. All things considered, he really didn't belong there.

'Go,' said the Great Malevolence to the Watcher. 'Fly to the very edge of our kingdom. Wait there, and when Crudford returns with the heart, bring them both to me.'

The Great Malevolence realised what it had said: *When Crudford returns with the heart.*

'When', not 'if'.

This is very bad, thought the Great Malevolence. I am becoming an optimist. There could only be one reason for it: Crudford, Esq. In some dreadful way, the demon's good nature was starting to infect Hell itself. The Great Malevolence could not allow this situation to continue. It decided that, once the heart had been returned to Hell, Crudford would have to be dealt with. When Mrs Abernathy's heart was cast into the icy Lake of Cocytus, there to remain frozen forever, it would have some company in its misery

Crudford would be freezing right alongside it.

Back in Biddlecombe, there was silence for a time.

'Who?' said Professor Stefan at last.

'Mrs Abernathy,' said Maria, and set about explaining as best she could. Professor Stefan and Professor Hilbert looked as if they didn't care to believe her, but it was hard to doubt Maria when everything she told them was being backed up by two demons dressed as elves and a third who was polishing his hat.

'She wants revenge,' said Crudford, when Maria had finished speaking. 'She's gone mad. She was always a *bit* mad, but when she travelled to Earth and the Ba'al bits got mixed up with the Abernathy bits, she went completely bonkers. If she's made a deal with the Shadows, then she doesn't care about the Great Malevolence or anything else: all she wants is a last chance to punish Samuel Johnson and everyone who stood alongside him. She will have her vengeance – at any cost.'

'And her heart is somewhere in there?' said Professor Stefan, indicating Wreckit & Sons.

'I think so,' said Crudford. 'I can hear it beating, but it's so loud that I'm not sure where exactly it's coming from any more. All I know is that the heart is close, and the toystore is the centre of power for all that's happening here, so my guess is that it's in there somewhere.'

'But how do we get in?' said Professor Stefan. 'I mean, there's an immense occult force field protecting the store. We can't go messing about with it. Somebody might get hurt. *I* might get hurt.'

Crudford removed his hat and took out his trusty notebook and pencil. He scribbled away frantically for a few minutes. Finally he shouted 'Eureka!',[54] and showed the results of his efforts to all.

The Great Malevolence would have been familiar with the looks of bafflement that met Crudford's display of his work, for it consisted only of this:

[54] *Eureka*, which comes from Ancient Greek, means 'I have found it', and is reputed to be what the Greek scholar Archimedes (287–212 BC) shouted after he stuck a foot in his bath and noticed that the water level rose. This was because he had realised that the volume of water displaced by his foot was equal to the volume of the foot itself. This meant that, by submerging them in water, the volume of irregularly shaped objects could now be measured, which had been impossible – or very, very difficult – before.

It also enabled Archimedes to solve a problem set for him by King Hiero II, who wanted to know if a gold crown that had been made for him was pure or had been polluted with silver so that the goldsmith could cheat him. Archimedes knew that he could now weigh the crown against a piece of gold of similar weight, and then submerge both in water. If they were of the same density, then they would displace the same amount of water, but if the gold of the crown had been mixed with silver then it would be less dense and would displace less water, and so the king would know that he had been cheated.

Archimedes was supposed to have been so excited by his discovery that he ran naked through the streets of Athens. You can only get away with this sort of thing if you're a genius. If you're not, they'll lock you up or, at the very least, give you a very stern talking to. You may also catch cold, or injure yourself on a gate.

'It's an arrow,' said Brian. 'What are we going to do, attack the shop with Indians?'

Crudford raised his eyes to the darkening skies in frustration.

'No,' he said. 'We're just going to do this.'

He squelched over to the occult barrier, reached down, and lifted up the bottom the way one might raise a curtain on a stage to peek at what lies behind.

'Simple,' said Crudford. 'I'd try not to touch the edge of the barrier as you crawl under. It'll hurt – if you live long enough to feel it.'

CHAPTER XXXIII

In Which Spiggit's Plays an Important Role.

The various dolls, teddy bears, and small battery-powered animals that had forced Samuel and the others up to the next level of Wreckit & Co. watched in silence as Crudford led Maria and the others into the store. The aftermath of battle was still visible. There were disembodied limbs lying on the floor, and teddy bears with their stuffing hanging out. A makeshift doll hospital had been set up close to the lift, and dolls wearing the uniforms of doctors and nurses were doing their best to reinsert arms and legs, and the occasional head, into the correct sockets. Some of the larger dolls still clutched knives, and a couple of stuffed toys snarled at the new arrivals, but none of the toys made any attempt to attack.

'What happened here?' asked Maria.

Nurd took in the Nerf bullets and sporting balls scattered across the floor.

'My guess is that this lot tried to attack Samuel and whoever else was trapped, and they got more than they bargained for,' he said.

Wormwood paused by the remains of a small black stuffed bear. Its head had been almost knocked from its body, and was attached to its neck only by a couple of thin threads. Carefully, tenderly, Wormwood picked it up and held it in his arms, cradling its head in his left hand. A large tear dropped from Wormwood's right eye.

'Is this what we have become?' he said. 'We have set human against teddy, doll against man, and this little bear has paid the price! All he wanted to do was give pleasure to some small child, to be his friend in times of joy, and his comfort in times of trouble. Oh, the humanity!'

He lifted the bear and placed it against his shoulder, its small black body stifling his sobs.

'Ow,' said Wormwood, then louder. 'Ow! Ow!'

'What is it?' said Nurd.

'The little swine is biting my ear!' said Wormwood.

He gave the bear a sharp tug, and its body separated entirely from its head. Unfortunately, the head remained attached to Wormwood's ear, its sharp teeth continuing to gnaw at the lobe.

'Get it off!' said Wormwood. 'It really hurts.'

Nurd tried tugging at the bear's head, but its teeth were firmly embedded, and he succeeded only in painfully stretching Wormwood's ear.

'That's not helping,' said Wormwood. 'You're just making it worse.'

'Well, you're the one who picked it up in the first place.'

'I felt sorry for it.'

'And see where it got you,' said Nurd. 'Maybe you can offer to help those dolls sharpen their knives next.'

Maria arrived with a pencil borrowed from Brian. She managed to jam it between the bear's jaws and prise them open just wide enough for Nurd to remove the head from Wormwood's vicinity. He held it in front of Wormwood's face by one of its ears, where it continued to snap at him, just as the elf had earlier tried to get at Nurd. Nurd considered this poetic justice. He didn't want to be the only one being bitten by possessed objects.

'He seems to have a taste for you,' said Nurd. 'Can't imagine why. I bet you taste awful.'

He tossed the head in the direction of the doll hospital, disturbing the final delicate stages of an operation to restore an arm to a Hug-Me-Hattie doll. Hug-Me-Hattie's arm slid under a radiator, and the doll doctors and nurses gave Nurd a look that could only be described as cutting.[55]

'Sorry!' said Nurd. 'As you were.'

The scientists, meanwhile, were watching the toys. With the exception of the clearly lunatic black bear that had nibbled on Wormwood, the toys still showed no desire to approach.

'Why aren't they attacking us?' asked Professor. Stefan.

'Maybe it's because we have demons with us,' suggested Professor Hilbert. 'It might have confused them.'

'They don't look confused,' said Professor Stefan. 'They just look hostile.'

💀 [55] Do you need me to explain that joke? No? Good.

257

'Why don't we see what happens if we try to leave?'

The two scientists, with Brian and Dorothy/ Reginald in tow, pretended to depart.

''Bye!' they said. 'Lovely meeting you! Good luck with everything!'

The heads of the toys turned to follow their progress, but no attempt was made to stop them, not even when Brian opened the main door and stepped outside. He might have kept going as well had not Professor Hilbert grabbed him by the collar and pulled him back inside.

'That's quite enough cowardice for today, Brian,' he said.

'It really isn't,' said Brian. 'I have loads left.'

But Professor Hilbert was not to be argued with, and Brian reluctantly trudged back into the store.

'Interesting,' said Professor Stefan. 'Mr Nurd, Mr Wormwood, perhaps you'd like to try, just out of curiosity.'

Nurd and Wormwood did as he asked, but as they approached the door the toys closed in on them, blocking their way with a wall of plastic and fur broken only by the odd knife.

'Ah,' said Professor Stefan. 'That would seem to answer the question, at least partly. Something wants you two to remain here.'

'We should have known,' said Wormwood. 'We were invited to the opening, and we never get invited to anything. Now it looks like the only reason we were asked is because something wants to hurt us.'

He and Nurd looked sad.

'Try not to take it personally,' said Maria.

'I'll try,' said Wormwood, 'but it's difficult.'

Crudford put one hand to the side of his head, even though he didn't have any obvious ears, and listened.

'Can you still hear the heart?' asked Professor Hilbert.

'It's definitely near,' said Crudford. 'I say we go up. It's clear that whatever we're looking for isn't here.'

Brian didn't want go up. He wanted to go out. He could not think of any reason why he should go deeper into this shop of horrors. At that moment, fate intervened – as it often will – to give him a push in the right direction.

'What is that noise?' said Professor Stefan. 'It sounds like music.'

A handful of Nosferati survivors, their ears jammed with dead mice to drown out the sound of the organ, had found the stairs out of the basement. They emerged from the stairwell with their fangs exposed, their clawed hands raised, and their bald heads shining under the emergency lights.

'Me first,' said Brian. He made it to the top of the stairs in record time. Brian might have been a scaredy-cat of the highest order, thought Professor Stefan, but he was very agile when he needed to be. He just hoped that 'me first' wouldn't be Brian's last words.

All of the pieces were on the board – almost. There were two missing, but they were on their way.

The demons called Shan and Gath were probably happier than they had ever been. In Hell, they had been strictly third-level staff: their main task was to tend the Eternal Fiery Pits of Doom, which wasn't very difficult as the Eternal Fiery Pits of Doom were never likely to go out any time in the near, or even distant, future. That was why they were called the *Eternal* Fiery Pits of Doom, and not the Temporary Fiery Pits of Doom, which doesn't have the same ring about it at all. Every so often they were sent on holiday to the Quarry of Grey Meaninglessness, where they broke rocks for two weeks, and were entertained in the evenings by the swinging sounds of Barry Perry on the kazoo.[56]

Then, during the attempted invasion of Earth, they had discovered the strange joys of a foul beer named Spiggit's Old Peculiar and had never looked back. For a while they had not looked anywhere at all, Spiggit's tending to cause temporary blindness and an overwhelming desire to be dead. Back in Hell, they attempted to brew it themselves, with mixed results, but they had never stopped trying. When they eventually managed to escape from Hell, their ability to consume large quantities of Spiggit's without actually dying, combined with their sensitive taste buds, had brought them the job of a lifetime: as chief tasters and beer experimenters at Spiggit's Brewery, Chemical Weapons, and Cleaning Products Ltd.[57]

💀 [56] Barry Perry had tortured crowds throughout the north of England for much of his life, taking innocent songs that had never done anyone any harm and murdering them with his kazoo. When he died and found himself in Hell, he also discovered that his kazoo had come with him, if only because someone had shoved it up his bottom before he was buried. Retrieving it from his bottom proved too difficult, though, so his shows in Hell tended to be a bit muffled, which was no bad thing.

💀 [57] In case you think this is an odd name for a company, and are wondering how Spiggit's could manage to create so many different products, let me set your mind at ease: it was all the same product, with varying amounts of water

Yes, they were demons. Even Old Mr Spiggit himself, whose eyesight was very poor, and who was generally regarded as a lunatic, could see from the start that Shan and Gath weren't your usual employees. On the other hand, they didn't stand out as much at the Spiggit's Brewery as they might have done elsewhere on Earth. Years of exposure to Spiggit's had caused biological changes to many of the company's employees. Mr Lambert in Accounts had to shave his hands at least twice a week, and had so much facial hair that the only way to be sure that you were talking to his face was to look for the bulge where his nose was; Mr Norris in Sales had a third thumb; and Mrs Elmtree in Quality Control had grown small but noticeable horns. They didn't mind, though, as Spiggit's paid well, and nobody else would employ them anyway because they looked so distinctive.

Shan and Gath had proven particularly good at looking after the more experimental brews, including the lethal Spiggit's Old Notorious, a beer so dangerous that a batch of its yeast had once stolen a car and held up the Bank of Biddlecombe. The yeast had never been caught, and was now believed to be living somewhere in Spain. Shan and Gath had put an end to that kind of nonsense. No yeast was going to cause trouble on their watch.

Very few things could lure Shan and Gath out of

---

added. Supplies rarely got mixed up, not since the Goat & Artichoke pub had received a delivery of weapons-grade Spiggit's by mistake. The pub had since been rebuilt, although some pieces of the landlord had still not been found.

their comfortable home at Spiggit's Brewery, but the invitation that had landed on their doorstep a few days earlier had contained the magic words 'FREE BEER', which was why they were now standing outside Wreckit & Sons wondering where the party was.

Shan approached the occult field. He suspected that it was dangerous, but he wasn't entirely sure. To test his theory he pushed Gath against it. There was a buzzing sound and the back of Gath's coat disappeared, leaving only a smoking hole where the material had once been.

'Hurh-hurh,' laughed Shan, as Gath put out the last of the flames.

'Hurh-hurh,' laughed Gath, before grabbing Shan's right hand and sticking Shan's index finger into the field. The finger promptly vanished, leaving only a smoking stump in its place.

'Hurh-hurh,' laughed Gath again.

'No, hurh-*hurt*,' said Shan.

He would have wagged his finger disapprovingly at Gath, who always took a joke too far, but he was still waiting for it to grow back. When it had done so, he looked again at the invitation.

'Beer,' he said, and pointed at the shop.

'Beer,' said Gath.

But between them and the beer stood the barrier.

Sometimes in life you have to lose a battle to win a war. Shan dug into one of the pockets of his coat and removed from it a black bottle. The bottle was encased in a titanium frame that kept its cork in place, and the following warning was written on the glass.

This bottle contains *Spiggit's Old Resentful.* Do Not Open. Seriously. Even creating this beer was a mistake, but all attempts to destroy it have proved useless. If you <u>do</u> open this bottle, you agree to give up all right to your health, and possibly your existence. Before opening, ask innocent bystanders to stand well back, or suggest that they move to another country. Do not open near naked flame. Do not so much as THINK of a naked flame in your head. Do not even smile warmly. Do not inhale. If inhaled, seek medical assistance within five seconds. If consumed, seek undertaker.

<u>INSTRUCTIONS FOR USE</u>: Open. Run away.

Shan and Gath had often looked longingly at the next-to-last remaining bottle of Spiggit's Old Resentful. It had been developed by Old Mr Spiggit shortly before people spotted that he was clearly as nutty as a nut-brown squirrel in a nut factory. How bad could Spiggit's Old Resentful be, Shan and Gath had wondered. The answer was probably very bad. Spiggit's did not issue such warnings lightly. If your regular beer has a biohazard symbol on it, even one with a smiley face, then the special stuff must be lethal.

And so Shan and Gath had long carried the bottles of Spiggit's Old Resentful around with them, hoping that the day might come when they would have cause to open them. Now, it seemed, that day was upon them.

Shan typed in the seventeen-digit combination on the bottle's lock, and the titanium cage sprang open. As if sensing that its time was upon it, something rumbled in the glass. Shan looked a bit worried. He looked even more worried as the cork began to remove itself from the bottle under pressure from whatever was inside. Like a man who suddenly finds himself in possession of a live hand grenade, he did the only sensible thing: he handed it to the bloke standing next to him, which in this case was Gath, and began backing away. Gath, meanwhile, might not have been very bright, but he wasn't entirely stupid. He tossed the bottle straight back to Shan, who caught it and sent it back to Gath, and so a game of Hot Potato continued until Shan saw that there was barely a finger's width of cork left in the bottle.

He threw the bottle at the occult field. The bottle didn't pass through but exploded on impact, showering the field with a dark brown liquid that looked like mud and smelled like low tide at a herring factory. Shan's eyes watered, and his nasal hairs caught fire. Gath fainted.

The occult field didn't have feelings, exactly. It was just an occult field generated by Hilary Mould's great engine, aided by the entities with which Hilary Mould had allied himself, but it did have a kind of awareness, for it was alive with dark forces. When the bottle of Spiggit's Old Resentful hit it and exploded, that awareness kicked into high gear, and the field made a swift decision to put as much distance between it and whatever was in the bottle as quickly as possible. The occult field vanished, retreating to another dimension where even the foulest of creatures had nothing on Spiggit's Old Resentful.

Shan slapped Gath on the cheeks to bring him back to consciousness. Once the smell had died down to a manageable level, they approached the shattered bottle. All that was left of the Old Resentful was some thick glass, and a large smoking crater in the ground.

Shan and Gath shook their heads sadly, and went to find their free beer.[58]

☠ [58] To return briefly to the subject of famous last words, which arose in connection with Brian the teaboy, it's a difficult job, coming up with a memorable farewell to life. If death comes unexpectedly, then last words may be something like 'Aaaarrrgggggh!', or 'Ouch!', or 'Of course it isn't loaded,' or 'That bridge will easily support my weight.' It's hard to be clever under pressure. The last words of the writer H.G.Wells were reputed to have been 'Go away, I'm all right,' which was unfortunate as he clearly wasn't. Arguably the worst last words ever spoken came from Dominique Bouhours, an eighteenth-century French essayist, and a big fan of correct grammar, who announced on his deathbed 'I am about to – or I am going to – die; either expression is correct.' I'll bet they were glad to see him go.

CHAPTER XXXIV

In Which the Great Size of the Multiverse is Revealed.

The first thing that struck Samuel as he reached the icy cold top floor was that he had suddenly developed two phobias: acrophobia, a dreadful fear of heights,[59] swiftly followed by astrophobia, the fear of space. Samuel had never been frightened of heights before, and he had always been entranced by the immensity of space. He could spend a happy hour lying on his back in the garden at night, Boswell sleeping beside him, just watching the stars and feeling as though he were adrift among them.

But the top floor of Wreckit & Sons was a different matter entirely, in part because there was no longer really a floor there, or a ceiling. The memory of them remained, the faintest outline of boards beneath his feet and plasterwork above his head, but they resembled little more than chalkmarks that were slowly being

---

[59] The word 'vertigo' is frequently used, incorrectly, to describe the fear of heights, but vertigo is a spinning sensation felt when someone is actually standing still. The correct term for a fear of heights is 'acrophobia'. Good grief, I sound like that grammarian bloke Dominique Bouhours, and he was really annoying. Sorry.

washed away by rain. Even as fear overtook him, Samuel wondered if this was what it was like to be a ghost: perhaps ghosts felt themselves to be real and substantial, and the world around them seemed pale and faded.

Beyond the near-vanished lines of the old store, and the fading shapes of trees, the Multiverse waited. It was a world of light and dark, of stars being born and stars dying, of clusters of swirling galaxies and gaseous columns of nebulae. Samuel could pick out the colours of the stars, shading from the blue of the new to the red of the old. He saw clouds of asteroids, and meteors turning to fire in the atmosphere of unknown worlds, and quasars, the brightest objects in the universe, their light powered by supermassive black holes. He saw universe layered upon universe, like panes of painted glass separated by distances simultaneously great and small. And he himself was both tiny and vast, for all that he saw seemed to revolve around him: he was suspended at the heart of the Multiverse.

The second thing that struck Samuel was a dwarf, as Angry, who had been leading the way, discovered that being a leader is only fun if you're collecting a trophy, or a cash prize. It's not fun if, as leader, you're the first person to put a foot where you expect a floor to be, only to find that a large number of universes have opened up in its place, and it looks like a very long way down. He slammed painfully into Samuel's stomach, knocking the air from Samuel with his elbow.

'Mind your step there,' said Angry. 'There's a bit of a drop.'

The others had paused on the stairs, aware that

there was some problem ahead, but now the steps behind them began to vanish, one by one, as the lower floors of Wreckit & Sons turned to mist and were gone.

'The stairs are disappearing, Samuel,' shouted Maria. 'We have to move up.'

But Samuel couldn't budge. His feet were frozen in place on what little solidity remained. He willed them to move in order to make room for the others to join him, but he couldn't. It was only then that he looked down and saw there was nothing beneath him after all but stars. He waited for himself to begin falling, like a character in a cartoon who manages to run off the edge of a cliff but doesn't start to drop until he realises what he's done, but Samuel did not fall, and he could definitely feel something solid under his shoes. Tentatively, he tapped with his toe. Whatever was beneath him felt like wood, and sounded like wood, which meant that it was, in all likelihood, wood.

Warily, testing the way before he took a step, he made room for the others to join him. Constable Peel was the first up.

'Oh, Lor',' he said, as he took in the view. 'I don't feel at all well.'

For a moment he appeared to want to turn back and take his chances with the vanishing stairs, but Samuel reassured him.

'It's OK,' he told Constable Peel. 'There's still a floor under us. You can see it if you look hard enough.'

Constable Peel didn't want to look. Looking meant seeing infinity, or as good as, waiting right beneath his feet. He stretched out a hand to balance himself, and Angry gripped it.

'It's all right, Constable,' he said. 'I have you.'

'If I fall,' said Constable Peel, 'I'm taking you with me. At least I'll die happy.'

With Angry's help, Constable Peel came to grips with the concept of a floor that both was and wasn't there. They repeated the process as the rest of the group joined them, until at last they were all standing together, alternating between fear and awe at the terror and majesty of the Multiverse, and at the one construction that really didn't seem to be belong in it, for standing before them was Santa's Grotto.

Samuel couldn't understand why they hadn't noticed it before. Maybe they'd been too concerned with not falling, and with taking in the view, but it was hard to ignore a little stone house with smoke pouring from its chimney and snow on its roof – real snow, because it had now begun to descend on them as well, tickling their faces before melting on their skin. The light flickering through its walls turned from white to orange as they watched, as though a great fire were raging inside.

The door opened, and Mr St John-Cholmondeley appeared.

'Look,' said Jolly, 'it's Mr Smokey-Chimney.'

'So it is,' said Dozy. 'Oi, we want a word with you about this job, Slimy-Chopsticks. We're starting to think that we might not want it after all; that, or you need to pay us more.'

Now it was Mr St John-Cholmondeley's turn to glow red.

'It's Sinjin-Chumley!' he screamed. 'How many times do I have to tell you? *Sinjin-Chumley!* It's just two words. How hard can it be?'

Even amid the chaos of the Multiverse, the dwarfs could see that he was annoyed. The dwarfs prided themselves on their sensitivity to the feelings of others.

'Sorry,' said Angry.

'Yes, sorry,' said Jolly and Dozy.

'Applidlespopop,' said Mumbles.

'He says he's sorry too,' said Angry.

'Sorry, Mr . . . ?' said Mr St John-Cholmondeley.

He cocked his head, and waited for a reply.

The dwarfs looked at one another. Somebody had to give it a try. Angry, who had decided that he'd had enough of taking the lead for one day, gave Jolly a nudge.

'Sorry,' said Jolly, 'Mr Slimjim . . .'

He ran out of steam. Dozy gave it a try.

'Sorry, Mr Soapy-Chandling.'

'Mr Slightly-Chafing.'

'Mr Singing-Chutney.'

'Mr Stinky-Cheesecake.'

There is a phrase sometimes used about people who are very angry: 'he was incandescent with rage'. An incandescent light, as I'm sure you know, is one with a filament that glows white-hot when heated. It does not, of course, mean that someone really glows white-hot when annoyed, or it didn't until Mr St John-Cholmondeley came along. As they watched, Mr St John-Cholmondeley's eyes turned bright red, and then changed from red to burning white before bursting into flames. He opened his mouth, and smoke and fire jetted from between his lips. His whole body shook as smoke poured from his sleeves, and the ends of his trousers, and the neck of his shirt.

'It's—' he roared, but he got no further. His suit ignited and his body exploded, but there was no blood or flesh, only bits of plastic. Mr St John-Cholmondeley was simply a showroom dummy in a cheap suit brought to life, and now that existence was at an end. His head, which had soared high into the air with the force of the blast, landed with a thud and rolled across the nearly unseen floor, where Angry stopped it with his foot.

The white light was fading from Mr St John-Cholmondeley's eyes, and his skin was assuming the hardness of plastic. The dark force that had animated him was leaving, but there was a little wretched life left in him yet.

'It's—' he began again, but Mumbles interrupted him.

'Sinjin-Chumley,' Mumbles said, pronouncing it perfectly.

'We knew all along,' said Angry. 'Serves you right for being unpleasant.'

Mr St John-Cholmondeley found the strength to make his eyes glow an angry orange one last time before the light vanished from them and all that remained was a plastic head. Two thin streams of pure darkness poured from his ears and flowed beneath the walls of Santa's Grotto, and that darkness seemed to be mirrored above their heads. More stars were snuffed out, swallowed by swirling clouds like thick black ink. Eyeless faces appeared in the void, but their very blindness made them more threatening. Long grasping fingers stretched out towards the Earth, and black tongues licked at lipless mouths, as though already tasting the planet's light and life before consuming it. But the barrier between the Shadows and the universe held, for now. The Shadows flattened themselves against it, but they could not penetrate. It would not hold for much longer, though. Already cracks were visible, shining red like streams of lava.

Nurd appeared at Samuel's right hand.

'All of this because of us,' said Nurd, and he sounded both amazed and terribly, terribly sad. 'She will sacrifice whole universes to the Shadows in order to avenge herself.'

'What if we just offered ourselves to her?' said Samuel softly, and if Nurd had been astonished by the lengths to which Mrs Abernathy was prepared to go to have her revenge, he was more astonished still at the boy's words, and he felt honoured that he could call such a person his friend. Billions of years in age separated them. One was human, the other demon. Yet in all his long life Nurd had never felt closer to another being than he did to Samuel. The Multiverse had brought them together, and they had both been changed utterly by the meeting. Samuel had crossed dimensions, and now understood something of the true nature of existence. He had confronted the greatest of evils, but he had also been saved by a demon.

And that demon had himself been saved by Samuel: had they not met, then Nurd would still have been living in exile in the bleakest, dullest part of Hell with only Wormwood for company, devising plots that would never come to pass. Nurd would just have been another failed demon, an entity not strong enough to be truly evil, but not strong enough to be good either.

Now this boy was suggesting that they try to lay down their lives not just for their friends but for humanity and for every other life form, known and unknown, that swam or flew or crawled in the Multiverse. As Nurd watched, Boswell, who had been standing just behind Samuel and peering through his master's legs at all that was happening, shifted position, and moved to Samuel's side, where he sat down with his weight leaning against the boy's right leg.

He hears Samuel, thought Nurd, who had long ago learned not to underestimate the little dog. He senses what the boy is thinking of doing, and he will not leave him. This dog will die with its master rather than abandon him. If a small dog is willing to stand beside the boy at the cost of its life, then what choice have I but to do the same?

'We can try,' said Nurd, 'but I fear that Mrs Abernathy is so insane by now that it won't be enough for her to see only us suffer, and she has made her bargain with the Shadows. They will not let her break it easily. Perhaps, though, we can appeal to her vanity. Even the cruellest of beings must sometimes show mercy. If there is a power in taking lives, there is a greater power in sparing them. If we can make her believe that letting humanity survive would better demonstrate her might than allowing the Shadows to consume everything, then we could have a chance.'

Samuel picked up something in Nurd's tone.

'But not a big chance,' said Samuel, and he managed a smile.

'Not really,' said Nurd, 'but that's better than no chance at all.'

Maria joined them.

'What are you two whispering about?' she said, but even as she spoke Lucy bustled forward and plonked herself between Maria and Samuel. Lucy might have been shallow, and very self-obsessed, but she was nobody's fool. She might not have liked Samuel as much as she once thought she did, and she certainly didn't understand him, but there was no way that she was going to let anyone else take him from her.

'He's *my* boyfriend!' she said.

'Er, I've been meaning to talk to you about that,' said Samuel, although it struck him that this probably wasn't the ideal time to bring it up. Then again, if the universe did come to an end, he didn't want to spend his final moments stuck in a doomed relationship with Lucy Highmore.

'*Excuse* me?' said Lucy.

Nurd took a discreet step back. It is said that Hell hath no fury like a woman scorned. Nurd had spent a long time in Hell, and he knew just how furious it was. If scorning Lucy Highmore was going to be worse than Hell, then Nurd didn't want to be stuck in the middle of whatever happened next. He managed to put Constable Peel and two dwarfs between him and the argument.

'Hey, wait a minute,' said Constable Peel, who might

have been dim at times but could see where this was going.

'You're a policeman,' said Nurd. 'You have a duty to protect.'

He kept a tight hold of Constable Peel's shoulders, just in case the policeman got any ideas about seeking cover for himself.

'Look, it's just not working out between us,' said Samuel. 'It's not you, it's me.'[60]

'How dare you!' said Lucy. 'You're saying that it is me!'

'No, I'm not,' said Samuel. 'At least, I don't think that I am. Hang on, I might be.'

'But nobody has ever broken up with me before,' said Lucy. 'I do the breaking up. I even have a speech about how we can still be friends, and how you must be brave, and all that nonsense.'

'Right,' said Samuel, and his mouth began working before his brain could catch up. 'Well, we can still be friends, and I suppose you have to be brave—'

Any further musings he might have had on the future of his dealings with Lucy Highmore were brought to a sudden end by the impact of her right shoe against Samuel's left knee.

'Ooooooooh!' said Lucy. 'Well, I'm glad I'm not going out with you any more! You're strange, you're too short, and your shoes sometimes don't match. And by the way, this has been the worst date of my life!'

---

[60] Please see footnote 13 in Chapter Five and then substitute 'me' for 'you', and 'you' for 'me' in the sentence above.

She turned to face Maria.

'You Jezebel!' she said. 'If you like him that much then you can just have him, and I hope he makes you as happy as he made me.'

She stomped away, then stomped back again.

'Just in case you didn't understand what I meant,' she told Maria, 'I was implying that he didn't make me happy at all, and I hope you're just as unhappy with him as I was.'

'I knew that,' said Maria. 'And I do like him. I think I may love him, actually.'

'Bully for you,' said Lucy. 'I don't want an invitation to the wedding.'

She stomped away for the second time, and stood beside Nurd and Constable Peel with her arms folded, simmering like a pot on a warm stove.

'What are you two looking at?' she said.

'Nothing,' said Nurd.

'Me neither,' said Constable Peel. 'I'm just minding my own business.'

'Just keep it that way,' said Lucy. 'Oh, men!'

Samuel, meanwhile, was staring at Maria with the confused expression of a man who has just learned that day is, in fact, night, and the moon is made of cheese after all.

'What?' he said, as he couldn't think of anything else to say.

'It doesn't matter,' said Maria, then added: 'You're an idiot.'

'What?' said Samuel – again.

'For a smart boy,' said Angry to Jolly, who had been

watching the entertainment and enjoying it immensely, 'he really is surprisingly stupid sometimes.'

'Look, I like you,' said Maria. 'A lot. I've always liked you. A lot. Do you understand?'

'What?' said Samuel, for a third time.

Maria kissed Samuel gently on the lips.

'There,' she said.

'Ah,' said Samuel.

'The light dawns,' said Angry.

'It's like watching a caveman discover fire,' said Jolly.

'Now,' said Maria, 'to return to the original question: what were you and Nurd whispering about?'

Samuel could taste Maria on his lips. His head was swimming. It was such a shame that he was either going to be killed or the Multiverse was about to come to an end, because he realised he had always loved Maria. He definitely didn't want to die now, and he rather hoped that the Multiverse might be saved without his death being part of the bargain, but then he also understood that there really is no sacrifice, and no bravery, unless there is something to be lost.

He put his hand against Maria's cheek.

'Nurd and I are going to offer ourselves to Mrs Abernathy in order to save the Multiverse,' he said.

'Over my dead body,' said Maria.

'That,' said a voice lubricated by poisons, 'can probably be arranged. Oh, and ho-ho-ho.'

CHAPTER XXXV

In Which We End on a Cliffhanger.

Samuel and Maria had seen photographs of Hilary Mould, but had obviously never imagined meeting him in the flesh, not that they had lost a lot of sleep over it. Even in life Hilary Mould had not been a very handsome man. He had fish eyes, a misshapen nose, and a chin so weak that a small child could have taken it in a fight. What little hair he had stuck up at odd angles from his head like clumps of bristles on an old, worn paintbrush, and his ears stood out at right angles from his head like car doors that had been jammed open. He was also so pale and sickly that he resembled a corpse that had recently been dug up and then forgotten about.

In a way, this should have meant that *actual* death was unlikely to make him any less appealing than he already was, but anyone hoping that might be the case would have been sorely disappointed. Hilary Mould now looked worse than ever, and his name seemed to suit him even more than it had in life since he was *actually* mouldy: something unpleasant and green was growing on what was left of his face, and he appeared to be at least thirty per cent down in the finger department. His skin had retreated from his fingernails, making them appear disturbingly long, and it was possible to see the tendons working through the holes in his cheeks as his jaws moved. His big eyes had turned entirely black, and wisps of darkness hung like smoke around his lips as he spoke. The fact that he was dressed as Father Christmas did not help matters.

'Mr Grimly, I presume?' said Sergeant Rowan. 'Or do you prefer Mould?'

'You may call me *Mister* Mould,' said Hilary Mould. 'I've been waiting a long time for this day. Now—'

'Excuse me,' said Jolly.

Hilary Mould tried to ignore him. He'd been walled up in the basement of Wreckit & Sons for a long time, even if his spirit had been able to wander in the form of a possessed statue infused with some of his blood, but that wasn't the same thing as being out and about. He had a big speech prepared. He wasn't about to let himself be interrupted by a dwarf.

'Now, my great—'

'Mister, excuse me,' said Jolly again. 'Still here.'

He waved his hand helpfully, but Hilary Mould was absolutely determined not to be distracted.

'NOW,' he shouted, 'my GREAT MACHINE has revealed itself to—'

'Really need to talk to you,' Jolly persisted.

'Mister, mister,' said Dozy, waving his left arm to attract attention, 'my friend has something to say.'

Hilary Mould gave up. Honestly, it was most frustrating. He'd created an enormous occult engine, and had sealed himself up at the heart of it, undead and not a little bored, waiting for the moment when dark forces might resurrect him, and just at his time of triumph he found himself dealing with chatty dwarfs.

'Yes, yes, what is it?' said Hilary Mould, as he tried to think of ways that the Shadows could make the dwarfs' sufferings last even longer as a personal favour to himself.

'Mister,' said Jolly, 'your hand has dropped off.'

Hilary Mould stared at his left hand. It was still there, minus most of its fingers, but after spending more than a century walled up in a tomb you had to expect a certain amount of minor damage. Unfortunately, when he switched his attention to his right hand he discovered only a stump. The hand itself – his favourite one, as it still had three fingers and a thumb attached – was now lying by his feet.

'Oh, for crying out loud,' he said.

He bent down and picked up the hand.

'You could try sticking it back on,' suggested Angry helpfully. 'I don't think glue will do it, but maybe if you wrapped it up with sticky tape . . .'

'It doesn't matter,' said Hilary Mould through gritted teeth, or through whatever teeth he had left to grit, which wasn't many.

'You could try a hook,' offered Jolly.

'If you wore the right kind of hat, people might think you were a pirate,' said Angry.

'Stop!' screamed Hilary Mould. 'I told you: it's fine. I have another hand. Just let it drop.'

Jolly detected the opportunity for a joke, but Hilary Mould saw it coming and cut him off before he could get a word out. He stuck the severed hand in his pocket, and pointed one of his remaining fingers at the dwarf.

'I'm warning you,' he said.

Jolly raised two hands in surrender – well, one hand. He'd hidden the other one up his sleeve.

Hilary Mould grimaced in frustration. This wasn't going at all according to plan.

'Mister,' said Dozy again.

'Look,' said Hilary Mould, 'please let me finish. I have a lot to get through.'

He fumbled in another pocket and extracted a tattered, folded sheet of paper. He started trying to unfold it, but he immediately ran into trouble due to a lack of fingers.

'Need a hand?' said a dwarf voice.

Hilary Mould didn't rise to the bait. He kept his temper, managed to get the paper open, and checked his notes.

'Um,' he muttered to himself. 'Yes, "waiting a long time for this day" – done. Laugh sinisterly. Move on to description of occult engine, tell them about ruling the world, laugh again in an evil way, hand over to . . . Okay, fine. Right.'

He cleared his throat.

'Ah-ha-ha-ha-ha!' he laughed.

'Mister,' said Dozy.

'WHAT? What do you want this time?'

'Do you wear glasses?'

Hilary Mould looked confused.

'Sometimes,' he said.

'Well,' said Dozy, 'I hate to break it to you, but you might have trouble with that in future.'

'Why?'

'Your right ear just fell off.'

Hilary Mould reached up to check. The dwarf was right. His right ear was no more. He saw it resting by his right shoe.

'Oh, blast!' he said.

He didn't want to leave it lying around. Someone might step on it. His hand, though, was barely managing to hang on to his notes.

'I'm sorry,' he said, 'but would somebody mind picking that up for me?'

Jolly obliged.

'I'll get the other one while I'm down here,' he said, for Hilary Mould's left ear, clearly pining for its friend, had detached itself from his head and headed south.

'Do you want me to put them with your hand?' asked Jolly.

'If you wouldn't mind,' said Hilary Mould.

'Not at all.'

Jolly squeezed the ears into Hilary Mould's pocket. Unfortunately, the pocket was already taken up with the hand, so Jolly had to use a little force to get the ears in there as well. He distinctly felt something snap and crumble as he did so: more than one something, as it happened.

'Do be careful with them,' said Hilary Mould. 'I'm sure there's a way of fitting them on again.'

'Don't you worry,' said Jolly, discreetly using the end of Hilary Mould's jacket to wipe bits of crushed ear from his fingers, 'you'll look a whole new man when they stick those back on.'

Jolly rejoined the others.

'He'll never wear glasses again,' he whispered to Angry. 'And I don't know how he's going to wind his watch.'

Hilary Mould was worried. He had just discovered one of the dangers of walling oneself up in a basement for a very long time: rot tends to set in. Even with a hint of Shadow essence coursing through his remains, he was in very real danger of falling apart entirely before the real business of the evening was concluded.

'I suppose you're wondering why I created my engine,' he said.

'We were, a bit,' said Samuel.

'I knew,' said Hilary Mould, 'that there was a great force of darkness somewhere out there in the vast reaches of space.'

He gestured grandly at the stars surrounding them. A finger flew off into the blackness.

'Just pretend that never happened,' said Hilary Mould. He continued: 'I felt this darkness calling to me. I heard the lost voices. And I knew what I had to build: an engine, a great supernatural machine in the form of a pentagram, and then the Shadows would come.'

'What did they promise you in return?' asked Nurd.

'Eternal life!' said Hilary Mould, and added a 'Bwa-ha-ha-ha-ha!' for effect.

'And how is that working out for you, now that you're falling apart?'

'It'll be fine,' said Hilary Mould,

His nose twitched.

'This decay is only temporary, I'm sure.'

There was definitely a sneeze coming. He could feel it.

'Blast this dust.'

Hilary Mould sneezed. His nose shot past Angry, who made a vain attempt to catch it but succeeded only in breaking it with his fingertips.

'If it's any help,' said Wormwood, 'I know just how you feel.'

'I am not worried,' said the now noseless Hilary Mould. 'The Shadows will restore me to my original form, and they will give me the Earth to rule as my reward.'

Samuel looked doubtfully at the Shadows looming above their heads, still waiting for their way into this universe to be revealed. He didn't think that they were likely to keep their side of the bargain with Hilary Mould. If they got through, there wouldn't be an Earth left for him to rule.

'But the engine didn't work, did it?' said Maria. She stood beside Samuel, seemingly fearless. She made Samuel feel braver too. 'Not like you thought it would.'

'There were, apparently, some problems,' Hilary Mould admitted. 'The Shadows still couldn't enter our world. There wasn't enough chthonic power, not in an engine designed only by a human. That was why I hid myself away in the basement, waiting for circumstances to change. The Shadows told me to be patient. They said that, in time, humanity's own inventions would weaken the barriers between dimensions. And they were right: that was precisely what happened, but still, still it was not sufficient. One final ingredient was required: a force greater than the Shadows, greater even than the most advanced machines of men. It was –'

'A heart,' said Samuel, finishing his sentence for him.

For the first time, Hilary Mould looked surprised, and also disappointed. This was to have been his big revelation, and now a boy had deprived him of it. The dwarfs had been bad enough, but this was just too much. He decided that, once the Shadows had entered the universe, he was going to have a long lie down and not talk to any dwarfs or children for eternity.

'Yes, a heart,' he said, making the best of the situation. 'A heart of purest evil; a heart capable of pumping its poison into my engine, providing it with the fuel that it required to break down the walls, to shatter the divide between universes; the heart of a demon with a hatred for the Earth to match the Shadows' own.'

He added another 'Bwa-ha-ha' for effect, but it came out sounding funny because of the absence of his nose.

'And what did you and the Shadows say that you would give to Mrs Abernathy in return?' asked Samuel.

'We promised,' he said, 'to give to her all those on Earth who had conspired against her. Most of all, we promised to give to her Samuel Johnson.'

'Then let her take me,' said Samuel, 'but spare my friends, and spare the Earth and the Multiverse from the Shadows.'

Maria took Samuel's right hand and held it tightly.

'If he goes, then I go.'

'Look,' said Hilary Mould, 'you're *all* going. Don't you understand? You're doomed, every one of you.

She doesn't want to bargain with you. She doesn't *have* to bargain. She gets what she wants, the Shadows get what they want, and I get what I want. I should say, though, that she has a special fate lined up for you, Samuel. Oh, a very special fate.'

'And what would that be?' asked Samuel. He was glad that his voice didn't tremble, although he was sorely afraid.

'She's going to cut out your heart and replace it with her own,' said Hilary Mould. 'You're going to become her new body, the carrier for her evil. And you'll know it, and feel it, because she'll keep your consciousness trapped in there with her like a prisoner locked away in a prison cell. She'll allow you to watch as she destroys your friends, but she'll leave your dog until last: your dog, and your demon friend Nurd. She's going to spend a very long time hurting them. Suns will die, and galaxies will end, but their pain will go on and on, and you'll be a witness to every moment of it.'

Boswell barked at Hilary Mould. He'd heard his name mentioned, and sensed that this dry, foul-smelling man meant him and Samuel no good. Boswell was on the verge of attacking him and depriving him of some more fingers, but Samuel held him back.

Nurd stepped forward.

'You're a fool,' said Nurd.

'And why is that?' said Hilary Mould.

'Because you trust the Shadows, and you trust Mrs Abernathy. When the Shadows come through, they'll smother you along with everything else in this universe, and Mrs. Abernathy won't protect you. She won't even be able to protect herself. The Shadows are the only entities in the Multiverse that the Great Malevolence could not bend to its will. They are its enemies as much as ours. If the Great Malevolence could not make them do its bidding, why do you think one of its lieutenants – a lieutenant, by the way, who has twice been defeated by a boy and his dog – would be able to succeed where it has failed?'

'She is strong,' insisted Hilary Mould.

'She is weak,' said Nurd. 'The Great Malevolence had turned its back on her even before Samuel and the rest of us tore her apart. She had failed the Great Malevolence, and it had no more use for her.'

An expression of unease flickered on Hilary Mould's rotted features. Nurd picked up on it immediately.

'Ah, she didn't mention that, did she? She didn't tell you that she'd been cast aside by her master. We are stronger than she is, and we always have been. You've been tricked, Mr Mould. When the Shadows come, your alliance with her won't save you. If you do get eternal life out of this, you'll spend it in utter darkness with the Shadows pressing down on you, and if I were you, I'd rather have no life at all.'

Hilary Mould's confidence was crumbling, just as his body was. He wanted to convince himself that Nurd was telling lies, but he could not. Nurd's words had the weight of truth to them.

'She was only ever using you,' said Nurd. 'That's what she does. She's clever and ruthless. When she's finished using you – and that should be pretty soon, I think – she'll cast you to the Shadows, and you'll wish you had just toddled off and died years ago instead of hanging about in old shops in the hope of ruling the world someday.'

By now, Hilary Mould had no doubts left. Nurd was right.

'The engine,' said Hilary Mould, as the dreadfulness of his fate became clear to him. 'The engine must be turned off.'

'How?' said Nurd.

But before Hilary Mould could reply, his lower jaw dropped to the floor. He knelt to retrieve it, but his left leg shattered below the knee and he toppled sideways. Samuel ran to him. He was thinking of Crudford. If Crudford could find Mrs Abernathy's heart and steal it away, the force powering the engine would be gone, and the Shadows would not be able to escape from their world into this one.

'Where is the heart, Mr Mould?' said Samuel. 'Tell us, please!'

Hilary Mould had only one finger left. He slowly unbent it from his fist, but before he could point it the grotto behind him began to fall apart. Samuel barely had time to get out of the way before the heavy stones fell on Hilary Mould, turning him to dust.

Samuel's ears rang from the sound of the clashing stones. His eyes and mouth were filled with dry matter, some of it almost certainly bits of Mould. He spat them out.

There was a thumping noise in his head: the beating of a heart that was not his own. It was almost as though Mrs Abernathy had already entered him, just as Hilary

Mould had threatened. He tried to find the source of the sound. It was coming from the group of humans and non-humans nearby.

It was coming from *inside* one of them.

The others seemed to realize it at the same time as Samuel. Slowly they moved away from one another – watching, listening – before grouping together again as they narrowed down the source, until at last a single figure was left standing alone, and the identity of Mrs Abernathy's host was revealed.

CHAPTER XXXVI

In Which Mrs Abernathy's Identity is Revealed.

The isolated member of their little band said nothing. It was left to Professor Hilbert to break the silence.

'Dorothy!' he cried. 'Er, and/or Reginald, of course. Can this be true?'

'Turncoat!' said the Polite Monster. 'Eight letters,' it added, "one who abandons one party or group to join another".'

'No,' said Samuel. 'I don't think Dorothy ever really existed at all.'

Professor Hilbert turned to Professor Stefan.

'I thought that you hired her,' he said.

'I thought that you did.'

'We need a more careful hiring policy,' said Professor Hilbert.

Dorothy/Reginald removed her false beard. What was revealed was a chin that had begun to blacken and decay. She tugged at her hair, and it came away from her skull in clumps until only a bald, spotted scalp remained. Her body started to swell, bursting through her clothing. Her arms and legs lengthened, and they could hear the grinding of bone against bone, and the snapping of sinews. She rose above them all as tentacles exploded from her back, their beaklike endings gulping at the air, as her black heart flooded the host body with its poison and transformed it. Her head expanded, horns sprouting from the bone, and her mouth grew larger and larger. Her human teeth were forced from her gums and replaced with row upon row of sharp incisors. She reminded Samuel of a huge black mantis, but there was a hint of Ba'al to her appearance, and more than a little of Mrs Abernathy. Her skin was slightly translucent, and the bones and muscles were visible beneath it, as was the dark heart that beat at the core of her being, protected by a thick, hard shield of keratinised cells.

But it was the eyes that drew Samuel's attention. They were large and still somewhat human in appearance, but any traces of real humanity were long gone: in their place was only absolute madness. Samuel thought that it was like staring into the centre of a storm, a thing of pure, relentless destruction.

'Hello, Samuel,' said the beast, and the voice was Mrs Abernathy's, and any lingering doubts were banished.

'Hello,' said Samuel, for want of anything better to say. From somewhere near his ankles came the sound of Boswell barking. Mrs Abernathy had once hurt the little dog badly. He had not forgotten, but he was not afraid. Instead, he seemed anxious to inflict some harm of his own upon her in return.

Above their heads, the Shadows converged, the weight of them pressing down upon the Earth. They sensed their time was near. Soon, this world would be theirs, and all other worlds would follow. They would swallow every star in the universe and leave it cold and black before moving on to the rest of the Multiverse. In time they would make their way to Hell itself and put out its fires, for the Shadows wanted no lights left burning. The Shadows wanted only darkness beyond imagining.

'Look at you all,' said Mrs Abernathy. 'Look how easily you were lured to me.'

She took in Dan and the dwarfs, and Sergeant Rowan and Constable Peel, and Shan and Gath, and Maria, even the Polite Monster, until finally her lunatic eyes fell on Samuel and Boswell, and Wormwood and Nurd.

'You!' she said to Nurd. 'Twice you have been my ruin. Twice you sided with humanity against your own kind. There will not be a third time.'

A great forked tongue unfurled itself from behind her jaws and coiled around Nurd like a snake. Holes opened on its surface, and each hole was a tiny, sucking mouth lined with teeth. The tongue came close to Nurd, but it did not touch him, and he did not flinch, until at last it was drawn back into her mouth.

'Not yet,' said Mrs Abernathy. 'That would be too quick, too lacking in agony. Mould was right: there are greater punishments in store for you.'

'He should never have trusted you,' said Samuel. 'If he'd given it even a moment's thought, he would have known that you'd kill him in the end.'

'Kill him?' said Mrs Abernathy. 'I didn't kill him. He was already dead. He just didn't want to admit it. And I could feel him turning on me. He was weak, like all of your kind. The Shadows would not have been kind with him: about that, at least, you were right.'

'They won't be kind with you either,' said Nurd. 'They hate demons as much as humans. They'll destroy you without a thought.'

'Perhaps,' said Mrs Abernathy, 'but they'll have to find me first. You know, in a way you did me a favour when you scattered my atoms throughout the Multiverse. Even I had not understood how powerful I was until then, for as my being imploded, as I felt pain beyond that experienced by any being before me, I was given a glimpse of the Multiverse in its totality. For an instant I saw every universe, every dimension, because I was part of them all, and the memory of that moment was absorbed by every atom of my being. I know the Multiverse: I know where it is weakest and where it is strongest. I know the holes between universes. I can stay ahead of the Shadows for eternity, for there will always be new places to hide.'

'And the Great Malevolence?' said Nurd. 'There will be no forgiveness for releasing the Shadows into the Mulitverse. You will have deprived it of its prize, of claiming the conquest of the Multiverse for itself, and the Great Malevolence will hunt you until the last star disappears from the sky.'

'I can stay ahead of our master too,' said Mrs Abernathy. 'I have knowledge beyond that of the Great Malevolence. The old demon has lived too long in Hell. It has grown weary, and slow. It knows only its own rage, but I have knowledge of every nook and cranny of the Multiverse. Perhaps, in time, other demons will come to me, and leave the Great Malevolence to its plotting and planning, its endless hurt. There are ways to defeat the Shadows. There are universes of pure light. Their greed will eventually lead them to such places, and there I will be waiting. The wait may be long, but I have time.'

She turned once more to Samuel.

'And you will be with me, Samuel: you will keep me company in my exile, and you will live with the knowledge of the hurt that you brought upon your family, your friends, and worlds beyond number because of your meddling.'

'Then take me,' said Samuel. 'I'll go with you willingly. You can do what you want with me, but spare the others. Spare all of these worlds.'

'No,' said Mrs Abernathy.

'You can take me too,' said Nurd. 'I'll suffer beside him.'

'You'll suffer anyway,' said Mrs Abernathy. 'You should have listened to Mould: you're not offering me anything that I don't already have in my grasp.'

'But why make them all suffer because of me?' said Samuel.

'Because I want to,' said Mrs Abernathy. 'Because it gives me pleasure.'

Samuel tried to recall what Crudford had said about playing on Mrs Abernathy's vanity.

'But wouldn't it display your power more forcefully if you were to hold back the Shadows, and allow so many to go on living?' said Samuel. 'Isn't there more greatness in sparing lives than taking them?'

Mrs Abernathy swatted away the possibility as though it were a fly, and a very small fly at that.

'No,' she said. 'No, it wouldn't.'

'Frankly,' said Jolly to Angry, 'even I didn't buy that one.'

'It was a long shot,' agreed Angry. 'It would be like telling us that it's better to pay for stuff than to get it for nothing by stealing it. I mean, it might be true, but you're not going to get anywhere by believing it.'

'You know,' said the Polite Monster to Mrs Abernathy, shaking with the kind of suppressed rage of which only the nicest people are capable, 'you really are a very, very rude – four letters, "ill-mannered or impolite" – demon.'

Mrs Abernathy roared, and foul-smelling spittle shot from her jaws.

'Enough!' she said. 'It begins.'

The stones from the collapsed grotto ascended slowly into the air, revealing the dusty remains of Hilary Mould, but also a very old, very battered wooden door. It hung suspended just a foot off the ground, and at its centre was a single lock.

'This is the last barrier, the doorway between the Kingdom of Shadows and this world,' said Mrs Abernathy. 'It needs only the key to open it.'

Her gaze flicked dangerously from one face to the next, until it came to rest on Maria.

'You,' she said. 'I feel Samuel's fondness for you. You will provide the key.'

As she spoke, two of the tentacles on her back lashed out, wrapping themselves around Maria and lifting her off the ground.

'You are the key,' said Mrs Abernathy, 'and the key is blood.'

The surface of the door rippled. Great splinters protruded from the ancient wood, each capable of spearing a human being like an insect on a pin. The keyhole changed shape, becoming a red-lipped mouth waiting to be fed. The last of the stars disappeared from above their heads as the Shadows merged into a single mass of blackness, a great face composed of many entities in one, and galaxies were swallowed in its jaws.

The dwarfs rushed at Mrs Abernathy, and she struck back with her tentacles and her long spindly arms, each ending in claws of spurred bone. Nurd and Wormwood went for her legs, trying vainly to overbalance her and pull her down. The policemen joined the attack, supported by Dan and the Polite Monster. Even Lucy came out of her sulk and joined the fray. They hit her with truncheons and fists, with cricket bats and tennis rackets, but the demon was too strong for them. All they managed to do was distract Mrs Abernathy, but at least they were preventing her from drawing closer to the door, and impaling Maria on its waiting spikes.

Samuel's voice sounded loudly, even amid the chaos.

'Everybody get back!' he cried.

Without thinking, the attackers did as he commanded, creating space around Mrs Abernathy.

'You put my girlfriend down!' said Samuel.

A single black object soared through the air towards Mrs Abernathy, its cork already popping as its contents struggled to escape. The newly-arrived Shan and Gath watched it go with great sorrow.

The dwarfs saw it too.

'Is that—?' said Angry, diving for cover.

'It can't be,' said Jolly, already trying to hide behind Sergeant Rowan.

'I thought it was just a myth,' said Dozy, who had decided that, if someone had to go, it might as well be the Polite Monster, as he would probably be too polite to object, and so had chosen to use him for cover.

'Spiggit's Old Resentful,' said Mumbles, and there was awe in his voice, as well as fear for his safety, for he seemed to be left with nowhere to hide at all. As a last resort, he curled himself into a small ball and prayed.

The bottle struck Mrs Abernathy in the chest and exploded into shards. The yeasty weapon of war sprayed her skin and immediately went to work on it like acid, burning through the shield that surrounded her heart. Mrs Abernathy screamed in pain and dropped Maria. Her tentacles and arms instinctively went for the growing wound as she tried to wipe the fluid from her skin. Instead it simply spread to her other limbs and began to scald them as well. Her screaming grew in pitch and volume, and then turned to a sound so agonized as to be barely audible, for the first of the Spiggit's had found her heart.

Just then, there was a wet popping sound from inside Mrs Abernathy, and her heart moved. It seemed to be forcing itself out of her damaged body, as though trying to escape its fate. At last it was entirely outside her, and it was only when a small gelatinous mass appeared behind it, black gore running down his sides, that the truth of what was happening was revealed.

Mrs Abernathy gurgled. She reached for her heart, but Crudford was too quick for her. He oozed out of reach as Mrs Abernathy's body, weakened by the trauma of her injury, collapsed. The life left her eyes. Just like Mr St John-Cholmondley, her human form had merely been a vessel for an essence of evil. Her foul heart continued to beat in Crudford's arms, for that was where all of her true power resided.

The wooden door collapsed in upon itself. The face of the Shadows opened its mouth in a soundless cry of frustration and rage, and then was gone. The divisions between the dimensions of the Multiverse were slowly concealed, falling upon one another like clear sheets of plastic dotted with stars until at last there was only one familiar set of constellations in the sky, and then even that was gone as the floors and ceilings and walls of Wreckit & Sons became visible once more. Samuel and the others were left standing beside the ruins of the grotto, and there was silence but for the beating of Mrs Abernathy's heart.

'Don't go anywhere,' said Crudford. 'I won't be a—'

And then he, and the heart, vanished.

CHAPTER XXXVII

In Which Mrs Abernathy Finally Gets Her Just Desserts.

A great host had gathered by the shores of Cocytus, in the chilliest, bleakest region of Hell. Jagged peaks towered above the lake, casting their shadows across its frozen surface. Nothing dwelt among their crevasses and caves: even the hardiest of demons shunned Cocytus. A bitter, howling wind blew ceaselessly across the lake's white plain, the only barriers to its progress being the bodies of those not fully submerged beneath the ice.

Cocytus was both a lake and a river, one of five that encircled Hell, the others being the Styx, the Phlegethon, the Acheron, and the Lethe. But Cocytus was the deepest and, where it entered the Range of Desolation, the widest. It was there that the Great Malevolence liked to imprison those who had betrayed it. The lake had four sections, each deeper than the next: those guilty of only minor betrayals were permitted to keep their upper bodies and arms above the surface; those in the second level were trapped up to their necks; those in the third were surrounded by ice, yet a little light still penetrated to where they lay; but the worst were imprisoned in the darkest depths of the lake, where there was no light, and no hope.

The Great Malevolence itself had once been a prisoner of the lake, placed there by a power much greater than its own, but it had been freed by a demon that had melted the ice with cauldrons of molten lava. Each load of lava would melt only an inch of ice, and before the next cauldron could be brought most of the ice would have returned again, so that every cauldron made only the tiniest fraction of difference. Yet still the demon filled its cauldron and carried it to the lake, working without rest for centuries, until finally the ice was weak and low enough for the Great Malevolence to escape.

That demon was Ba'al, later to mutate into Mrs Abernathy.

The Great Malevolence was not a being familiar with sadness or regret. It was too selfish, too wrapped up in its own pain. But Mrs Abernathy's betrayal had hurt it more than it had ever been hurt before. Now it was forced to condemn to the lake the demon that had once saved it from this same ice. Had there been even one atom of mercy in the Great Malevolence, it might have found some way to forgive Mrs Abernathy, or make her punishment less severe, as a reward for her help in times past.

But the Great Malevolence was entirely without mercy.

It had instructed all the hordes of Hell to gather at the Range of Desolation and witness Mrs Abernathy's fate. It would be a lesson to them all. The Great

Malevolence demanded loyalty without question. Betrayal could lead only to the ice.

Arrayed before him were the jars containing the various parts of Mrs Abernathy. At a signal from the Great Malevolence, the jars were emptied on the ice and Mrs Abernathy – part human, part Ba'al – was reassembled until only the space for her heart remained empty. Finally, Crudford appeared accompanied by the Watcher, and carrying the beating black heart in his arms.

'Well?' said the Great Malevolence.

'The Shadows have withdrawn, Your Awfulness,' said Crudford. 'They will threaten you no more.'

The Great Malevolence did not share Crudford's optimism. The Kingdom of Shadows would always be a threat, although the Great Malevolence did not say this aloud: it would display weakness, even fear, and it could not be weak or fearful in front of the masses of Hell. Beside the Great Malevolence, the Watcher fluttered its bat wings briefly, the only sign it gave that it too understood the danger posed by the Shadows.

'And the boy?' said the Great Malevolence. 'What of Samuel Johnson?'

'He fought her,' said Crudford. 'He broke the shield around her heart. Without him, she might well have managed to complete the ritual, and the rule of the Shadows would have begun.'

'Such strength,' said the Great Malevolence. 'Such bravery. Perhaps, in time, he might be corrupted, and we could draw him to our side.'

Crudford very much doubted that, but he knew better than to say so.

'And the traitor Nurd?' said the Great Malevolence.

'He remains on Earth with the boy.'

'He should be here. He should be frozen in the ice like all these others who have betrayed me.'

Again, Crudford said nothing. He felt the Watcher's eight black eyes examining him, waiting for Crudford to make an error, to condemn himself with his own words, but Crudford did not.

The Great Malevolence waved a clawed, bejewelled hand.

'Place the heart in its cavity,' it instructed.

Crudford did as he was ordered, and was glad to be rid of the horrid thing. Instantly the heart began to fuse with the flesh around it, and the disconnected parts of Mrs Abernathy's body started to come together. Atoms bonded, bones stretched, and veins and arteries formed intricate networks.

When all was complete, Mrs Abernathy's eyes opened, and she rose to her feet.

'Master,' she said.

'Traitor,' said the Great Malevolence.

'All that I did, I did for you.'

'No, you did it for yourself. You sided with our enemies. You called the Shadows to your cause. You would have given them the Multiverse, and eventually Hell itself, all to avenge yourself on one human child.'

'It's not true,' said Mrs Abernathy. 'It was all a trick on my part. I had a secret plan . . .'

She was frightened now. The ice was already burning her bare feet. She looked to Crudford for help.

'Tell our master, Crudford. Tell it of my loyalty.'

But there could be no comfort from Crudford. Mrs Abernathy was appealing to the only demon in Hell who was incapable of lying. Before she could speak again, the Great Malevolence's right hand closed around her body, and it lifted her high above the lake.

'I condemn you,' said the Great Malevolence, and its voice echoed from the mountains as every demon in Hell looked on. 'You are a traitor, and there is only one punishment for traitors.'

And with all the force that it could muster, the Great Malevolence flung Mrs Abernathy at the ice. She hit the surface and broke through, and the ice gave way before her as she plummeted deeper and deeper into the lake. At last, when she was lower than any of the others condemned to its cold grip, her descent slowed, then ceased entirely. The ice closed above her head, and she was lost to view.

There was only one task left for the Great Malevolence to complete, for there was one demon that most definitely could not be allowed to roam freely throughout Hell and the Multiverse any longer, spreading his optimism and good cheer. There was space in Cocytus for Crudford as well. Looking on the bright side was also a betrayal of all that the Great Malevolence stood for.

But when the Great Malevolence reached for Crudford, the little demon was already gone, and he was never again seen in Hell.

CHAPTER XXXVIII

In Which There is a Parting of the Ways.

In the silence of Wreckit & Sons, Samuel and the others stared at the spot from which Crudford had popped from one dimension into another.

'Well, we won't see him for a—' said Jolly, just as Crudford appeared once again. Jolly was ever so slightly unhappy. He'd been hoping to keep Crudford's hat.

'All done,' said Crudford. 'Can I have my hat back please?'

Jolly obliged with as much good grace as he could summon, which wasn't a lot.

Beside them, the mutated form that had, until recently, housed Mrs Abernathy's black heart was already starting to rot. All traces of Nosferati, and spiders, and sinister clowns had vanished. There were toys scattered across the floor below, but they were no longer intent upon inflicting harm on anyone. They were simply toys, although Samuel had the feeling that he'd never look at a teddy bear in quite the same way again.

'Where's the heart?' asked Nurd.

'Back in Mrs Abernathy's body,' said Crudford.

'And where is that?'

'Frozen somewhere near the bottom of Lake Cocytus.'

'Ah. So the Great Malevolence wasn't very pleased to see her then?'

'Oh no, it was pleased,' said Crudford, 'but only because it meant that the Great Malevolence got to freeze her in an icy lake for eternity. I think it would have liked to have imprisoned you there with her, Nurd. I think it would have stuck me in the ice as well if I hadn't made myself scarce.'

'Tut-tut, and after all that you've done for the old miseryguts,' said Nurd. 'Some demons have no gratitude.'

'It's all for the best,' said Crudford. 'I never really fitted in down in Hell. I didn't want to torment people, or be horrible. I always felt that there might be something better around the next corner. There wasn't, of course: there was just more of Hell, but I never gave up hope. Unfortunately, Hell has no place for optimists. Well, it *does* have a place for them, but it's at the bottom of a lake.'

'So you can't ever go back?' said Samuel.

'I don't want to go back,' said Crudford. 'I know my way around the Multiverse, just like Mrs Abernathy. I know all the little back entrances, all the cracks and holes. I think I might just explore it for eternity. After all, there's a lot of it to see. It's a wonderful place, the Multiverse.

'And I'm not the only demon who has escaped: there are thousands of demons scattered all over the Multiverse, and only some are vicious and evil. Lots of them are perfectly lovely, with an admirable work ethic. Mr Comestible, for example, has set himself up as a baker only a couple of universes from here. His cinnamon rolls are worth crossing dimensions to try.'

'With all of your knowledge, I don't suppose you could help me to get home?' asked the Polite Monster. 'Not that it isn't nice here, but I left a pot boiling on the stove – five letters, "an apparatus for cooking and heating" – and Mother will be starting to worry. Oh, and I have a crossword puzzle to finish.'

'It would be my pleasure,' said Crudford, and he meant it.

'I'd like to come too,' said a voice. 'Actually, *we'd* like to come.'

It was Nurd who had spoken. Samuel stared at him in shock.

'What?' he said. 'You're leaving? Why?'

Nurd looked at the boy. Samuel was his friend, the first friend that Nurd had ever had if you didn't count Wormwood, which Nurd didn't, or not aloud. (He didn't want Wormwood to think that Nurd might need him. He did need him, and Wormwood knew that he needed him, but it didn't mean they had to get all soppy about it.) Samuel had made Nurd a worse demon, but a better person. For that Nurd would love him forever.

'I don't belong here,' said Nurd. 'I've tried to belong, but I'm still a demon, and I'll always be one. If I stay here, I'll have to keep my true nature hidden forever: if I don't, they'll lock me up, or try to destroy me. Even if I avoid discovery, I can never be myself. I'll just be that strange-looking bloke who lives with the Johnsons, him and his even stranger-looking friend.'

'That's me,' said Wormwood, unnecessarily.

'And what am I to do as you get older?' Nurd continued, having slapped Wormwood semi-affectionately on the back of the head. 'Do I continue living with your mum? Do I come and live with you? How will you explain me to your wife, or your children?'

'So you're running away?' said Samuel. He fought his tears, but they won, and he hated them for winning. 'You're leaving me because of something that hasn't even happened yet, something that might never happen?'

'No,' said Nurd, 'I'm leaving because I have to make a life for myself. I spent so long in Hell, and then you gave me a place here. You showed me a new world. More than that, you gave me hope. Now I want to see what I might become out there in the Multiverse. And you have to make a life for yourself too, Samuel, one in which there aren't two demons peering over your shoulder, always needing you to protect them.'

'Don't,' said Samuel. 'Please don't go. Don't leave me.'

Now Nurd was crying too, weeping big wet tears that soaked his elf costume. It was hard to be dignified while dressed as a large elf.

'Please understand,' he said. 'Please let me go.'

Samuel's face was contorted by grief.

'Go, then!' he shouted. 'Go on and wander the Multiverse. You were only ever a burden to me anyway. All I did was worry about you, and Wormwood just made things smell when he wasn't setting them on fire. Go! Find your demon friends. I don't need you. I never needed you!'

He turned his back on Nurd. Maria tried to comfort him, but he shook her hand off and stepped away.

Slowly, giving Samuel space in his sadness and anger, the others lined up to shake hands with Nurd and

Wormwood. The dwarfs even managed to hug them without trying to steal anything from them. When their farewells were completed, Crudford drew a circle in the air with his finger, and a hole opened. On the other side lay a red ocean, and anchored upon it was a white boat with a yellow sail.

'Where is that?' asked Wormwood.

Crudford shrugged.

'I don't know. Let's find out.'

Crudford and Wormwood waved goodbye as they stepped though the portal and into the boat. Only Nurd remained. He reached out a hand as though he might somehow bridge the distance between Samuel and himself, the space both emotional and physical that had opened between them, but he could not. His let his hand drop. A new universe beckoned. He touched the sides of the portal. They felt solid. He used them to support himself as he placed his right foot into the waiting world.

A finger tapped him on the back. He turned, and Samuel buried his face in Nurd's chest. The boy wrapped his arms around him, and it seemed that he would never let go. Samuel was sobbing, and could barely speak, but Nurd could still make out the words.

'Goodbye,' said Samuel. 'Goodbye, friend. I hope you find what you're looking for. Come back to me someday. Come back and tell me of your adventures.'

Nurd kissed him gently on the top of the head, and Samuel released him. Nurd stepped through the portal. Before he could look back it had closed behind him, and his friend was gone.

CHAPTER XXXIX

In Which We Step Forward in Time.

There is a house on the outskirts of a town far from Biddlecombe, a house old and full of character. Its gardens are neatly tended, but there is space in them too for ancient trees and blackberry bushes, for a little chaos amid the order. On this day the sun is shining, and the house is filled with people. There are children, and grandchildren, and even some great-grandchildren. A man and woman, both still lively and bright despite their years, are celebrating their 50th wedding anniversary. There will be cake, and songs, and laughter.

A small table has been cleared in the living room, and on the table sits their wedding album. It contains all of the usual photographs that one might expect to see from such an occasion: the bride arriving, the ceremony, the couple leaving the church in a cloud of confetti, the hotel, the dinner, the dancing. Here are the parents of the bride and the parents of the groom, basking in the happiness of their children; there, guests cheering and raising glasses. It is a record not only of one day, but of many lives lived until that moment, of friends made and not forgotten.

The final photograph is a group picture: all of those
in attendance are gathered together, row upon row:
tallest at the back, shortest at the front. Most people
who leaf through the album just glance at it and move
on. They have seen enough photos by then. There is
food to be eaten, and champagne to be drunk. There
is even some beer, for Spiggit's has brewed a special ale
for the occasion. It is called Spiggit's Old Faithful, and
those who have tried it swear that it is very good once
their memory has returned. The brewers are here somewhere too. They are giving rides on their backs to small
children, who don't care that they smell odd and can
only say 'Hurh!'

But those who take the time to look more closely at
this last photograph in the album might pick out what
appears to be a small, gelatinous being in the bottom
right-hand corner. He is wearing a top hat, and has
borrowed a bow tie for the occasion. To his left, wearing
a suit with one sleeve on fire, is a man disguised as a
ferret, or a ferret disguised as a man. Whatever he is,
he is grinning broadly, mostly because he has not yet
noticed the flames.

The bride and groom stand in the middle of the front
row. Maria looks beautiful, and Samuel looks like a
man who knows that the woman beside him is beautiful,
and that she loves him, and he loves her. At their feet
sits a small dachshund. He is not Boswell, for Boswell
has gone to another place, but the son of Boswell, and
the spirit of his father lives on in him.

To Samuel's right is a figure dressed in a very elegant
dark suit. His skin has a slightly greenish tinge to it,

although that might just be a problem with the camera. His chin is very long, and tilts upwards at the end so that, in profile, he resembles a crescent moon. He has a white flower in his buttonhole, and he is content.

Let us leave the album and move back into the sunlight. The oldest of the trees in the garden is a spreading oak. Beneath it, shaded by leaves and branches, is a bench, and two friends are seated upon it. Nearby, Wormwood tends the garden, aided by Crudford. Wormwood, it has emerged, is a skilled gardener, perhaps the greatest the Multiverse has ever known. A dachshund digs beside him, hoping to unearth a bone. This is the great-great-great grandson of Boswell.

His name, too, is Boswell.

There is much of Samuel the boy in Samuel the older man as he sits on the bench, a glass of champagne by his side. His hair, now grey, still flops across his forehead, and his glasses still refuse to sit quite evenly on his nose. His socks still do not match.

Nurd's appearance has not changed. It will never change, for he will never age. He once used to worry about what might happen when Samuel died, for he could not imagine a Multiverse without his friend, but he worries no longer: he has learned the secrets of the Multiverse, and has seen what lies beyond death. Wherever Samuel goes, Nurd will go too. When the time comes, he will be waiting for his friend on the other side.

Waiting along with a host of Boswells.

'Tell me a tale,' says Samuel. 'Tell me a story of your adventures.'

He has heard all of Nurd's tales many times before, but he never tires of them. It is not just in appearance that he resembles the boy he once was. He has never lost his enthusiasm, or his sense of wonder. They have carried him through difficult times, for it is not only Nurd who has led an exciting existence over the years. Samuel's life, too, has always been enjoyably odd and there are stories about him that may yet have to be told.

And as the sun warms them, Nurd begins to speak.

'Once upon a time,' he says, 'there was a boy named Samuel Johnson . . .'

Acknowledgements

My thanks to Sue Fletcher, Swati Gamble, Kerry Hood, Lucy Hale and all at Hodder & Stoughton; Emily Bestler, Judith Curr, Megan Reid, David Brown and the team at Atria Books; and all my foreign publishers and agents who have supported these odd little books. As always, I'm indebted to my agent Darley Anderson and his staff, without whom I wouldn't have a career at all. Finally, love and thanks to Jennie, Cameron and Alistair.